WAKE

A LOST SAVAGES MC NOVEL

CILLA RAVEN

Cover art and design by
Nichole W. - Rainy Day Artwork

Get new release updates and exclusive content when you sign up for my mailing list!

I dedicate this book...

To Topsail Island, North Carolina

To my great, amazing, fantastic, wonderful, awesome husband, who inspires me each and every day,

To every person that dreams of that fairytale kind of love that seems impossible to find,

And to every person who has ever had to learn to fear a loved one,

This book is for you.

CONTENTS

CHAPTER 1

KALIYAH

Sorry to whoever wrote the scripts for the fairytales I grew up watching in movies as a kid, but bro, you got it *all* wrong.

Fabulous, floor-length gowns and fairy godmothers don't appear out of nowhere, promising to fix your problems when you're at your lowest, crying on a bench in a torn dress.

Even if they did, corsets are some of the most uncomfortable garments in the world, and I have no idea why anyone would subject themselves to hours of not being able to breathe just to have an hourglass figure and perky tits.

Random animals have never cleaned anything I've ever owned, and although I would bend over backward to have a pet dragon that breathes fire, the best I can hope for is a small bearded dragon. Unfortunately, those don't fly.

And they certainly can't carry me away to long-forgotten islands filled with buried treasure, unbroken seashells, clam bras, and unmarried, loyal princes.

Knights in shining armor, on the other hand... can be real, but they don't appear out of nowhere, either. They don't ride in on a white horse, reaching a gloved hand down so they can whisk you away into the sunset.

They drive up on Harleys, hand you a helmet, tell you to hold on tight, and fuck your world up in the best way possible.

Too bad I had to go through a certified villain before I learned this... before I finally woke up to reality.

~

*W*hen I was little - and regrettably, also well into adulthood - I was pretty naive.

Like so many other girls in my generation, I had it in my head that life would play out like a fairytale. I mean, those princesses were my proof, the shining example of what 'true love' was supposed to be.

I romanticized the idea of being in love, never even considering the fact that it takes two to tango.

No one ever told me that by falling in love with whomever the guy would be in my fantasy love equation, I would inadvertently be giving him the power to make or break my fantasized notions... and me.

So instead of proceeding with caution or asking myself what I truly wanted out of love in the first place - or life in general for that matter - I focused on the white dress I'd wear on my wedding day.

I planned a reception where all my friends would be in attendance, accidentally meeting the men of their dreams over shared shrimp cocktail appetizers because, of course, my future husband's friends would be perfect matches for mine.

I imagined the accepting sadness that would be on my father's face as he lifted my veil, the unshed tears my mother would have in her eyes as I said, 'I do.'

I thought about the kiss my fiancé would secretly steal the night before our wedding because he just wouldn't be able to help himself.

However, in the early morning hours of the day before my actual wedding, I was sitting on the bathroom floor of a luxury downtown apartment in Chicago with the door locked, crying my eyes out as I read through the messages on Cam's phone, wishing I wasn't reading what was so clearly spelled out in front of me.

They say hindsight is twenty/twenty, that you can only see things clearly once you're looking back and aren't in the heat of the moment anymore, and though it hurts like hell to ride the wake of learning things the hard way, I have to say I agree.

I'm not proud of how hard or how quickly I fell for Camdyn Fletcher.

I'm certainly not proud of how completely I lost myself in our relationship, either.

But he'd been an intriguing anomaly...

The heartthrob that only had eyes for me, the shy girl who wanted to become an author, even though he'd thought it was a useless, time-consuming endeavor.

He was the business mogul's son who, at first glance, seemed down to earth - the quintessential rich guy who didn't care about money.

Sure, he'd had his life handed to him on a silver platter and had a tendency to be a bit snooty, but he worked hard too, and something about all of his consistent inconsistencies had me falling head over heels before I really knew him.

Honestly, I felt like I'd *never known* him as I read those texts he'd sent to my only friend in the world at the time, Cassie... like the past six years had been nothing but the worst lie ever told.

Somehow though, despite what I was feeling, I was able to

pull myself together enough to step out of the bathroom and quietly plug his phone back in without waking him.

I didn't really have a plan or anything; my tears had just dried up at some point, and it seemed like my thoughts had stopped altogether... like I was numb all over.

I just stood there, staring down at him like some sort of nutjob, and really, I probably was a bit crazed right then.

Those messages between Cam and Cassie had spanned the entire two years we'd been living together in Chicago, and even though we were supposed to be getting married the next day, he still had plans to go see her when he woke up.

He'd been texting other women too, but since Cam and Cassie were the only people I had left in my life after my parents died, the fact that he was cheating with *her* was especially painful.

It was times like those when I really wished I could call my parents and cry everything out to them, but they'd died the year before within months of each other, and I still couldn't think about them without feeling like a hole had been ripped through my chest.

They'd always taken my side, no matter what, and I knew they would've been there with a, 'We're here for you,' rather than a, 'We told you so,' even though their real feelings for Cam had left much to be desired.

To have someone, anyone really, to spill my heart to at that moment would've been better than nothing.

I mean, Cam was still asleep in front of me, but that didn't matter... I was completely alone, and I knew it.

I zombie walked to the other side of the bed and climbed in, pulled the covers up to my neck - though the movement offered little comfort - and gazed at the skyline through our floor-to-ceiling windows, right as Cam's alarm started going off.

He began to stir, and I fully expected my feelings from earlier to come back with a vengeance when I faced him, for my nerves about the situation to make themselves known, but they remained utterly silent.

When Cam sat up after a few minutes of his alarm going off, without thinking, I sat up too.

He cut it off, half-turning toward me, but he didn't say a word as he got up to get ready for work.

That wasn't unusual for us, not speaking to each other. Still, after learning everything I had, his closedoffedness added insult to injury - like he could've at least made an *effort* at hiding his callousness.

I still felt numb as I sat there watching him move about the apartment, stuck in my own head the whole time, oscillating between disbelief and heartbreak.

Surprisingly, I found myself studying his features... and judging them harshly, something I'd never done with anyone since looks have never been that important to me, but I couldn't find it in me to care.

As I watched him, his chiseled chin was just too sharp, his movements a bit too practiced, and for the first time in our six-year relationship, I noticed his eyes were utterly soulless.

His black hair was ruffled from sleep, and I knew he'd rather die than let anyone 'important' see him that way.

Our apartment was open-concept, so you could see everything no matter where you were, and I watched shamelessly as his naked body stepped into the glass shower.

The first time I'd seen him naked, I remember thinking how perfect he was, how toned and statuesque, but as his muscles moved while he washed, all I could think about was the number of hands that had felt those muscles... how Cassie had felt them.

Revulsion rolled through me from the thoughts, but otherwise, I still felt nothing, and I couldn't explain why.

When he was finally ready to go to 'work,' he stopped at the foot of the bed to say, "I'll be staying at Brandon's tonight for my bachelor party, so don't wait up," before he sighed, turned around, and left.

I think those words were what snapped me out of whatever fog I'd been in because as soon as he walked out the door, I rushed after him on silent, bare feet and stared out the peephole, hoping against hope he wouldn't head to Cassie's apartment across the hall.

However, whatever teensy bit of hope I'd had left shattered as he walked right past the elevators and knocked quietly on Cassie's door.

Back when we moved in, I'd thought it was such a stroke of luck that the only other apartment on our floor was rented by a woman my age with whom I could become friends. But when she opened her door and started kissing Cam, right there in our shared hallway, as if I weren't less than fifty feet away from them, the proximity didn't seem nearly as appealing.

In fact, the whole situation made me sick to my stomach.

I turned around, putting my back against my door after they'd disappeared behind hers, and waited for my dinner to come back up.

I waited for the tears and the heart-wrenching pain I knew were inevitable too.

I'd given up everything I'd ever hoped for in life just so I could be with Cam, and as I replayed our relationship in my head, it was like I was looking at my life through a different set of lenses... like I was seeing myself through someone else's eyes.

From the first time he kissed me in college, to when I dropped out during my fourth year, giving up my dream of becoming an author so I could move with him to Chicago, promising to be the trophy wife he'd always wanted.

From the way he made me feel like the most perfect being he'd ever laid eyes on, to the day he told me I looked like I was six months pregnant and needed to go to the gym.

From the first time we ever made love my freshman year, to the first time his hand landed on me in anger six months later.

Every detail seemed punctuated and highlighted, but as I waited for the tears, I was thoroughly shocked when none came.

Some emotion even stronger than sadness and sorrow was pushing them back. It was rage - anger so intense it painted my vision red and forced all rational thought from my mind.

Storming out of our apartment, I made my way to Cassie's, hearing a telling moan before I could even raise my hand to knock, but I ignored it as my fist banged on the door harder than I'd intended.

I don't know what I expected... maybe for Cam to rush out and apologize, for him to grovel at my feet and beg me to stay with him, but just like the contrast between fairytales and reality, what he actually did came nowhere close to what I'd imagined.

He opened the door in a fucking towel as if he called her place home, then had the nerve to look down at me as if *I* were the one who wasn't supposed to be there.

However, as I took in his dead eyes and uncaring demeanor, I just couldn't get any words out.

All the questions I thought of, I already knew the answers to.

I didn't need to ask how long it'd been going on; I already knew.

I didn't wonder what he thought he was doing; he knew perfectly well what he was up to and obviously didn't give a rat's ass.

There was no point in calling him names; it wouldn't phase him.

So after standing there, fuming with my fists at my sides for a solid minute, I simply turned around and tried to stomp back to our apartment.

I didn't make it halfway before he grabbed me by the arm and turned me around to face him.

Apparently, I'd gotten his attention.

A small spark of life lit his eyes as he said, "This changes nothing."

I think I was more shocked by those words than I was when I found out he was cheating in the first place.

My mouth flew open, and without much thought, my arm jerked out of his grasp, and my hand went flying toward him.

I slapped him with an open palm that sent his face sideways, a satisfying smack lingering in the hallway as I said, "This changes *everything*."

My voice was calm but firm, sounding surer than I felt, but as his eyes slowly slid back to mine, a familiar sense of fear and dread began welling up inside me again.

I knew what he was capable of; I'd walked on eggshells for most of our relationship so I could avoid that side of his personality.

Shit, I'd covered more than a handful of bruises with makeup during our time together, and I knew how he'd react to any unwanted outburst from me.

I just hadn't been thinking.

I was too upset to think, and as his hand gripped my bicep again to pull me back into our apartment, I knew what I had coming.

However, whereas in the past I'd always felt like I deserved what he did to me for one reason or another, made up excuses for his behavior, or given him the benefit of the doubt, this time I already knew I wasn't going to put up with it anymore.

I knew in my soul that I was leaving.

I might not have known where I was going, how I was going to get there, or what my life would be like once I left, but I did know Cam wasn't going to be a part of my life anymore if I had anything to say about it; I was done.

I just had to make him believe I was staying so I would have a chance of breaking free.

If I didn't, if I let him know I was leaving him, he'd kill me to convince me otherwise; he'd said as much the last time I threatened to leave him.

And if there's one thing you should know about Camdyn Fletcher, it's that he always keeps his word.

CHAPTER 2

KALIYAH

*F*ighting Cam off just wasn't an option; I'd tried before and come up remarkably short, making things way worse than they would've been had I just submitted to his demands and been compliant.

If I wanted him to leave so I could escape, I had to play by his rules, bend to his will, and take whatever he dished out gracefully.

However, it was still a hard pill to swallow after the night and morning I'd had, allowing him to push me down on the couch and stand over me, bending his body down to put his face right in front of mine so he could chastise *my* behavior. As if I were some child who needed to be taught a lesson rather than the fiancé who'd just caught him cheating.

It might've been considered weak, codependent, needy, or whatever other psychological catchphrase people would use to describe my behavior for me to stay with him after he put his hands on me the first time, but I never said I was perfect.

I knew it was wrong.

Deep down, no matter what excuse I made for him, I knew what he did was crossing a line, but here's the thing I'd always told myself...

Everyone decides where to draw their own lines.

For some people, physical violence is a hard limit, which is perfectly reasonable. Others draw their lines at something as simple as how their partner hangs up a towel in the bathroom or puts dishes away.

Violence, demeaning and obsessive behavior, borderline psycho moments where I genuinely thought he was making a bigger deal out of things than he needed to... stuff like that hadn't been a boundary for me *until* I realized he'd been cheating.

Apparently, *that* was the line I wasn't willing to let him cross; go figure.

I don't judge where other people draw their boundaries, and I don't see a need to defend where I drew mine back then either, especially now that I know it was a skewed and detrimental point of view to have.

What I will say is that love has no reason behind it. It doesn't care if someone is toxic and bad for you. It's naive and, quite honestly, desperate. It wants what it wants, to hell with any and everything else that should really be considered.

If someone makes you feel like you are their everything, like you are the center of their universe, and you fall for them because of it, their love has the ability to make you do things you thought you never would. It can allow you to put up with a lot of stuff you swore you'd never tolerate just so you won't lose them.

Such a perspective might've been a crazy way to look at the situation, but when Cam was impassioned by me for whatever reason, whether it came out as good attention or bad, I was just happy that *I* was who he was focusing his attention on; I soaked that shit up like a sponge. And as unhealthy as it may have been, I justified his behavior by thinking that he *had* to love me, *had* to care about me if it drove him to resort to violence.

However, when I realized that coveted attention had been focused elsewhere, I was disgusted *by myself* for what I'd allowed him to do to me over the years, because by that point, all the 'sacrifices' I'd been making so willingly for his 'happiness,' made me feel like a clown... and that's putting it nicely.

But what I think was most surprising of all was just how quickly my love for him had vanished. It was like as soon as my tears had dried up while reading those texts, so had all the love I'd ever held for him.

His fingers wrapped around my thighs, squeezing hard enough to leave a mark as he said, "You will be at the church tomorrow to marry me, do you understand?"

I didn't need to search for the answer. I knew what he wanted me to say, so I nodded and said, "Yes, I'll be there," before dropping my eyes to the floor between us in submission, even though the words alone made me want to vomit.

Luckily, that was all he needed to hear to quiet whatever fears he'd been having.

He was convinced I'd honor my word because I always had.

He didn't think twice before he nodded in satisfaction and got ready for work again, actually heading to work after leaving that time, rather than going across the hall.

However, I had no intention of living up to his expectations anymore.

He was going to be gone all day and night, and if I got my mind to start working again, I could be long gone before he ever even realized I wasn't there.

~

*W*hen he finally left, it felt like I could breathe again for the first time since I'd picked up his phone early that morning.

Yet, anger still simmered just below the surface.

I tried taking a few deep breaths, but the effort was wasted since it didn't calm me down at all. I made myself a cup of tea, but no amount of the steamy liquid affected anything I was feeling.

The only thing that did seem to help was trying to think my way out of Cam's life.

However, I was inexplicably linked to him in almost every way. Hell, he'd even made sure the bank account that held my inheritance from my parents' deaths and the sale of their small dairy farm had his name on it.

Still, I knew if I let myself think of all the reasons it would be a problematic break from him, I'd be too scared to go through with it, and the idea of staying with Cam for even another second was too much already.

That thought was the kick in the ass I needed, and when I saw our tickets for our honeymoon lying on the counter beside the espresso machine, that kick in the ass suddenly had direction.

He'd wanted to go to Hawaii or Cancun, somewhere expected like that, but I'd dreamed of getting married on Topsail Island, North Carolina, ever since I was a little girl.

Growing up on a small farm in the middle of nowhere, Kentucky, didn't afford my family many vacations. In fact, we only went on one vacation outside the state during the entire time I lived with them, and it was to Topsail.

I think I'd been around six or seven years old at the time, and I'm pretty sure my mom had won the vacation at bingo or something, but I remember just falling in love with the place once we got there.

I'd been playing in the sand while my dad swam in the ocean. My mom had been sitting in her lawn chair, applying way too much sunscreen to her pale skin. I remember looking up and seeing this lady in a flowy white gown getting married on the beach, not half a football field away from us.

Her blonde hair had been left to hang loose in long waves, and she wore a crown of flowers rather than a veil over her face.

There were only a few people there to watch her ceremony, but it was so beautiful that even at that young age, I'd made up my mind that that's where I wanted to get married too.

However, Cam wouldn't even hear of us getting married outside of Chicago, outside of his mother's Catholic church.

I pressed the issue though, something that had been remarkably out of character for me at the time, and he'd compromised for the first and only time in our relationship. I'd marry him in Chicago, but we would honeymoon on Topsail.

Really, I think he caved just so he could get me to shut up, but he'd said, "Fine, book it. Plan the whole stay, whatever, but put it on your card. I'm not paying for two weeks on some island no one's ever heard of."

It was the only argument I'd ever won against Cam, and I'd planned the two-week stay of my dreams, complete with a full itinerary without batting an eye.

As I stood there, staring at those tickets for a solid few minutes, I couldn't believe I was actually considering going on our honeymoon without Cam.

I also had no idea what I would do afterward, but those hesitant thoughts didn't last long when I compared them to how terrible my life would be if I did end up marrying him.

As difficult as it is to admit, I didn't trust myself to stick to my guns where Cam was involved; he had too strong of a hold on me. The apathy I felt for him was too new as well, and I had no idea how long it was going to last.

It was like the difference between being sober and being blackout drunk.

Sober Me has always been equipped with a working brain, a heart that empathizes, and a go-to demeanor that can best be described as being nice to everyone.

Blackout Drunk Me though... well, she's only really equipped with a vagina and an attitude.

Every time I know I'm going to be drinking, Sober Me sets up Drunk Me for a night of fun that she can enjoy while also putting fail-safes in place so that even if Drunk Me turns into Blackout Drunk Me, she still won't go too far. Things like telling the bartender when I get there that I'm only allowed to have four drinks, setting alarms on my phone to remind Drunk Me that it's time to go home, and I always made sure Cassie was there to ensure Drunk Me made it back safely.

The drive I had to leave Cam felt pretty solid, like it wasn't going anywhere any time soon, but I needed to be sure my resolve wouldn't crumble later like it had before.

I needed to go, and I didn't need to overthink anything too much.

I just needed to make a plan and stick to it.

If I slowed down to ask myself the big questions other people might ask themselves if they were in my situation, like what I was going to do with my life, where I was going to live, how I was going to pay for things... I didn't trust myself not to back out entirely and just deal with the consequences.

It'd happened before when I'd thought about leaving.

So while I had my resolve and anger pushing me forward, I was going to use every bit of it to get away and stay away.

And if Future Me had a sudden change of heart, it would be too late.

I would already be gone, and she would have no other choice than to deal with what I'd set up for her.

~

*T*hat different set of lenses I was seeing our relationship through was working overtime while I packed in a hurry.

When I went to my closet, it was like I was seeing it up close for the first time.

I'd never realized how many of my clothes had been picked out by Cam, things I would've never chosen to wear myself.

The same thing happened when I looked at the shoe rack.

It was nearly full, but when given the choice of what I was going to bring with me, and Cam's preferences weren't considered, only one pair of flip flops and one pair of boots made the cut.

Packing was easier than it had ever been before since I was only grabbing the things I actually wanted, and in no time, my two duffels and a carry on were full of nothing but the necessities.

I'd even had room to pack my laptop, journals, favorite pens, and sticky notes... all my favorite writing must-haves, even though I hadn't written a thing since I'd moved to Chicago.

I don't know when the idea had popped in my head, but as soon as I thought up an image of me sitting on a balcony on a lazy morning, looking at the beach down below with a laptop under my fingertips and a cup of hot tea beside me, I was more motivated to get to Topsail than I'd been before. As if finally writing again was just as much, if not more of a motivator than leaving Cam was, to begin with.

I hadn't even left yet, and already a smile was plastered across my face just thinking about it.

Pretty soon though, I was standing by the door, both tickets in hand as I took a good look around the apartment I'd spent the last two years of my life in.

Even though I only planned on using one of the tickets, I

certainly wasn't going to leave Cam's there, just in case he decided to follow me.

I didn't know for sure that he would, but there was no doubt in my mind that once Cam found out I wasn't where I was supposed to be, his anger would make him unpredictable, and I didn't want to take any chances.

There were a few things still left that I didn't want to live without, and I was worried about what Cam would do to what I left behind, but there was no way I could take everything with me.

Things like my hefty book collection, the printed manuscripts I'd written in college, the dresser that I'd had since I was a kid that had somehow ended up fitting with the design Cam allowed, and the other small things that one collects over time just had to stay there until I came up with a better plan.

Unfortunately, that meant I had to leave some of my most prized possessions behind.

My mother had made four photo albums of my childhood for me while she'd been fighting breast cancer, but I could only fit one in my bag. Leaving the other three behind ripped my insides apart because I wasn't sure I'd ever see them again, but I didn't have another option on such short notice.

I was able to grab the fat teacup my father had painted for me when we went to paint pottery together the last time he visited before he died. It was purple on the inside and white on the outside. He'd scribbled, 'The days are long when we're not together, but every time you drink from this, just know I'm wishing I were drinking next to you,' in black paint all around the outside of the cup.

The words barely fit, and he'd had to make the letters smaller and smaller as he went just so he could get all of them on there, but as messy as it was, it was the best present I'd ever gotten in my life... especially since he'd passed just two months later.

His sentiment had taken on an entirely different meaning after his death, and there was no way on earth I was going to leave it behind.

The cup was tucked away, wrapped up in my clothes so it would survive the journey, but I still worried about it. However, it was the best I could do right then, and as I took a deep breath, I let that worry slide away so I could focus on what I needed to do.

Our flight wasn't supposed to leave until the next day after our wedding, but I was hopeful that I could get them to move up my departure time if there was any space available on an earlier flight.

I'd already checked the flight schedule from Chicago to Raleigh and seen that there was only one more planned for that day, and I knew if I didn't hurry, there would be no way to catch it.

With that in mind, I walked from the apartment to the elevator in the hallway, ruminating over canceling Cam's ticket altogether once I got to the airport when I heard movement coming from Cassie's apartment.

My heart sank.

I didn't want to face her right then for so many reasons, and I found myself wishing the elevator would hurry up just in case she decided to come say, 'Hi,' as if this morning and the past two years had never happened.

Luckily though, I was already on the elevator with the doors closing before her door opened, and as it took me safely down to the ground floor, I breathed a sigh of relief so loud it even surprised me.

However, if I knew Cassie - and by all accounts, I'd thought I had - if she wanted to talk to me, she would definitely be the kind of person to follow me downstairs.

Hailing a taxi was a forte of mine though, so as soon as I

stepped off the elevator, I didn't waste any time heading outside and flagging one down.

I also didn't even bother with putting my bags in the trunk. I just opened the door, slid inside, asked the driver to take me to O'Hare, and slammed the door as I saw Cassie step out onto the sidewalk.

She looked upset and worried, but it was too late; the cab was already moving, and I wasn't about to tell it to stop.

CHAPTER 3

KALIYAH

*A*lmost as soon as I left, my phone started ringing in my jacket pocket, and I had to shift all my stuff around just so I could pull it out.

The name Cassandra Hossgrove was plastered across my screen, and when I saw it, another surge of anger spiked through me.

What? Sleeping with my fiancé and chasing me out of my apartment wasn't good enough? She had to call me too? Not just send a text that I could ignore like a normal human?

That girl would not quit.

I declined her call and shoved my phone back in my pocket with a huff; I was not ready to deal with her shit yet. The ride to the airport was surprisingly relaxing, and I didn't want to ruin it by talking to Cassie.

Granted, there was an enormous amount of anxiety spreading through me about what I was going to do with my life, and questions continued to pop into my head about what I was going to do once I got to Topsail Island, but with every bit of resolve I had left, I planned on *not* making a plan until I got there.

I could decide what to do with my life from the rental house on Topsail; thinking about it beforehand would've just made me second guess myself, and I couldn't do that.

Within almost no time by Chicago's traffic standards, the taxi was pulling up in front of the airport, and my brain basically shut off as I went through the mindless tasks of paying the driver, walking inside, and standing in line.

My phone had gone off a few times while I'd been waiting, but I never even bothered checking who it was before I hit the volume button, lowering its incessant ringing.

However, by the fourth call, I'd had it, so I silenced the whole thing, turning off all notifications because I wasn't in the mood to deal with anyone.

When it was my turn to step up to the counter, I handed my tickets over to the lady, and her face pinched as she glanced at me with sympathy.

"I'm sorry, but these tickets are for tomorrow, and that flight has already been canceled. Weren't you notified?"

"Wait, what?" I asked.

"I can try to move you and your other passenger to the next flight to Raleigh, but I have to warn you, we've already been canceling flights there due to the hurricane."

"What hurricane?"

Apparently, I'd been living under a rock by the way the woman peered over the counter at me, but she answered nicely enough.

"Hurricane Sirus. It's supposed to hit somewhere on the east coast later tonight, and flights for tomorrow are already being canceled because they think it's going to linger for a while. I can see if there's room for two on the next flight out though?"

"Just for one," I told her, thinking as quickly as I could. "My fiancé isn't coming, and I was hoping I could cancel his ticket while I was here."

"Oh. Well, that's no problem at all," she said as she started clicking away on her computer. "I just need to see your ID and the card you booked the flights with."

I handed everything over to her and tried not to think about how much my hands were sweating.

If she couldn't get me on a flight that day, I'd have no other choice than to go back to our apartment until I came up with some other plan, and that would just make things worse.

That flight was my only available 'out,' and as the lady continued to not let anything show on her face, good or bad, my nerves kept fraying with every second that passed.

However, a short time later, she put me out of my misery when she said, "You're in luck," her voice obnoxiously upbeat. "The last flight we have to Raleigh is still a go, and there's been a cancellation. There's one seat left if you'd like it?"

I nodded, but she barely glanced at me before she continued, "It'll be leaving in about an hour. Do you have everything you need with you now?"

I nodded to her again and gestured to my bags before she said, "Alright, great. Give me just a second, and I'll get everything sorted for you."

She checked my bags and gave me my new ticket, and after eventually making it through security, I made it to my gate just as they started boarding.

Overall, I have to say that was one of the easiest experiences I'd ever had dealing with an airline, and something about it just seemed fated to me - like I was meant to be on that plane, heading to North Carolina on my own.

However, I'd been so wrapped up in getting on the next flight - and worrying about what would happen if I couldn't - that it wasn't until I was already strapped into my seat and the plane was taking off that I finally processed the fact that she'd said 'hurricane.'

~

*T*rying like hell to convince myself that not all hurricanes are Katrina level lethal, where everything gets fucked, I pushed the incoming storm to the back of my mind and settled into my flight - a feat made much easier by the fact that the older guy next to me seemed to have no inclination to strike up a conversation either.

Speaking to strangers was never something I'd been good at.

A social butterfly, I am not.

Beyond the weather, which was already being purposely shoved aside in my mind, I just never knew what else to say to people. They'd always say things where the only answer I had in response was a noncommittal, 'Uh-huh.'

Most would take that as a sign to move on, but the worst ones kept going even after I was obviously not interested in talking.

The guy next to me didn't seem like the type, but I still put my earbuds in and closed my eyes anyway, in case he decided to change his mind.

About halfway through the two-hour flight, I was dozing, stuck in that limbo between being asleep and awake, when the turbulence hit. One particularly violent patch jostled me the rest of the way awake and left me feeling like my belly had jumped into my throat.

The fasten seatbelts sign flashed on a few seconds later, and the guy next to me spoke up for the first time.

"You look scared, but you don't need to worry," he started, and I just stared at him because I had no idea what to say in response. "This is just a regular storm."

I didn't know what he was talking about, and as the plane

bucked again, my hands shot out to both armrests, gripping them tightly as if they would somehow protect me if things went sideways... or down, as it were.

"I mean, this storm isn't attached to the hurricane, so we're much safer than you might think. I'm just trying to ease your mind," he said, his voice a bit higher than I would've expected.

"Uh-huh. Thank you. That's very kind of you," I said eventually as the plane evened out.

"No worries," he chuckled a little. "My granddaughter is afraid of flying, but she doesn't want to hear about how everything's going to be alright. She wants the hard facts, and that's it." He smiled like he was thinking about her, and I didn't respond as I looked out the window, leaving him to his thoughts so I wouldn't have to talk anymore.

The rest of the flight was just as harrowing, but I managed to keep the fear from my face, for the most part.

Once we finally landed, I breathed a bit easier, thankful I was on solid ground and states away from all my worries back in Chicago. I knew Cam was probably still at work, oblivious to the fact that I'd even left, and something about that made me smile to myself.

I disembarked, finding my way to the baggage claim area with few problems, and my bags were some of the first ones on the conveyor belt.

Again, I had that feeling like everything was falling into place, as if even the universe itself thought this was the path I needed to be on, and as I headed over to the rental car agency's booth, the feeling just got stronger.

There were hardly any problems switching my reservation until the guy double-checked the date I'd be returning the Jeep I was renting.

I'd had to make a quick decision right then that I hadn't been expecting I'd need to: whether I was going to be returning to Raleigh or not.

The drive from Raleigh to Topsail Island was a little over two hours long.

Yes, there'd been closer airports I could've flown into, but flying into those smaller airports meant layovers and a higher-priced ticket, so when I'd booked the trip, I'd had it in my head that Cam and I would have a little road trip together as well.

With little more than a gut feeling guiding the choice, I decided I wouldn't be returning to Raleigh.

It was really my first 'post-Cam, new-life' decision, but I was happy with it since it got me further and further away from the life I'd lived with him.

I'd thought, 'Fuck it. I might as well just see where this hair-brained idea takes me,' and told the guy I'd need to drop the rental off somewhere closer to Topsail Island.

He set me up with the address of a place in Jacksonville, which I already knew from making all of our travel plans was about half an hour away from the island. He handed me the keys and told me where to find the Jeep, and with a pep in my step, I made my way outside.

The rental cars were all in a line in the parking garage, and the little red Wrangler stuck out like a sore thumb.

I loved it instantly.

When I finally threw my bags in the back and got in, I just sat there for a minute while I wrapped my mind around every-thing that had happened in the last twenty-four hours.

Breathing deeply, I relaxed for the first time in a while and set my mind to finishing the last leg of the trip to Topsail.

Pulling out my phone to find the rental house's address, I ignored all twenty-one voicemails and thirty-seven text messages.

Cam had to have already realized I was gone... it was the only reasonable explanation.

Although that thought freaked me all the way out and my hands started shaking, I couldn't let myself focus on it.

I just had to get the address and plug it into the Jeep's GPS; I could worry about handling Cam later.

Once I was finally on the road though, the anxiety from not listening to the voicemails and reading the texts was eating me up inside.

I tried really hard to fight the temptation to check them, I did, but eventually, there was no way I couldn't.

The rain was easing to a slow, lazy drizzle, and I had the cruise control set as I picked my phone back up and pressed play on the voicemails.

It was the worst decision I'd made all day.

The first one was from right after I'd left the apartment.

Cassie's voice rang through my ear, and I fought the wave of nausea that flooded through me as I heard it.

"Kaliyah, hey. I don't know what to say that'll make this any better. I'm really sorry. You don't have to leave…"

I took the phone from my ear and pressed delete. I didn't want to hear that shit.

The next one was Cassie too.

"Hey, I know I messed up, but really, I need you to call me back. Cam called and asked me to check on you, but when I told him you'd left, he started freaking out. He's on his way back from work right now. Please call me back."

I pulled the phone away and just kind of stared at it for a second as my brain worked to process what I'd just heard.

I'd hoped I would be able to keep Cam in the dark all the way up until he was standing alone, waiting on me to walk down the aisle the next day… I know it was a bit heartless and dramatic, but I was upset and petty… I thought he deserved to be left at the altar after what he'd done.

However, if Cassie had already told him I'd left, my safety net of time wasn't just dwindling down - it was already gone, shot all to hell.

Deciding to listen to the rest before I let myself freak out completely, I deleted that one and pressed play on the next.

It was Cam.

"What the fuck is this I hear about you leaving with bags, huh? What did I tell you the last time you tried this shit? You better get back to the apartment before I do, or so help me, you will not live it down."

Delete.

Play.

Cassie.

"Oh my god, girl, just answer your damn phone! Cam just got here and tore through both of our apartments looking for you!" She paused for a breath before she said, "Girl, I'm worried. Cam looks... I don't even know how to describe it. Just call me back, please."

Delete.

Play.

Cam, his voice calm, low, and dangerous.

"I told you to be here before I got back, and look at that... you're nowhere to be found. I'm going to tell you one more time. Get your ass home right now."

I couldn't listen to any more messages.

I just couldn't.

So without overthinking the decision, I deleted all the voicemails that were left without even listening to them. I opened the text history with Cam and Cassie so it wouldn't show me any unread notifications, but I didn't read those either.

Well, not intentionally, anyway.

Cam's last message was in all caps, and I just couldn't *not* see it.

CAM: *I WILL FIND YOU*

CHAPTER 4

DECLAN

"Hey Dec, where should I put these?" Nash asked, holding up the new signs and banners he'd taken down from where they'd been hanging outside the shop.

"Just lay 'em out on the counter," I told him as I headed back outside to grab the display stands for the surfboard and kayak rentals.

Prepping for a hurricane wasn't that easy, and it certainly wasn't my favorite part of living on the east coast, but I'd grown up dealing with them, so it wasn't anything new to me.

Nash came outside to help after he'd handled what he needed to get done out front, and in no time, everything of value had been tucked safely away inside.

"We shuttin' up the windows next?" he asked with his hands on his hips as he looked around, trying to see what all we still needed to do.

"Yeah, then we gotta get all the things in here up as high as we can get 'em in case the water decides to come up over the dunes again."

Nodding with that happy demeanor of his, even though his face was pinched tight in thought, he said, "Alright, I'm on it," as he headed out the back doors.

The kid was only nineteen, but he already had a strong ass work ethic, never complained about hard labor, and loved the shop and the water just as much as I did.

I headed out with him while rock music drifted through the bluetooth speakers, and as we started pulling all the shutters down and tying up any other loose ends, we fell into that rhythm we'd gotten so accustomed to while we worked together.

It was quiet work for the most part, but Nash was still talking my head off just like it was any other day.

I didn't mind though.

He reminded me so much of my younger brother Tristan that even though he got on my nerves sometimes, I could never find it in me to call him out on it; I missed Tristan's incessant talking too much to shut Nash down.

I just listened, answered when I had to, grunted when I didn't, and it all seemed to work out well for us.

I hadn't planned on taking on any employees back when I moved to Topsail Island and bought the building two years ago. Still, when Nash heard through Topsail's grapevine that I was turning the downstairs section into a surf shop, he'd knocked on my door every day asking for a job, and eventually, I'd caved.

I've never regretted it.

There was no way I could've gotten everything up and running as fast as I did without his help, and it was nice to have someone to watch the shop while I had errands to run or whatever.

He was taking online classes through the college up in Jacksonville, so he could work full time and didn't have to foot the bill for the gas it would take to drive all that way every day, but I didn't mind that either.

He was too smart not to get an education, and I always insisted he got his schoolwork done while he wasn't busy in the shop, paying him for his time whether he was doing school or working, whether he liked it or not.

Nash had tried to fight me on that at first, but I wouldn't hear it.

Even his mom, Mrs. Wallace, had come up here and given me an earful about paying him for the work he wasn't doing, saying I was paying him to run the shop, not to go to school, but when I wouldn't budge for her either, she'd let it go too, smiling softly as she left.

Now, after two years, the kid was like a little brother to me.

He had a real savings account and enough cash on hand to help his mom out whenever she needed it, which was a lot more these days, now that her age was catching up with her.

"This one's stuck, Dec," he called out to me from the upstairs deck. "You mind bringing me that long flathead you got? I think I can fix it if I get the right leverage."

I glanced up at where he was perched on the ladder so he could reach the attic window and hollered up to him, "Yeah, one sec."

My tools were tucked away in my apartment above the shop, so it took me a minute to get up there and find the screwdriver he needed, but before long, I had crawled up into the attic and jerked the window open so I could hand it to him easier.

"Fuck," he said as he grabbed the ladder for dear life. "You scared the hell outta me! I thought you were gonna come out here to give it to me, not jump out this dumbass window."

I laughed at him and said, "But then I wouldn't be able to see the look on your face when you thought the boogie man was coming for you."

"You're a dick," he said as he took the screwdriver from me, but he was smiling as he said it, so I knew we were good.

I sat on my knees because there wasn't much space in the attic, and I watched him try to get the sliding shutter to work.

"Who the hell puts a full-size window in an attic anyway?" he asked, jamming the flathead into the part that was supposed to turn but wasn't. "It's not like there's enough room up there for someone to admire the view."

"People who know that if it looks like there's a third story, they can sell it for more money," I answered right back, and he humphed in response as I heard something click loose on the shutter.

"Got it," he said triumphantly, handing the flathead back to me.

I took it from him easily and started reaching up to close the window when he slammed the shutter down, plunging me into darkness in seconds.

"Who's the dick now, huh?" I yelled through the window, hearing his laugh sound back to me as I started crawling to the foldout ladder, being careful to keep my weight on the center floorboards so I wouldn't fall through the ceiling and into my apartment.

We both got back to work after that, each of us going about our tasks in separate parts of the building until everything was just about wrapped up.

When the prep was all finished, I stood by the double glass doors that led from the shop out onto the ground floor's back deck, and Nash met up with me, coming around the corner in a hurry so he could stash the ladder inside and grab his stuff before I locked it and pulled down the shutter over it.

"Looks like ol' man Stevens is renting out his house during a hurricane again. Hot chick just pulled up in the driveway and went inside," he said as I held one of the doors open for him.

He leaned the ladder up against the wall and started making his way behind the counter to grab his bookbag.

"That man is an ass," I said, thinking about the prick that didn't care about the property he owned next door to the shop or who he let stay in it during a hurricane.

That stingy fucker only cared about the money it could bring him, but he was already so loaded, he never even bothered sending a crew out to prep it for the storms we'd get because he could make up any cost for damages over one summer with the rates he charged his tenants.

He never stayed in the house himself, lived up in Maryland somewhere I think, and other than once a year when he was forced to come down to check the rental out for insurance purposes, I never saw him.

Switching my train of thought, so I didn't get pissed off about ol' man Stevens putting people in danger for money, the other thing Nash said piqued my interest.

"Your age or mine?"

I was only thirty, not too old for it to be a problem, but where women are concerned, that's a pretty decent age gap.

He laughed a little. "More like yours, I think."

I'd been staring at the wall, but when I glanced over to him at that, my whole body went stiff as I saw what he was doing.

"We should move these from under the counter," he said, and for a second, I couldn't fight the panic I felt at seeing someone touching mine and Gavin's cuts and Tristan's dog tags.

I rushed over to him, and when he handed it all to me reverently, I could only barely appreciate the sentiment through the emotions I felt.

"I've told you before not to touch these, Nash." They were the only words I could get out, and as I stood there, holding my dead brothers' things and my old leather, patch-filled cut, I felt like I couldn't move… I was stuck in that position like a dumbass.

Nash came around the counter slowly with his bookbag slung over one shoulder and patted me once on the back.

"Go hang 'em up upstairs. They don't belong down here under a dusty countertop that might get flooded out."

I didn't have control over my own fucking mouth as words just fell from me. "They'll be too close to me there."

Nash didn't hesitate for a second before he said, "That's where they're supposed to be, dumbass," and pushed me toward the stairs in a move I should've punched him for.

"Watch it," I said as I half-assed turned around to face him, Tristan's dog tags clattering to the floor in the process.

We both stood there for a second, and I could see the fear in Nash's face as he looked at me, but it quickly morphed into something else as I reached down to pick up the necklace.

"I've got an idea," he said as he dropped his bookbag and took off up the stairs to my apartment, and I sighed.

That boy tested me sometimes, but with the storm headed right for us, and with how badly I'd lost my shit over the stuff getting even a little wet last year, I knew the kid had a point, and I needed to put it all up higher.

I just had to swallow my pride and bury my emotions again to do it.

Nash ran halfway down the staircase a few seconds later with a hammer and some nails in hand. Before I could say anything, he was putting a hole in my pallet wall.

"What the hell do you think you're doing?" I asked as I started making my way over to him. I didn't like how much like my stepfather I'd just sounded, but there wasn't much to be done about it at that point.

"You'll see," he said as he finished with one hole and started on another, a step down from the first one.

"Boy," I warned, but he wasn't listening.

"I know it doesn't make sense yet, but it will, I promise."

He took another step down, starting on yet another hole, and I almost lost it.

"Nash!" I yelled, "Stop fucking up my shop!"

"This is the best place for them, okay? Just watch."

Having finished, he ran up to me and held his hands out for me to give him what I was holding, but he didn't rush me, just stood there patiently with his face lit up like a Christmas tree.

Carefully, I handed him everything, and he took it all gently, carrying it up the stairs to the nails he'd thrust through my perfect pallet wood paneling.

From my vantage point on the ground floor, I watched as he hung Tristan's dog tags up on the bottom nail first, then my cut on the middle one, and finally, my older brother Gavin's cut on the top one.

When he was finished, he looked at me hesitantly, as if he were afraid of what my reaction would be as he made his way back down the stairs.

However, when I saw them hanging there, almost like they were on display for all to see, I couldn't deny just how right they looked.

I saw it on Nash's face when he knew I wasn't gonna bite his head off, and as he passed me with a smile, I said, "You're gonna get yourself killed one day, I swear."

The kid just blushed as he picked his bookbag up, and I followed him out, trying not to think about the fact that Tristan had died in those dog tags, and that Gavin had been killed in and for that cut.

I pushed those thoughts from my mind as hard as I could as I gave Nash a ride home like I did every Saturday, but it was still just as hard for me to do as it had ever been before.

*M*rs. Wallace, or Moms, as we called her, was waiting for us on the porch when we pulled up to their home on the south end of the island on my bike.

Nash took his helmet off and stashed it in the bin outside their garage, and I tucked mine into the bag I had strapped to the seat before I followed him up the stairs.

"You boys get everything settled at the shop?" she yelled down to us from the front deck.

She was standing there in what she called her housecoat, dragging her IV beside her as we made it to the top of the stairs, that worried set to her brow, evident like it always was whenever a storm was coming.

"Yes, ma'am," Nash said as he kissed her on the cheek before he slid the glass door open and walked inside, the smell of whatever it was she'd been cooking, wafting out to tease my senses.

"You're too good for us, woman," I said as I kissed her cheek too. "How many times do I have to tell you to let Nash or me make Saturday dinner every now and then, huh? It smells incredible."

"Oh, you big flirt," she teased as she blushed and shooed me inside, stepping through the door behind me. "Quit your complainin' and set the table. I'll quit cookin' when you boys quit needin' to eat so damn much."

There was no telling her 'no' about anything.

She cussed like a sailor when she was angry, had never touched a drop of alcohol, and had taken in strays her whole life from what I knew.

There was always a bowl or two of food and water left outside her house for the occasional wayward animal that found her doorstep, and when she'd met me, she treated me like I was her own too, just as she had when Nash had come to stay with her when he was little.

He'd been taken from his bio parents when the cops found

out he was living in a crackhouse, and she'd taken him in, no questions asked, and adopted him not too long after that if I had the story straight.

Luckily, or unluckily, depending on how you looked at it, I'd met her back before she started getting sick all the time, and even I knew she had been a force to be reckoned with.

She still was, but she wasn't nearly as mobile as she used to be.

Moms was basically stuck inside her house every day because of her age and the illnesses that kept creeping up on her, so when she refused to be still or take it easy, Nash and I just let her be and thanked her for it, knowing whatever she did for us would make her happy. She wouldn't listen if we told her not to anyway.

"You know she's never gonna listen, Dec. Might as well enjoy it," Nash said as he grabbed plates down from the cabinets.

"I know, I know," I said as I got all the silverware together.

It had become almost like a tradition for us to have dinner together on Saturday nights.

I know most guys our ages would usually be out chasing ass or falling all over ourselves like the Marine guys down at the meat market do, but Saturday nights seemed to be the loneliest nights for Moms, and for the most part, we always tried to be there for her.

Mr. Wallace had died a few years back, and he'd apparently taken her out every Saturday night throughout their whole marriage. Even though I never met him, I still felt like I knew him by the way she and Nash both talked about him.

We talked about everything and nothing over the steak and potatoes she'd made that night, and Nash and I subtly checked that everything was okay with her like we always did.

Pretty soon though, dinner was over and, after helping with the cleanup and making sure they didn't need anything to ride out the storm, I gave Moms another kiss on the cheek and told Nash I'd see him the next day after the hurricane had passed.

I still had a few last-minute things to get, so I was ready when it rolled in later. I wanted to be back in time to catch the swells that were gonna be coming in with it, so I headed to the grocery store with my Harley roaring beneath me as the first drops of rain started pelting down on my helmet.

CHAPTER 5

KALIYAH

*A*bout halfway through the drive to Topsail, I hit a patch of sunshine and rainbows - like there was quite literally a double rainbow arching across the highway as the skies ahead began to clear.

There were still clouds everywhere, and I could definitely see the outer edges of the hurricane after a while, but that 'this is right' feeling had dug itself deep inside me, and I couldn't help but think those rainbows up ahead were ushering me into the next chapter of my life.

Okay, maybe I was being a bit dramatic, but that was exactly what it had felt like.

Freedom.

Invigorating and stringless freedom. Finally.

I breathed deeply, letting all the stress and 'what ifs' leave my body and mind entirely.

There was nothing but the trees lining the highway, my

station of choice blaring out the speakers, and a house by the water waiting for me at the end of my journey.

It took me a second to realize it, but everything I was feeling actually had a name.

I was happy.

For the first time in what seemed like forever, a smile was on my face that wasn't forced, my heart didn't feel like it was trying to beat inside a vice, and my soul felt lighter than it had in a very long time.

When I noticed the change, a girly little giggle escaped my mouth, and I wore the lingering smile that followed it all the way to Surf City on Topsail Island.

It wasn't until I got to the cute two-story house that I finally remembered I hadn't changed the dates for it yet. Still, with how relatively smoothly everything else had gone on up to that point (not counting the voicemails and text messages, that is), I was optimistic when I called the guy renting it to me.

"Hi, this is Kaliyah Bennett. I'm supposed to be renting your house in Surf City for the next two weeks, starting tomorrow," I said after the man answered the phone.

"Yeah, yeah. Is there a problem? You not stayin' now 'cause of the storm?" he asked with an attitude I chose to ignore.

"Well, no. I'm calling because I was wondering if I could stay in it tonight as well."

He didn't answer right away, so I rushed to say, "I just want to get in and settled before the storm comes, you know, and I'm kind of already here. If it's booked, I understand, and I can find a hotel or something, but if it's not, I don't mind paying for the extra night."

"I don't think that'll be a problem," he said in a much more upbeat tone than he'd had only seconds before. "The key's under the mat; just let yourself in."

"Alright, thank you," I said, relieved.

"Mmhm."

He disconnected the call quickly, but I didn't let his lack of manners mess with me at all; I just climbed out of the Jeep and grabbed my bags.

The house was a pretty sort of greenish-blue color. It sat on stilts at the front of the house and had a garage on the backside. You could park underneath the house in the area in front of the garage, and it reminded me a lot of a carport.

I didn't bother trying to pull the Jeep into the garage since I hadn't gone inside yet, and I knew I would have to go back out for dinner, but as I walked under the carport to have a look at everything, I didn't think parking it in the garage to keep it safe from the storm would be that much of an issue when I came back.

Other houses on the street were shaped the same way, and I even saw where someone had strung up a hammock between their stilts; it was cute as fuck.

The house sat right beside the most adorable little surf shop I'd ever seen, and when I'd booked the trip, I'd thought it would be perfect, seeing as how we could just walk next door to rent almost anything we could want to play with in the water.

Well, 'I' would be more accurate... *I* could rent whatever I wanted to play with in the water.

I headed up the stairs at the side of the house, luggage in hand, and smiled again when I got on the front porch. Two his-and-hers rocking chairs were sitting off to one side, and a sign with the name of the house, 'Sea Breeze Dream,' was hanging from the front door.

The key was exactly where the guy had said it would be, and even though the door got stuck and I'd had to throw my hip into it to get it to open, it was exactly like the pictures online had made it out to be.

The kitchen and living room were what you walked into from the front door, while the two bedrooms were upstairs.

The whole place had a homey feel I loved, and I wound up

standing at the back door on the second floor for a little bit, just watching the waves crash on the shore.

Out back on the first floor, there was just a covered patio, but upstairs, right off the bedroom I was staying in, there was a screened-in porch with a fantastic view of everything outside.

I badly wanted to drop everything and run out onto the beach despite the choppy waves and the dark clouds overhead, but I forced myself to wait on that activity, at least until I'd unpacked.

Not fifteen minutes later, the drawers in the bedroom were full of what I'd brought with me, my empty bags had been stashed in the closet, and my laptop and other writing things had been placed on the desk in the bedroom.

I plugged my laptop in to charge while I went in search of dinner, smiling as I thought about all the words I was going to write while I was there.

My stomach was complaining about not having eaten since the day before, so I decided to wait on exploring the beach until after I'd eaten.

I took my dad's teacup and my mom's photo album down to the kitchen as I left, setting them out on full display like they deserved, however temporary their new home might end up being.

Heading down to the Jeep, I looked up 'food near me' on my phone but was a little disappointed by the limited options available without driving to Wilmington or Jacksonville.

Apparently, Topsail Island sat right in the middle of the two larger cities. They were each about thirty to forty-five minutes away, and Topsail didn't sport anywhere near the kind of amenities they did.

It didn't matter too much though, since I remembered passing a few places that looked promising on the way in.

After tucking my phone back in my pocket, I climbed up into the Jeep again, heading back the way I'd come.

That optimistic viewpoint I'd had since I left the airport was starting to fizzle out fast though, as I passed one place after another that was closed in preparation for the storm.

Honestly, it was a shock to my system to have so few options.

Having come straight from downtown Chicago, where you could find almost any type of cuisine you wanted within walking distance, Topsail Island stood in stark contrast since I hadn't found even one food place that was still open.

I tried my best not to let it phase me, but my patience started to wear thinner as my stomach grew louder.

Eventually, I caught sight of a place called Swingbridge Beer & Wine, and though I knew they probably wouldn't have the food I was craving, I knew they would undoubtedly have the alcohol I was going to need.

And they were open; that alone had been a happy surprise to find.

I parked and headed inside right as it started to rain again, and no sooner had I rushed through the door than a man and a bird said, "Hello," at the same time.

"We were just about to close up," a woman said excitedly as she walked up to the counter from the back of the store, carrying a cardboard box in her hands. "You made it just in time! I'm Heather, and this is my husband, Chris. Let us know if you need help finding anything."

"Uh, thanks. I will," I said as I tried to blend in with the wooden shelves. It wasn't like there was anything wrong with the man, woman, and bird, but again... I'm not a very social person.

I perused the racks for a while, and they had such a good selection that the decision for what I was going to be getting plastered with that night so I could sleep through the storm, ended up being a pretty hard choice.

Eventually though, I just grabbed what I knew - two bottles of Lambrusco - before I headed back up to the front.

The big glass windows that spread across one whole side of the store hid nothing from where I ended up standing at the register, and I couldn't help but notice the rain had picked up considerably while I'd been lost in the wine section.

Already the green field across from the store beside the marina was starting to flood.

However, as I sat the bottles down on the counter, Chris, a tall, long-haired hippy guy with the tie-dyed t-shirt, met me with a smile that eased some of the tension in my shoulders as he asked, "Will this be all for you?"

Heather was beside the man breaking down the box I'd seen her carrying earlier, the bird perched on her shoulder.

"Yep," I squeaked out, reaching for my wallet as my mouth started to run like it always does whenever I'm in front of people I don't know. "I'm surprised you guys were still open; everywhere else looks shut up tight for the storm. Also, that is just an adorable bird," I said as I slid my card in the machine.

At hearing my voice, the bird in question said, "Hello, Sophia," startling me and making me jump.

Heather smiled and laughed out a small, light-hearted giggle as she reached up to stroke the bird down its back. "This is Sophia. Apparently, she wants you to know that."

I found myself smiling at her and the bird, most of my social anxieties forgotten with the whole... unexpectedness of it all.

People aren't that welcoming back in Chicago, or even back in Baltimore, where Cam and I had gone to college.

Their demeanor was much more like what I'd grown up with in my small hometown in Kentucky, but I was so far removed from that time and those people that it still came as a bit of a shock.

"Well, hello Sophia," I said. "It's nice to meet you."

"Who's a pretty bird?" Sophia asked.

A full-on laugh spilled from me at that because she sounded like such a diva as she asked the question, and without hesitation, I said, "Well, of course, it's you; you're the pretty bird."

Sophia made a contented sound that made me think it was a bird's equivalent of a cat's purr, and the man handed me my receipt.

"Thanks for stopping by!"

"Thank you," I said as I took the receipt and jammed it in my wallet before I grabbed the wine.

My stomach chose that moment to growl so loudly I think it even startled Sophia, and at its prodding, I asked, "Hey, do you guys happen to know of any place where I can get some food? I mean, from a place that might still be open? I just got into town, and there's nothing in the rental where I'm staying. I haven't seen anything open on the island yet other than this place."

The man nodded though I could see some concern written on his face. "Igan Grocery is just across the street. Our two businesses stay open longer than anyone else's because we know how these things go, and I'm sure if we're still open, Roxy hasn't closed up yet."

"Alright, thank you so much."

After saying goodbye to the friendly shopkeepers and Sophia, I sprinted back out to the Jeep and climbed in, already soaked through by the time I got in.

"Well, that's just great," I said, taking in my wet clothes. I ignored how they stuck to my skin, as hard as that was to do, and started looking for the grocery store.

It was right where Chris had said it would be, and I drove over quickly, hoping to be in and out and back to the rental house before the rain really started coming down.

Rushing inside even though I was already dripping, I peeled hair out of my face before I grabbed a basket and headed for the freezer section.

I may have been raised on a dairy farm, but it had been so

long since I'd cooked anything that I didn't even know if I could boil water anymore.

Yeah, Chicago had spoiled me.

Before I'd left him, I would've said it was Cam that had spoiled me, but after everything that had come to light, I wouldn't let myself think that anymore.

I couldn't.

The whole Cam subject was not at all where I wanted my head to be, but as I traveled down the aisle, selecting a few frozen dinners he never would've allowed me to eat, my anger at him and the life I'd lived with him was making me all jerky in my movements.

It was like I was filling my basket with hate-filled spite instead of frozen entrees, and by the time I figured I had enough to last me a few days, I nearly slammed the freezer door, I was so angry.

I whipped around, picturing Cam standing there in a towel at Cassie's door, and ran right into a fucking brick wall of a man, causing my whole basket to tumble from my hands, spilling the contents all across the floor.

~

I saw nothing but chest.

A black t-shirt, stretched over muscles that were obviously hidden underneath, registering in my brain a millisecond later.

Then his eyes captured mine as I looked up.

They were the deepest, brightest blue I'd ever seen in my life, and instantly my lips parted of their own volition.

His hair was dirty blonde and disheveled, toeing that line between looking like it had been done on purpose and like it had been the result of hat hair - and damn if it didn't toe that line perfectly.

His jawline was chiseled but not sharp, and the lips that sat on his face were fucking captivating, the top one just slightly thinner than the bottom.

I was shocked into stunned silence, and I suddenly couldn't think around the man in front of me, almost as if no words could form in my brain, which, for a girl who fancied herself a writer, was saying something.

Slowly, I came back to my senses while the guy backed up a step so he could kneel down.

I had no idea what he was doing at first, but when I saw my frozen meals scattered around our feet, I remembered what had happened and was instantly mortified at how dumb I'd probably just looked.

It set my nerves on edge, knowing my face was flushed, and anger at myself was starting to make my skin buzz.

"Don't worry about it," I snapped, not thinking the words through before they flew out of my mouth as I leaned down to right the basket.

The guy tried to help anyway, throwing cold boxes of premade mac'n'cheese in the basket for me, but his help just felt humiliating for some reason, like I shouldn't have been so scatterbrained and distracted by Cam that I ran into the guy in the first place.

Him helping was just drawing attention to my clumsy ass incident and making it last longer; I didn't want his attention on me for a reason so dumb as that.

I tried not to think about all the reasons I *would* want his attention on me, but they popped in my head anyway without permission.

"It's not a big deal," the guy's voice pulled me up short, my eyes glancing up to his while my body became as stiff as the frozen food that was still in my hands.

Has anyone ever been turned on by someone's voice alone? Like, does that shit happen in real life?

I'd only ever read about it in books, but when that guy spoke, it was like his words just slid over me in the best way possible, setting my already frazzled nerves on fire.

"What?" he asked, snapping me out of my stupor, forcing me to realize I'd probably been staring at him like I was insane.

"What?" My voice came out at him, slashing like a knife. "Maybe if you weren't walking so close, none of this would've happened," I said as I painfully tore my eyes from his and focused my energy back on picking the boxes up.

I have no idea why I was acting that way. I mean, I knew I was really the one at fault, bumping into him first between the tiny aisles, but I just couldn't seem to calm myself down and act like a rational human being.

"Woah," he said as he leaned back, hands raised as if I really did wield a knife. "You crashed into me, not the other way around."

I didn't want to admit how right he was, and as I stood up, picking up the basket as I moved, I glanced down at him one more time.

I'll never get the image of him kneeling before me with his hands up out of my brain; that shit isn't going anywhere.

Ignoring how deeply seeing that man had affected me, and all the crazy-ass emotions that were flooding my system because of him, I didn't say another word before I turned around and stormed off, my cheeks reddening more with every step I took.

I could feel his eyes on my back as I made my way down the aisle, but no matter how much I wished I could curl up in a ball and die, I'd be lying if I said I didn't strut a little as I moved.

When I finally turned the corner, heading anywhere other than the frozen food section, I released a breath I hadn't known I'd been holding.

What was with me all of a sudden?

I'd never acted like that in my life, never once snapped at a stranger… especially a hot as fuck beast of a stranger that was simply trying to help me.

I wandered around, hoping he would leave soon so I wouldn't have to face him again, but I could already hear the rain pounding down on top of the store, and I didn't want to risk not making it back to the rental house safely.

Pulling my shoulders back and lifting my chin in the air on the off chance I'd see him again on my way out, I walked over to the cash register as if nothing had happened.

However, the man was just getting his change back from the cute girl behind the counter when I strolled up.

He glanced back to see me, and I swear I saw his eyes drift down my front, but it was so fast I barely caught it.

"I hope you have a generator," he said to me before he turned back to the cashier. "I'll see you later, Roxy. Don't keep this place open so long you get stuck here."

"I'm closing up right after you guys leave, I swear it, Declan," the girl, Roxy, said with a smile that made it a little too obvious she was into the guy.

'He looks like a Declan,' I'd thought to myself with an attitude.

He didn't seem to care about Roxy's flirty smile though. He smiled back at her all friendly-like, took his bags, and walked over to the doors, where he picked up a motorcycle helmet I assumed he'd stashed there when he'd come in.

'Of fucking course, he drives a motorcycle in a hurricane,' I'd thought as I dropped my basket on the conveyor belt, trying to wrap my mind around what he'd meant about having a generator.

"Will this be all for you?" Roxy asked, pulling all my attention from the blue-eyed biker guy to her.

"Yes, this is it."

Once my focus had shifted, I took in her blonde hair and her nose ring. She had two sleeves of tattoos poking out on her forearms from where the sleeves of her hoodie had been pushed up, and I thought it was odd she was wearing a hoodie at the beach.

It was early August, and even though the wind was making a brisk breeze, it certainly wasn't hoodie weather.

However, when she stepped back to answer the phone when it rang, I saw she had on some shorts with it, and it all made sense to me.

She tucked the phone between her ear and her shoulder so she could continue ringing up my items while she answered.

"Igan Grocery," her voice came out as if she were the picture of professionalism. However, that front disappeared quickly once she knew who was calling.

"Dusty, stop fucking worrying, alright? I've got time to close down and check on Mama before it really gets bad... Yes, I'll call Mya too... Just don't head back down 'til it's passed, okay? I've got this... Uh-huh... Love you too, asswipe."

She hung up right as she got done ringing everything up for me, and I swiped my card while she took the basket I'd been using back over to the stack by the door.

"Sorry about that. My brother went up to see his friend in New York, and he worries, you know?"

I smiled and nodded while I waited for the machine to ask me for my pin when I heard a loud ass motorcycle tear off down the street.

"You ridin' out the storm or headed outta town last minute?"

"I just got here, actually," I said, waiting for the word 'approved' to flash across the screen.

"Oh."

I could see a worried expression fall over Roxy's face as she considered what I'd said.

"No offense or anything, but like... have you ever experienced a hurricane like this one? It's a Category 4."

I'd experienced a couple that had come up and petered out,

back when I lived in Kentucky, but I knew it was nothing like what I was about to face. However, I didn't want the girl to worry… she already seemed like she had enough people to worry about.

"No, but I'll manage, I'm sure."

Roxy stood there, holding my receipt hostage as she looked at me.

It was a little unnerving, to be honest.

"Look," she said as she finally handed me the scrap of paper. "This one could get really ugly, and I don't want to scare you or anything, but most of the locals have evacuated if they could. You need to take this seriously."

I thought she was trying to help, I did, but I also couldn't get past the offense I took to what she'd said, like what was it about me that made it seem like I couldn't handle some heavy wind and rain?

"I don't know what you see in me that makes you think I'm not taking this seriously, but I can assure you, I am."

Roxy looked like she didn't believe me for one second, but rather than try to argue with her when I obviously needed to get back to the rental house, I huffed and grabbed my bags from the counter, planning to head out the door without looking back.

However, her next words softened me a bit before I walked out.

"Just be safe, okay? If you need anything, call the cops or something. I just don't want anyone to get hurt."

I could tell she didn't mean to be offensive at all, in anything she'd said, but it had still rubbed me the wrong way, and as I ran out to the Jeep, I attempted to get my emotions back in check.

When I finally thought it through, I knew I didn't hold Roxy's concern against her, really. If anything, I needed to take her advice and make sure I stayed safe through the hurricane.

So with a renewed sense of worry, I pulled out of the

parking lot and started driving back to the rental house, avoiding the giant pools of water that had already started standing on the road as best I could.

~

I barely made it back to the house.

Okay, maybe that was an exaggeration as well, but fuck if that drive back from the grocery store wasn't scary as hell.

To even think about some biker driving around in that mess on purpose... I'd just hoped he'd made it, that's all I'm saying.

The wind had been whipping that little red Wrangler around like it'd done something to personally piss off the gods, and keeping it between the lines, when for a good part of the drive I couldn't even see any lines, had been nearly impossible.

I'd gone around a curve at one point where I'd had no idea where the road was because a huge ass lake was starting to form right over the road.

I was lucky the Jeep had high ground clearance.

Somehow though, I'd made it back, and as I sat under the safety of the house, I thanked whoever was listening that I was still alive; the drive had scared me that bad.

The house's key didn't have a garage door opener with it, but I knew it would probably be better if I could park the Jeep inside to protect it from the storm.

I might've had my parents' inheritance to lean on money-wise, but nobody wants to pay for damages on a rental.

After pulling myself together, I got out and walked up to one of the garage doors.

Using the only key that came with the rental house, I tried to unlock it, but it didn't turn out to be the same one that worked on the house.

I tried the other door with no success either, eventually

deciding the Jeep would have to stay in the carport area, storm or not.

I got my bags out and, carrying everything I'd bought in one go, I ran up the flight of stairs to the safety of the house.

The fucking power was out when I got there.

None of the lights flipped on, and suddenly Declan's comment about a generator started making a lot more sense.

I had the fleeting thought that there might be a generator in the garage, but there wasn't a door inside that led down to it, and since I couldn't get in there with the key I had, it was an almost useless thought to have.

I was a fucking idiot.

Only buying microwavable food so I wouldn't have to actually cook when a hurricane was coming through?

I definitely should've known better.

No wonder Roxy had seemed so concerned.

I hadn't bought candles or a flashlight or anything.

There was still some light, just enough to see by, coming in through the windows and doors, but I had no idea what time it was or how much time I had left before everything was going to be pitch black when the worst of the storm hit.

I pulled out my phone, hoping I might be able to find somewhere that was still open so I could get some supplies, but I didn't even get a chance to see the time before the thing died in my hand at the worst possible moment.

"Fuck!" I yelled as I barely kept myself from chucking the bitch into a wall.

I'd been ignoring the voicemails and text messages that had continued to come in all day, mad that Cam and Cassie were still blowing my phone up when it should've been painfully apparent that I was avoiding them. I couldn't help but blame all their messages for draining my battery life when I needed it.

I could usually go days without charging it because I hardly used the thing, and since I hadn't even checked my social media accounts on it all day, I knew it had to have died because of them.

I didn't have a car charger; there was no need for one in Chicago since we either walked or took a cab everywhere we needed to go, and I hadn't thought to pick one up while I'd been gone because I'd naively thought I'd have power in the rental house.

I knew the stores I'd already been to were closed by that point, so no matter how desperate things were turning out to be, it was looking more and more like I would just have to ride it out.

Simmering in my own anxiety, I stood there in the middle of the living room, trying to get my head straight so I could think through what my other options were, but it was entirely too quiet.

Even with the wind and the rain that I could hear, the whole house now felt eerily silent.

There was no hum from the refrigerator, no low rumble from the air conditioner, and there certainly weren't the noises I'd grown used to hearing in downtown Chicago at this time of day... whatever time of day it may have been.

I took a steadying breath, but it came out all shaky.

By that point, my nerves were thoroughly shot.

The thought entered my brain that I should get moving to do something, anything to get my mind off everything that was going wrong, so I started putting all my useless, frozen dinners in the freezer, making sure I shut the door to keep them as cool as possible for as long as possible.

Once that was done, and the wine was set out on the counter next to my dad's teacup and my mom's photo album, I remembered I'd plugged in my laptop before I'd left, and a spark of hope lit inside me.

Knowing I could check the time and the weather forecast on it, I ran up the stairs as best I could in the low light. However, when I finally got my laptop open and tried to turn it on, it stayed just as off as my life seemed to be.

The power had been off for a pretty good while if it hadn't even charged the thing enough for it to turn on while I'd been gone.

I slammed it shut, trying to think of anything I could do that would make the swirling ball of panic and uneasiness in my chest go away, but nothing was coming to mind.

I'd left my entire life behind, flown like a thousand miles to get away from it, and technically, I was still supposed to be getting married the next day.

I had a gazillion text messages and voicemails just piling up on my phone, and now I had no way to listen to them until the power got turned back on, whether I could handle what was in them or not.

I was in a house I didn't know, on some island I'd only ever visited once as a kid, all by myself, with no friends, fiancé, husband, or anything.

I'd made a fool of myself in front of some biker guy in a grocery store, and I couldn't understand why the interaction had messed with me so bad, why his face was still stuck in my head.

There was a Category 4 hurricane headed right for me, the power was out, my phone and laptop were both dead as fuck, I hadn't slept any the night before, and I wasn't just tired; I was also fucking starving.

I needed food and sleep and something to drink and a flashlight and…

Gah, I needed so much right then, and it seemed like everything was so messed up, I might not survive whether there was a hurricane coming or not.

It was too much.

I was officially Future Me, and I was definitely having

second thoughts, wondering if everything I'd done that day had been one gigantic mass of mistakes.

The first batch of tears started flooding my eyes as I stood there with my hands on the back of the desk chair.

As they started to fall, a crack of thunder tore through the air so loud it shook the house I was standing in.

It startled the hell out of me, and I looked out the bedroom doors to the screened-in porch, catching an eyeful of dark clouds and raging seas.

However, when I looked closer at the water, I almost couldn't believe what I was seeing.

All the sorrowful thoughts I'd been having fled my mind entirely as I stepped out onto the porch to make sure my eyes weren't seeing things that weren't there.

But as I got to the best vantage point I could get to, there was no mistaking the fact that some dumbass was actually surfing in the waves down below.

"What the actual fuck?" I asked myself as I watched a guy in a wetsuit ride a wave the whole way in like a pro.

I didn't know shit about surfing, but I was pretty sure the guy had a death wish if he was out there surfing in all that.

However, like a train wreck, I just couldn't peel my eyes away from him as he paddled back out through the choppy waves to catch another one.

He was a good football field or so away from me, but even from that distance, I could see he was tall and slender, but still bulky enough muscle-wise to power himself against the current, and it was both disturbing and captivating to watch.

However, after a couple more successful rides, I saw the next swell coming in right as he did, and it made a shiver slide down my back.

The guy didn't seem scared though; he just started paddling like I'd seen him do before, if with a little more gumption than he had on the other waves.

There was no way for me to tell what had gone wrong, but I could feel it all the way up on the deck, that something wasn't right.

Maybe he wasn't paddling fast enough, or maybe the wave crashed before he thought it would... I don't know.

What I did know was that when that huge wave crashed down on the surfer, and he disappeared below the water, I saw two pieces of his board come back up while he didn't.

I waited to see his head pop up out of the water, but after a minute or so, panic seized inside my chest, and without thinking, I found myself running through the house and out onto the beach to see if I could help him.

CHAPTER 7

KALIYAH

$\mathcal{D}$eclan was nuts; there was no doubt about it.

He was also my safest bet until the storm cleared, and I knew it.

I'd been sitting on the couch in the living room when the first window blew in from an insanely large gust of wind, or a piece of debris, or something... I didn't know what caused it.

Fortunately, I'd been covered in a blanket, trying to hide from the storm, so none of the glass ended up penetrating my skin or anything; a few pieces just landed on top of the blanket, and some dispersed across the floor.

Still, it scared the ever-loving fuck out of me, and I couldn't help the scream that ripped through my throat as it shattered, which, I'd found out later, was what had made Declan charge over like some kind of knight to a princess's rescue.

I'd gotten up, being careful not to step on any of the glass, and ran upstairs thinking the bedroom would be safer, but no sooner had I sat on the bed and taken a few calming breaths as surprising as it might be, fucking someone new every week did get old after a while.

Her face was still drifting through my mind as I grabbed the bag of battery-powered candles I'd bought, but I ignored her intrusion as best I could, blaming it on the fact that I hadn't been laid in about a year as I went upstairs to get changed into my wetsuit.

I ignored the new home for my brothers' and my things as I passed them on my way up.

Those dog tags and cuts were blatant reminders of the past I'd left behind, and I certainly didn't need any more reminders since my brothers and the club were always on my mind anyway.

It's why I'd tucked the stuff that was so painful to see up under the countertop of the shop downstairs in the first place... so I wouldn't have that ache in my chest every time I saw them.

A short time later, all but forgetting the woman's face and the old but gaping wounds from my past, I pulled down my favorite board before heading out to the beach right as the good swells were in full swing.

The only times the waves got really big on the island like that was when hurricanes were passing through, and as horrible as it might sound, I've always gotten excited when they've come in because it meant I could ride the bigger waves.

It reminded me of the waves on Oahu, where I'd learned how to surf with my dad and my brothers when I was younger.

Way back before my brothers and I were even born, my dad had helped start the Lost Savages Motorcycle Club in Savannah, Georgia.

But as life goes for knuckleheads, the heat had been getting too close to my dad after a while.

When I was six, the cops or feds or whoever, had something on him specifically, and not really knowing what else to do, my Uncle Lyn had suggested that Dad join the military to get them off his trail, promising to save his seat for him when he came back.

He joined right after that and got stationed down on Oahu for the last four years of his life, which happened to be the best four years of mine because everything was right in the world while he was in the military.

He was home every night and weekend up until he got deployed, there were kids for us to play with on base, and Mom was still Mom... it had been the dream life for a kid my age.

While he'd been home, Dad had taken Gavin, Tristan, and me out early every morning to go surfing at White Plains, and the waves we rode there might as well have been monsters compared to the ones Topsail would get.

However, as I rode one wave after the next, it was almost like every one of the men I'd lost in my life were out there too, surfing those waves right alongside me.

I knew they weren't really there, I wasn't crazy, but whenever I was surfing, it just felt like they were, and I never passed up an opportunity to feel that if I could help it.

The water was warm, but it had a chill to it because of the hurricane, and the waves were making real cones before they crashed up onto the beach. Rain was coming down in sheets, and it was starting to get worse, but I didn't care; I was already wet.

I got a few good rides in, the undertow pulling harder than I'd been used to for some time, but I knew I was strong enough to combat it for at least a little while longer.

So when I saw a beast of a wave coming up from behind me, I smiled and started paddling, pumping my arms as hard as I could to catch it, imagining my dad and brothers were out there egging me on.

However, right as I was about to stand up, I missed my footing and fell forward as the wave broke right over my head.

I felt my board break as I got rolled, the weight and pull of it from my ankle strap suddenly feeling a lot lighter than it had before, but I knew what to do in that situation.

Holding my breath, I didn't fight where the water wanted to move me; there was no way I could've fought against it if I'd wanted to anyway.

I just held my breath and kept my wits about me.

As soon as I felt the undercurrent starting to pull me backward, that's when I started swimming sideways from where the beach was, so I wasn't swimming against the current, but at the same time, I also wasn't letting it pull me out to sea.

It took a while, and my lungs were burning by the time my head finally breached the surface, but it had been such a rush, I was still smiling as I gulped in the air I'd needed.

The current brought me a good hundred yards down the beach from where I'd entered the water in front of the surf shop, so I climbed out holding the half of my board that was still attached to my ankle and started walking back against the force of the wind.

When I finally looked up, my steps faltered as I saw the girl from the grocery store standing there with her feet in the water, holding the other half of my board in her hands as she searched in front of her with a worried expression on her face.

I wondered what she was doing there, where she'd come from, what she'd look like when she smiled... all kinds of things I had no business questioning, in quick succession as I got closer to her.

However, it didn't take her long to notice me.

If looks could kill...

Her long dark hair was matted against her head, neck, and shoulders from all the rain, and her clothes were soaked through completely, clinging to her short, tight frame in mouthwatering ways I couldn't help but pay attention to.

But it was her face that really caught my eye again as it switched from one of concerned worry to disbelief and anger.

I hadn't gotten ten feet from her before she started yelling, and I couldn't really tell if she was shouting so I could hear her or just because she was so mad.

"You again? Of course, it would be you. Who the fuck else drives motorcycles and surfs in hurricanes?"

Smiling from the adrenaline pumping through my veins and the look on her face, I said, "It's fun. You should give it a try someday."

But she did not see my humor.

"Try it? I don't have a death wish like you, thank you very much. Here's your dumbass board you broke," she said as she shoved the board toward me. "You know, it might still be whole if you weren't out here during a hurricane! I mean, the stupidity!"

The woman was adorable when she yelled like that, rain falling in her face and dripping off her chin.

I couldn't keep my smile from widening as I said, "You know you're out in a hurricane too, right? Yellin' at a stranger who's been nothin' but nice to you?"

The look she gave me was fucking hilarious as I called her on her bullshit, and I saw when her hands turned to fists at her sides.

"You be safe now," I said with a grin before I turned to head back up to the surf shop, leaving her to stand and fume behind me.

I would've given anything to watch her stomp back up to whichever rental house she'd come from, but I didn't want to lose the mic drop moment I'd just had because it felt too good, so I kept my face forward and kept walking.

However, a few seconds later, I did catch sight of her as she ran past me to climb the stairs to ol' man Stevens' rental, huffing the whole way.

'So she's the chick Nash was talking about earlier,' I thought as she disappeared from view and I made it back up to the shop.

'Looks like this could get pretty interesting.'

∽

hank fuck I still had enough hot water to shower even though the power was out.

I might've loved to surf, but I hated having sand in places it shouldn't be, and when you live at the beach, that problem becomes a constant nuisance.

I showered quickly by the light of the battery-powered candles I'd posted up on the sink and got dressed by the same light a short time later.

Single life on the run could get pretty dull, especially when there was no one around to distract me and no power to allow tv or the internet to pass the time.

Despite that though, I'd always considered myself reasonably resourceful, so a short time later, I was sitting on my screened-in back porch with a beer in hand, watching the force of the hurricane as it fully made its appearance.

The rain was coming in through the screens, but if I stayed in the middle of the porch, I could stay dry and watch the storm without getting wet again.

Some people may not like them, but I'd always loved watching thunderstorms, no matter how intense they got.

There was just something about them - the world purging its anger on everything that crossed its path - that spoke to my soul on some level I couldn't rationalize.

While it was raging, I was calming; watching them had always had that effect on me.

My mind wandered as I watched it, drifting like seafoam on a wave, riding the current wherever it saw fit to carry me.

The woman from next door glided to the forefront of my thoughts, and for a moment, I allowed myself to imagine what she'd do if I saw her again.

Would she yell at me for something else? Or would I happen to catch a smile on that face?

What if I caught her in a moment of happiness?

Or pleasure?

What if I could be the source of both her happiness and her pleasure?

Immediately, I sat up straight from where I'd been lounging back, scrubbing a rough hand down my face.

There was no way I needed to let those thoughts grab ahold of me.

She was a tourist, and I was on the run, living in hiding, and no part of that equated to something even remotely sustainable.

Not that I was looking for a relationship anyway, but even if I were, it definitely couldn't be with her, no matter how appealing she was to me.

The shocking sound of glass shattering and a high-pitched scream from the Stevens rental slapped me right out of my daydreaming madness, and instantly, I was on my feet, grabbing my piece without a second thought as I rushed down the steps from my apartment.

I had no way of knowing what had broken or what had caused whatever it was to break, but judging by that scream, the woman was in trouble, and I wasn't just gonna sit around and hope she was okay. That just wasn't the kind of man I was.

I ran up to her door and banged on it, but no one answered, and I had a moment where I wasn't sure what my best option was.

Even so, when I heard more glass shatter and a scream sound from her a second time, I didn't care about societal niceties anymore and tried to turn the doorknob, growling internally at the fact that it wasn't locked.

I pushed through the door, pistol in hand, and started clearing rooms one by one like I'd been trained to do.

It was dark as fuck inside the house, but I could make out

just enough to move around the space without too much difficulty.

The living room and kitchen were clear, and so was the first-floor patio out back.

Turning on my heel, I started making my way up the carpeted stairs when whimpering sounds of muffled crying reached my ears.

I'd heard plenty of crying in my life, but it had never affected me like her tears did.

The sound gripped my soul like someone was squeezing my heart inside my body, but I kept moving anyway, unable to comprehend why I hated the sound of that particular woman crying so much.

Slowly, I moved into the bedroom I thought she was in, but as soon as I walked inside, another blood-curdling scream tore through her throat when she saw me.

It didn't take me long to realize there was no one else in the room causing her harm, and I lowered my gun when I realized I was what had scared her that last time.

She was sitting on the floor in the corner of the bedroom, knees tucked up to her chest as she stared at me like I was the crazy one.

"What the hell are you doing here? And with a gun, too? Get out!"

She must have found her nerve once she knew I wasn't gonna shoot her because she stood up, that same anger from earlier, slapped right back in place on her face despite her drying tears.

"I heard glass breaking and a scream, so I came over to make sure you were okay," I said, though my voice came out a bit gravellier than it usually sounded, probably because of the adrenaline.

"Well, yeah, the fucking window in the living room blew in,

and it scared the hell outta me! Then the one in the bathroom up here did the same thing."

I could tell she didn't know whether to be relieved or angry at me, and the fact that she even questioned it to begin with did something to me.

"Ol' man Stevens, the guy that owns this place," I started as her eyes kept sliding between me and my hand where I held the gun, "He hasn't storm proofed this house in at least the last two years I've been here. I'm not surprised the wind finally took out some of the windows."

Seeming to catch on to the dangerousness of that failure immediately, she asked, "Is that even legal? Like shouldn't he *have* to stormproof it if he's renting it out?"

I just shrugged because I didn't know the answer to her question, and without asking, I turned around and walked across the hall to the bathroom to see the damage.

Sure enough, there was glass everywhere, and rain was pouring in from outside, landing in the tub and splashing everywhere.

"What are you doing?" the woman asked, but I ignored her as I walked back downstairs carefully in the darkness.

I knew she was following me, and as I saw the same kind of damage downstairs in the living room that I'd found in the bathroom upstairs, I didn't even stop to look at her before I said, "Get your stuff together. You're staying with me until the storm is over and we can get this cleaned up."

Some part of me wondered why the living room window being shattered hadn't registered in my mind when I'd gone through there earlier, but I dismissed the thought soon after because the woman was just standing there, not grabbing her stuff like I'd wanted her to.

When she didn't move or answer me, I turned my head to look at her.

I couldn't judge how she felt because I couldn't really see her face in the low light.

"Go," I ordered. "The storm is only going to get worse, and I'm not cleaning up your stubborn dead body tomorrow when it's supposed to be my day off."

I knew I was being an ass, that I could've asked her nicer than that, but the seriousness of the situation made it clear to me that I couldn't leave her with any other options. There was no way she could stay in that house safely when the worst of the storm hadn't even hit yet, and already windows were being blown out.

Honestly, I wouldn't have been surprised if I woke up the next day to find the place wholly destroyed and missing a roof by the lack of care put into it by Stevens.

To the woman's credit, and to the detriment of my last nerve, she didn't move a muscle, other than to clench her fists again - a movement I was only able to catch because a flash of lightning lit up the room for a split second.

However, I wasn't about to take 'no' for an answer.

"I will drag you from this place if I have to. Don't test me," I said after I turned to face her fully.

Again, I knew I probably should've been gentler with her, but I was desperate to get her out of there, and my ability to placate her feelings had disappeared entirely, if it'd ever even existed in the first place.

"Why the hell would I go with you, huh? You're not exactly safe either. I mean, you're reckless, and fuck, you just barged in here and pointed a gun at me! So thanks, but no thanks. Now, get out! I'll be fine."

My anger was thoroughly piqued at that, and I stepped up to her.

"I was sweeping the house because I thought there was someone in here hurting you. I wasn't pointing this thing at you. But you know what?" I grabbed her wrist and put my piece in her hand.

"Here," I said. "Now you've got all the power. Just get your stuff so we can get the fuck out of here."

If she'd thought I was crazy before, it was nothing compared to the look she gave me after I put the gun in her hand... like utter confusion and surprise mixed with a hint of something deeper.

In what almost looked like muscle memory to her, she took those stormy eyes off of mine and checked to see if the gun was loaded perfectly, as if she'd been doing it her whole life, before she dropped her hands to her sides, pistol in hand as she leveled me with a glare.

In my shock at having misjudged her slightly, I sighed, harnessing whatever niceness I could in that moment as I said, "I've got food that isn't frozen."

She might've huffed as she turned around without saying a word, but I caught the grin she couldn't hide completely, and I breathed out all the relief I felt as she started grabbing things off the counter in the kitchen.

I did it quietly so she wouldn't hear it - not that she really could've heard it anyway, given the fact that the wind and rain were so loud in the house from the broken windows.

Gun still in hand, she thrust a teacup and a thick book of some kind into my chest, and I took them as she said, "I'm going to grab the rest of my stuff. These matter more than my life, so don't drop them."

"I doubt that," I said as I nodded that I wouldn't let anything happen to her stuff, but I don't think she saw it before she headed back up the stairs.

A few agonizingly long minutes later, she finally came back down with two duffels in one hand, a backpack looking thing slung over her shoulder, and my gun in her other hand.

Sighing again, I took the duffels from her, ignoring her when she tried to protest.

"Just keep up," I said as I turned and started running out of her rental house, down the stairs, across the small lawn between our residences, and then into the street side door to my apartment.

I climbed the staircase, and when I knew she'd made it through the door behind me, I said over my shoulder, "Lock that door before you come up."

I heard a low growl escape her as I crested the stairs, but all that did was make a smile form on my face.

Dropping her bags beside my couch, I thought, 'I knew this was gonna get interesting.'

CHAPTER 7

KALIYAH

*D*eclan was nuts; there was no doubt about it.

He was also my safest bet until the storm cleared, and I knew it.

I'd been sitting on the couch in the living room when the first window blew in from an insanely large gust of wind, or a piece of debris, or something... I didn't know what caused it.

Fortunately, I'd been covered in a blanket, trying to hide from the storm, so none of the glass ended up penetrating my skin or anything; a few pieces just landed on top of the blanket, and some dispersed across the floor.

Still, it scared the ever-loving fuck out of me, and I couldn't help the scream that ripped through my throat as it shattered, which, I'd found out later, was what had made Declan charge over like some kind of knight to a princess's rescue.

I'd gotten up, being careful not to step on any of the glass, and ran upstairs thinking the bedroom would be safer, but no sooner had I sat on the bed and taken a few calming breaths than the window in the bathroom across the hall shattered too, sending me scrambling to the corner of the floor in fear.

'Fuck my life,' I'd thought as tears finally busted free from my eyes, and I sobbed into my knees.

So many things had gone wrong since I'd left Chicago, and though I'd had a few moments of peace while I'd traveled, they'd been stomped on and broken apart by almost everything else that had happened since I'd arrived on Topsail.

Then Declan had shown up, creeping through the house like a ghost.

I hadn't seen or heard him at all until a flash of lightning lit up the room, and there he was, appearing out of nowhere with a gun raised in front of him.

He was absolutely terrifying in that moment, his whole body readied for battle by the looks of him.

However, once I'd known he wasn't there to murder me in my sleep, my fear slid to a back burner in my mind as a seething kind of anger took its place at the forefront, and I directed every bit of it toward him.

He didn't let the harshness of my tongue affect him though; he just explained why he'd come over, all nonchalantly as if I should've expected him to do such a thing.

When we were downstairs, and he'd ordered me to get my stuff and stay with him, I'd had a whole moment standing there where I didn't know whether to slap the taste out of his mouth or to just do as he said.

My entire relationship with Cam flashed through my mind instantly - especially the parts where he would order me around regularly for nothing other than his own amusement, and those times when he wouldn't consider how I felt about anything before he'd make decisions for the both of us.

I don't know when the change happened exactly, but I wasn't willing to be bossed around by anyone anymore.

It was a new thing for me, a new mindset... and it seemed fragile and delicate, like I was only holding onto it by a thread.

I'd had it for less than twenty-four hours, and already it seemed like I'd let one controlling person go, only to have another one thrown right at me.

I'd called Declan out after thinking that, highlighting the fact that he was reckless and that he'd pointed a gun at me, feeling some kind of empowerment simply because I was standing up for myself for the first time in what felt like forever.

However, when he got right up next to me and spoke, telling me he wasn't pointing the gun at me, but was instead coming to make sure I was okay, my brain short-circuited and I didn't know what to do.

Cam's orders had never been for my own protection or safety; they'd been for his benefit, always.

Yet, as Declan stood before me, unwavering in what he was demanding, something about his commands had an entirely different effect on me than Cam's ever had.

There'd been a shot of sensations straight to my girly parts at his intensity, from the way he looked at me while he spoke, and it took everything in me to hide the surprise and arousal I felt from showing on my face.

When he'd put the gun in my hand, it was like I just couldn't pin him down.

I didn't understand the man standing before me; I'd obviously never met someone like him. I was thoroughly intrigued, but I wouldn't admit it.

On instinct, I'd checked the gun, just like my dad had taught me.

When I saw it was loaded with one round in the chamber and looked back up, Declan's eyebrows shot up as if he hadn't expected me to know how to handle a weapon like that.

I didn't want to think about how much I liked the fact that I'd impressed him, but as the words, "I've got food that isn't frozen," flowed from his mouth, all my anger and confusion disappeared in an instant.

I could hardly fight the laughter that wanted to bubble up from inside me, but I didn't want him to see that reaction because I wanted to hold on to my anger.

I turned around quickly, hoping he didn't notice the change in me.

After gathering all my stuff together, I followed him over to the surf shop next door but kept my eye on him the whole time, just in case he did turn out to be the psycho I'd first pegged him to be.

We didn't go in through the front door like I'd thought we would because it was covered with a big storm shutter.

We went through this other door beside the front entrance, and as soon as I ran in, drenched in rainwater, I saw a staircase leading up to the second floor.

I closed the door and locked it behind me when he told me to. Even though I was following his orders, I really did feel like I had all the power because I still had his gun in my hand.

I also had no intention of letting it go until I was sure I was safe with him.

The stairs were all wood from what I could see, lit by electric candles that were sitting at both the bottom and the top, creating a warm glow to see by.

Once I walked into his apartment, I had to admit, I didn't expect him to have his space so well set up. Call me crazy, but the impression I'd had of him since our collision at the grocery store hadn't painted him in the same light as his apartment did.

There were those same electric candles set up everywhere, almost as if he'd done everything in his power to ensure there were no dark corners anywhere.

The beach/surfer themed furniture and decor fit the place perfectly, and I had a sneaking suspicion he hadn't done it all himself.

All the windows were covered by the shutters, but he hadn't covered the sliding glass door that led out to his screened-in back porch, as if he couldn't keep himself from watching the storm as it passed.

"You can drop your stuff here. I'm Declan, by the way."

Again, the smooth sound of his voice pulled me up short, and as I walked over to him slowly while I processed it, his eyes held mine captive.

"I'm Kaliyah," I said, reaching out my hand to his.

He hesitated briefly before he stuck out his hand to shake mine, and I couldn't help but think he was just as caught up in me as I was in him.

However, as soon as he dropped my hand and stepped around me, heading to the kitchen, I dismissed that wayward thought because I was obviously seeing things that weren't there, overthinking things as usual.

"I might not have the best food in the world, but I can put somethin' together pretty quickly as long as you're not picky," he said as I dropped my bookbag and turned to face him.

"I'd eat anything at this point," I found myself saying, unsure why words continued to spill from my mouth when I was around Declan. "I haven't eaten since yesterday, and by now, I'm pretty sure my stomach thinks my throat's been cut."

His laughter spilled out into the apartment while he pulled things from the refrigerator and set them on the counter.

It was a great laugh if I'm being honest... so light-hearted and welcoming, my feet started bringing me over to the barstools at the island without me telling them to move consciously.

"Well, I can try to fix that."

As I sat on one of the stools, I watched him pull out a small camping stove before hooking it up to a tiny green tank on the island's countertop.

"Why do you have that in your cabinet like you use it every

week?" I laughed a little as he pulled a cast iron skillet from the same cabinet.

He smiled over at me and asked, "You really have no idea how to act during a hurricane, do you?"

I felt my cheeks get hot, and I looked down at the pistol in my hand, shocked to see it was still there.

I'd nearly forgotten all about it.

"Not really, no," I finally said, glancing back up at him.

Declan was seasoning what looked like chicken over by the other counter and spice rack, so I took in his toned form while he wasn't looking.

He had on a different black t-shirt than the one he'd had on when I met him in the grocery store, but the one he was wearing fit him just as well. It clung to his frame, and I had to admit, Cam had nothing on Declan as far as physiques went.

"Where are you from, anyway?" he asked as he continued to work with his back turned toward me.

"I grew up in Kentucky," I started, letting my gaze travel down his backside while I talked. "Went to college in Baltimore, and then moved to Chicago." His jeans were sitting loosely on his hips and had that look about them that screamed, 'I care about how I look, but not really.'

"Now, I'm here."

He turned around, and I had to shoot my eyes back up to his to hide what I'd been doing.

"You plan on staying?"

I thought there was a hopeful tone in his question, but I could've also just been hearing things. Ignoring that thought and wondering why I was so focused on this guy, I answered as best I could.

"I don't know yet. So far, all I know about Topsail, other than what I saw as a kid and what I Googled before coming here, is that hurricanes are scary as fuck."

Again, he laughed as he turned back around to put the meat in the pan.

The storm outside was still raging, but for some reason, I wasn't jumping when lightning struck anymore. Though I knew it probably had something to do with Declan, or maybe even the power I felt by having the pistol in my hands, I didn't want to admit that either he or the gun affected me in any way.

"There's only a few storms a year, and most aren't this bad. Don't hate Topsail just because you booked a trip when a hurricane was coming," he said with a smile before his eyes rose to meet mine again.

I felt stupid under his gaze... like I couldn't make my brain form the right words because I was just so nervous in his presence.

My face was hot, and my hands were sweating. A million words were flowing through my head, but none of them got a chance to fully form before another set was sliding through, bumping the others out of the way.

I ended up just sitting there, not answering him right away.

Which, in turn, made me feel even more embarrassed, and by the time my mouth had finally started to move again, I thought I might have offended him or something.

"It's been booked for about a year. There was no way I could've known." My voice came out sounding all sad and whatnot because I couldn't deny the pain in my chest as a flash of why I'd initially booked the trip skittered through my brain.

"Non-refundable tickets?" he guessed as he focused on making whatever it was he was 'puttin' together.'

I sighed a little before my mouth said too much again.

"Well, no. I'm supposed to be getting married tomorrow, but I found out he was cheating this morning, so I decided to go on with our honeymoon, and the rest of my life, without him."

It was Declan's turn to have his eyes dart up to mine, and as he did, his whole face looked surprised, his eyebrows sliding up under his hair a little while his eyes got bigger.

"Wow," he said, and I fought the blush that wanted to erupt all over my body. "So you're leavin' him at the altar? Sweet."

I did not expect him to say that, nor could I prevent the smile that formed on my face as he said, "Remind me never to piss you off. That's cold-blooded."

I huffed a bitter laugh.

"Him cheating on me with my only friend in the world is what's really cold-blooded. I'm just making the best out of a bad situation."

He smiled to himself before he looked down to finish putting some food on the plate he'd pulled down.

Walking around the island and getting close to me again, he sat the plate in front of me, saying, "Well, I'm glad you're here and you didn't marry him then."

I didn't want to think about why him liking the fact that I was here did something to me, and I couldn't for the life of me understand why I was so caught up on Declan when I'd literally just met him, not to mention all the shit I'd just left back in Chicago.

It was nowhere near the right time for me to be looking for anything with anyone new, but apparently, my body didn't care at all about any of those things.

Like love though, the vagina wants what it wants, to hell with any and everything else that should really be considered.

After handing me a knife and fork as well, he headed back around to start cleaning up what little mess he'd made, and all I could do was compare him to Cam in that moment.

Already, I knew Declan was a different breed, an entirely different person than what I'd been used to with Cam... they could almost be opposites of one another.

Cam had never cooked in the entire time I'd known him, nor would he have ever gone out of his way to help anyone other than himself. He certainly wouldn't have handed me a gun and let me have even a smidgen of power over him.

Yet, Declan had handed it over without blinking, and as I finally looked down at the food he'd made for me, I knew instantly, the boy could cook too.

When I cut off a bite of chicken and put it in my mouth, I nearly moaned at how good it tasted.

Yes, hunger is a great spice, but he'd made a meal that would've cost an outrageous amount of money back in Chicago, and all on a camp stove during a hurricane, no less.

"Do you like card games?" he asked once he was done cleaning up, and my food was nearly gone.

I nodded, but the only thing going through my head was that I would have to be careful with Declan.

He looked like the kind of guy a girl could lose herself in all too quickly, and after everything I'd been through, I had no intention of losing myself to anyone else any time soon... I'd done enough of that shit with Cam.

CHAPTER 8

DECLAN

"Alright, look," I said, laughing as I tried to explain the game of Rat Trap to her again.

Kaliyah, such a pretty name, with such a beautiful laugh, was laughing right along with me as she threatened to throw all her cards in my face.

"The point is to get all the cards."

"I've got that part, thank you," she said, her sass all too enticing.

"Do you want to learn how to play or not?"

We were both smiling as she feigned being offended by my words, but she relented and nodded, so I continued my lesson, rearranging myself under the table as subtly as I could so she wouldn't notice the movement.

"You flip out a card when it's your turn, and what you're lookin' for is a face card."

She rolled her eyes and sat her chin on her hand as she stared up at the ceiling. "Uugghhh," she groaned. "Yeah, yeah,

yeah, I know that too. When I lay a face card down, you have a certain number of chances to lay one down too, or I get every-thing underneath it."

"That's right," I said as I got to the part she was still having difficulty with. "Jacks give one chance; queens, two; kings, three; and aces, four chances for the other person to lay down a face card."

"If those are the rules, then why did you slap the hell outta that last one then, huh?" she asked like she was proving a point.

"Because you can slap on doubles and take everything under them."

"Oh my god, this game... I think you're just making up rules as you go," she said, but she regripped her cards a few seconds later with a determined look on her face like she was ready to go again.

"I promise, I'm not," I laughed as I flipped a jack out.

"Aaahhhhh," she nearly yelled as she realized she only had one chance. "You're cheating, I swear it."

It was adorable as fuck.

"No, there's just more than one jack in a deck, sweetie. Come on, let's see what you got."

Her eyes met mine over the table, and I swear to god my heart started racing at the same time my dick jumped.

The look she was giving me was challenging and sexy, and I couldn't help but match her stare with one of my own.

She flipped out her card, and though I saw it was another jack, I didn't move a muscle while I waited for her to remember the rule I'd just taught her.

When the light bulb clicked on in her head, her eyes got big as she whipped her hand out to slap the double jacks.

I sent my hand out to them too but didn't make it there before she did, and as she dropped all her cards on the table, saying, "Booom! Doubles bitch!" I nearly fell over with laughter.

We played for nearly an hour, and the whole time, she kept surprising me over and over again.

Where she'd been somewhat shy and tight-lipped at first, it seemed like the longer we played, the more comfortable she got with letting more of her personality shine through.

Her looks were already unique and distracting; her bright green eyes sat perfectly above her tiny little nose, and her long brown hair nearly reached her lower back. All that paired with what seemed like a bottomless, untapped well of awesome personality, and my attraction to her flew off the charts, growing with every second that passed.

I had to check myself a few times while we were playing, telling myself not to read too much into it, not to appreciate her good qualities too much because even though she said she didn't know if she was staying on the island, I knew the chances were probably very slim that she would.

When it was getting late and Kaliyah yawned, I stretched, smirking when I saw her checking me out as I moved.

"It's getting late. Let me go grab you a blanket and a pillow for the couch," I said as I stood up.

She got a smartass look on her face and said, "A gentleman would offer to sleep on the couch and give the girl his bed."

I chuckled a little because I could tell she hadn't meant to say that, given how red her face had gotten after she said it, but I could admit she played it off well afterward.

"I'm no gentleman, Kaliyah. Might as well get that out of the way right now," I said as I headed to my room to grab what she needed, smiling as I went.

She was pouting or embarrassed, I couldn't tell which one, when I came back into the living room, but she didn't say anything as she walked over to me.

I dropped the items on the couch for her, and the air in the room got too thick as she approached, the atmosphere instantly turning from flirty and casual to intense and a little awkward.

I didn't know what to say exactly, but at least she seemed to be having the same problem.

Taking a step back as she took a step forward, I watched her slide onto the couch. After some jostling to get the blanket over her, she looked up at me with big eyes.

"I don't want to seem ungrateful. Thank you. You didn't have to do all this, and I really do appreciate it... Even if you are making me sleep on the couch."

Laughing again, I turned my back to her, saying, "Goodnight, Kaliyah," over my shoulder as I walked to my bedroom.

Leaving her out there was hard, and I had no idea why I felt like that, but as I stripped down to my boxers, I chalked it all up to simple happiness about having company.

I never had anyone over other than Nash, or occasionally Dusty, because I didn't usually want anyone getting too close to me. But Kaliyah had been fun to hang out with, so I couldn't hate on myself too much for enjoying the night we'd had, hurricane and broken windows, notwithstanding.

As I laid down, her face kept playing through my thoughts... I felt like a kid who just couldn't fall asleep.

My brain wouldn't stop coming up with reasons for me to go back out there... things like getting a glass of water because I was thirsty, going to empty my bladder because I hadn't before I went to bed, or just outright checking on her to see if she was comfortable.

Eventually though, I really did have to piss, so I got up and walked right past my en-suite half bath to make my way to the living room so I could use the one out there.

She was tucked up in the corner of the couch like a little ball with the blanket wrapped around her, and the only part of her that I could really see was her face.

She'd been staring out the back doors at the storm when I walked out, and as she saw me, a scared look marred her usually soft and happy features. Still, she tried to cover it up quickly as I walked past her.

The image of her sitting in the corner of the bedroom next door with tears running down her cheeks flashed through my mind, and I began to wonder if she was just going through a lot or if she was actually that scared of the storm.

Don't get me wrong, the hurricane was definitely getting worse outside, and there was a genuine need to take it seriously, but I didn't think it warranted the fear I saw in her eyes.

Unless that is, she was already afraid of storms, to begin with.

Tristan had been that way, terrified of even the smallest of thunderstorms, but even so, he'd been one of the toughest men I'd ever had the pleasure of knowing, and I never gave him shit for it.

It was worse when we were little, but it never really went away for him.

I'd seen her jump at the claps of thunder a few times like Tristan would when she first got here, but as the night wore on and I kept distracting her, she'd gotten more comfortable. By the time I'd gone to bed, she hadn't been jumpy at all.

I'd hoped I'd eased her worries enough that she could fall asleep, but I was obviously wrong about that.

Making up my mind, I washed my hands and went back to the living room.

I stood outside my bedroom door and said, "Alright, I guess you can sleep in the bed with me if you want," and added, "But no funny business," with a pointed finger at her a second later.

Her mouth dropped open, but I didn't hang around to see what she decided to do; I just left my door open and climbed into bed, leaving the decision up to her.

Waiting in the darkness, pretending I didn't care whether she joined me or not, was nerve-racking and made sleep impossible, but I stayed there, unmoving regardless.

I desperately wanted her in my bed, and not just for the things I wanted to do to her sexually. It shocked the hell out of me to realize how badly I wanted to stay close to her.

I knew I'd really just met her, and that she was a tourist, and all the other factors that should've kept her on the couch, but I also couldn't care about any of that as I laid there, hoping she'd slide into the bed with me.

She'd blown in with the hurricane and hit me just as hard as one, her presence already seeping into my system, and as I heard stirrings of movement from the living room after a particularly loud crash of thunder, a smile spread over my face.

~

"*J*'m laying down with you because this hurricane is freaking me the hell out, but I still have your gun, and I'm not afraid to use it."

I was lying with my back to where she stood on the other side of the bed, but at that, I leaned my head back to look at her out of the corner of my eye.

"Oh, I don't doubt that," I said as she set my pistol on the nightstand, looking just as nervous as I felt before she peeled the covers back and hesitantly climbed into bed with me.

Turning my head back, so I wasn't facing her at all, I said, "My younger brother used to be scared of storms too. I'm not judgin'."

I barely heard her tiny gasp over the sound of the wind and rain outside, and I felt when her head turned to look at me, but I kept facing away from her, offering her the space she seemed to need while also trying to put her mind at ease.

"How'd you know?" Her voice was low, almost as if she wasn't sure she wanted me to hear her question or not.

"Your face. And the way you jumped at every crash of thunder when you first got here."

She sighed and pulled the blanket up higher, making it fall onto my neck, but I didn't mind.

"I'm sorry. I'll be still, I promise," she said, confusion and concern washing over me instantly.

Slowly, I rolled over onto my back, so I could look at her.

"Why would you apologize for being scared? I don't mind you being jumpy; like I said, my brother used to do it all the time. I kind of miss it, actually."

She looked at me in the low light offered by the single electric candle I'd placed on my dresser, and the surprise she felt at my words was unmistakable; so was the embarrassment that flooded her face not three seconds later.

Sighing again, she admitted, "My ex, Cam... he gets really mad when storms freak me out, makes me go lay on the couch if I can't be still. I guess I'm just used to that kind of response now."

There were a million things I wanted to say right then about how shitty a person had to be to act like that, but I kept my mouth shut as I forced that anger down and focused on what Kaliyah needed.

Gently, I turned to face her and slid my hand under her pillow, stopping when I got close to her, just in case she wanted to tell me to stop.

Her mouth was parted, and I could still see the fear in her eyes, but I could also see the relief in them too, as she nodded and rolled over, allowing my hand to slide under her head.

I only hesitated for a second before I slid in behind her the rest of the way and lightly wrapped my arm around her middle.

She didn't pull away, nor did she reach for the gun, so I figured I was in the clear to hold her.

However, her hand did land on my forearm, sending sparks of electricity through me as a smile played at my lips.

Her hair was all kinds of in my face, but she smelled so good, like fresh rain and flower shampoo, that it was all I could do to keep myself from sending my nose to her neck to breathe her in.

Instead, I relaxed around her, feeling her relax into me as well, and before I knew it, I was fast asleep, holding the very girl that danced through my dreams that night.

When I woke up the next morning, we were still in nearly the same position we'd fallen asleep in; the only difference was that Kaliyah was on her back in my arms, her eyes closed with her face turned toward me.

The storm had obviously passed at some point during the night, since early morning sunlight was streaming in as it rose above the ocean, through my back porch, and into my bedroom, where it landed squarely on each of us.

'Ah, fuck,' I thought.

No matter how tough I was on the outside, and despite all the messed-up shit I'd done in my life, I fucking knew I was a closeted and hopeless romantic... I couldn't help it, and as I stared at Kaliyah's sleeping face beside me, I knew I was in trouble.

'This girl is gonna fuck my world up, and I'm gonna enjoy every second of it.'

CHAPTER 9

KALIYAH

I woke up because Declan was trying to get out of the bed without disturbing me, but all his thoughtfulness did was pique my subconscious mind, making me think Cam was trying to sneak out.

It probably took me a solid minute to remember everything that had happened, but once reality sank in as I watched Declan creep into the attached bathroom and close the door, a new and nervous set of feelings settled over me.

There was quite a bit of relief from the fact that the storm had passed, but there was also embarrassment from how weak I'd probably seemed to Declan the night before.

Panic over all the life-changing decisions I'd made was driving a steady current of anxiety beneath everything else I was feeling, but outshining even that was a sense of contentedness.

Yes, this was supposed to be my wedding day, and no, I didn't have a plan, but as I got up and made my way to look out the back doors, I didn't doubt my ability to come up with one, so long as I thought everything through carefully.

The screen on Declan's back porch was ripped and torn in a few places, and the two chairs he'd had out there were tipped over, having slid all the way over to the edge of the porch during the night.

Otherwise though, the space looked like it'd survived the storm alright.

However, as I stepped outside to have a better look at everything, my mouth dropped open when I saw all the damage that had been done within my line of sight.

The dunes were just... gone, completely, and there was virtually no beach left to speak of.

Where the dunes had been so high the day before, sitting tall and proud right up against the edges of all the houses, protecting them, they were now nowhere to be seen, as if they'd never existed in the first place.

Smooth Rides Surf Shop had sported a back deck, a walkway over the dunes, and a staircase down to the beach on the other side when I'd looked at pictures of the place online.

However, in the wake of the hurricane, the staircase had been ripped clean off the walkway's end, and the walkway itself was in three separate sections, each inaccessible from the rest.

Waves were coming up dangerously close to Declan's building, nearly reaching the stilts directly below me since there were no more dunes to hold them back at what looked like high tide.

Splintered and broken wood littered the waterline as far as the eye could see both ways down the beach, and debris was strewn about everywhere, but it was the house next door that really captured my attention.

The first thing I noticed on the rental house I'd been staying in was the jagged and shredded back patio that I'd stood in front of, literally hours before. Broken pieces of decking were sticking out this way and that, as if the water had pushed up the floorboards, nails and all, without even trying.

The next thing I saw was that pieces of the siding were missing.

All the windows I could see from Declan's back porch were broken too, and as I took in the entirety of the rental house, I noticed that the whole damned thing was leaning haphazardly toward the road at an angle, looking like it could fall apart with the faintest gust of wind.

My eyes trailed down below, settling on the sand-filled carport, driveway, and road that were painfully explaining where all the sand from the dunes had gone.

The little red Wrangler was sitting there in at least two feet of sand, and had been slammed into the stilt at the corner of the front of the house, breaking the stilt and causing the house to lean precariously to that side.

Immediately, thoughts of calling the rental car agency, insurance claims, and money flying from my pockets assaulted me, but I took a deep breath and tried to recenter myself because I did have the security of insurance to help me.

Still, my brain couldn't comprehend the level of damage I was seeing for a moment because it just didn't match up with the night I'd spent at Declan's.

As I stood there in disbelief, I couldn't understand how all of that had happened while I'd been eating, playing cards, and sleeping soundly through the night. It didn't make sense.

When Declan joined me shortly after that, his calm threw me even more.

"Are you okay?" I asked timidly, not knowing him well enough, or at all really, to know how he was going to react to everything.

He nodded as his eyes assessed what he could see, but he didn't say anything.

His jaw was set tightly, and his thumbs were hooked in the waistband of his boxers.

I got the distinct impression that he was very upset even though he wasn't showing it on the outside, so I prodded again, asking, "Do you need a minute? I can go make coffee on that camp stove thing or something." But rather than answering my questions, he just shook his head and walked to the other side of the porch to see the damage that had been done over there.

"Aren't you upset? Or worried? You could tell me if you were."

Still, his mouth stayed shut.

"I mean, why aren't you freaking out right now? There's so much damage everywhere!" My tongue got the better of me because his calm and accepting silence was driving me insane.

Finally looking at me for the first time that morning, he smiled and said, "From what I can tell, the damage isn't that bad. I still have to go out and check everything I can't see from here, but so far, so good."

"What the hell do you mean, 'so far, so good?' The rental I was staying in," I said as I gestured with my hand to indicate the house next door, "is about to fall the fuck over!"

His bright blue eyes glanced over to the house in question, then back to me.

"Yeah, but no one was in it when the foundation shifted, and no one is in it now, so all that's left is the cleanup. I'm sure Stevens will send out a crew to assess it for damages and fix it as soon as the island opens back up."

My thoughts stumbled through what he'd said, trying to pick out the parts that threw me for a loop, but it seemed like everything he'd said, plus the way he'd said it all casually as if it were just another Sunday morning, was enough to make my head spin.

"How are you so calm about this? No, no one was in there,

but the thing is fucked up, and most importantly, what do you mean by, 'as soon as the island opens back up?'"

His smile was soft, and the look on his face was understanding, while I felt like I might burst out of my skin from all the anxiety coursing through me.

"Come on, I already have a pot of coffee brewing. It should be done by now," he said as he walked past me to go into the house.

I had no other choice than to follow him.

"To answer your questions," he said as he started pulling out mugs from his cabinet, "I'm calm because I need to be; it's the only way *to* be when shit hits the fan."

Pouring the steaming liquid into the mugs in front of him, he added, "I can see the damage that was done, but honestly, I've seen worse... far worse."

Declan handed one of the coffees over to me.

"If I were gonna freak out about every piece of wood or siding that needs to be replaced, then I definitely chose the wrong place to live, and I should hightail it outta here ASAP.

Hell, I might as well not even go back outside because I'm sure almost everything got damaged, at least to some degree, during that storm.

But to me, the most important things in this situation aren't things; they're the people that were here when it hit and who have to live through the cleanup.

Making sure everyone is safe is my first priority because things can be replaced, but people can't.

Also, I've just never been one to worry unless I knew I needed to.

I have people I need to check on today, but I helped all of them prep for the storm before it got here, so I'm already pretty sure they're okay, and there's no real need to worry."

I was torn between rolling my eyes or nodding my head in embarrassment.

Rolling my eyes because, of course, I knew the lives of the people here were the most important thing, and nodding in embarrassment because checking on those people hadn't been the first thing I'd thought of.

Instead of either reaction though, I chose to blow on my coffee, which was hot enough to burn my face off, and let Declan continue to explain things as he took the percolator off the camping stove, setting it on one of the cold burners while he pulled out the cast iron again.

"I checked the news on my phone when I got up and heard they've closed the roads on and off the island to anyone but emergency personnel. It happens sometimes, but they only do it when it's necessary."

"What kinds of things would make that necessary?" I asked as I watched him cut into a package of bacon.

"Well, if it's anything like the last one where they closed the roads off, it's because of downed power lines and parts of the road that are too covered in sand for people to drive through. Other parts might have water too deep to drive through too. But last time, it only took like two days or so for the water to go away, I think. I'm not sure though.

For the sand, like what we have here covering the road, that will probably take a bit longer."

Rather than freak out like I wanted to, I tried to stay calm despite what I was hearing.

I'd paid for two weeks on the island, so I was going to be here for that long, sand in the roads or not, but this new development put a damper on things, for sure.

This wasn't the picturesque vacation I'd planned, and though I was upset, I also knew there was nothing I could do about it.

So with that in mind, I shifted my focus from all the stuff I usually would've freaked out about and ate the awesome breakfast Declan made, trying not to worry about the things I couldn't change since I didn't have any other choice anyway.

⌒

*D*eclan practically inhaled his food as soon as it hit his plate, standing on the other side of the kitchen island, leaning one hip against it, while he shoved huge bites of bacon and hash browns into his mouth.

He wasn't a messy eater or anything, just fast, like he was in a hurry.

"I need to get ready and go check on some people. You're more than welcome to come with me if you want," he said after he'd eaten and cleaned up after himself.

Meeting new people, especially right after a hurricane had hit that might have severely impacted their lives, was not at the top of my priority list by any means.

But there was something about the way he'd asked me, almost like he was afraid I'd tell him 'no,' that made the introverted side of me shut the hell up, and I found myself telling him I'd be happy to go along with him and help if I could.

It wasn't a decision I would typically make, but by that point, none of the decisions I was making fit with who I'd been when I was with Cam, so I decided to just go with whatever felt right and see what happened.

He'd smiled at my answer and left me to finish eating while he went to shower and change, but he did that way too fast too.

No sooner had I finished my meal and washed my plate than he was walking out of the bathroom in a black towel, water droplets clinging to his tat-covered skin as he made his way into his room to get dressed.

I shifted my gaze to the floor quickly, berating myself for devouring him with my eyes on what should've been my wedding day to another man, but snapped them right back up to Declan as he stuck his head out his bedroom door.

"Shower's free," he said. "It's cold because there's no hot water, but you're free to use it if you need to."

"Okay, yeah. That'd be great, thank you."

"There's towels under the sink."

"Alright," I said, fighting the smile that crept onto my face as he started to close his door.

Opening it back up quickly, he said, "Oh, and you can just leave your dirty clothes in there until the power gets turned back on; I'll wash 'em."

"You really don't need to do all that," I said, but he answered me with a look that said I shouldn't fight him on what he was offering, shutting the door between us without a word.

Sighing, I grabbed my hygiene bag and the clothes I was going to need. In no time at all, I was showered, dressed, and my hair had been towel dried to the best of my ability.

I wasn't about to put on makeup since I had no idea what we would be seeing when we left.

Given all the destruction I'd seen that morning and the fact that my emotional state was already balancing on a tightrope, I knew myself well enough to know that if I saw anything that pulled at my heartstrings, tears would probably follow soon thereafter. I didn't want to have mascara streaks running down my face all day.

I looked about as good as I was going to get with no power to help me out, and when I finally came out of the bathroom, Declan was sitting on a barstool waiting for me.

"Hey, do you have anything you need to charge? My phone just died, so I'm plugging it into my solar charger while we're gone. I can connect more than one thing to it, so I thought I'd ask."

"Yes, actually," I said as I walked over to my bag again to pull out my phone and its wall charger.

I had to fight off the fear of the messages and voicemails that I knew were waiting for me whenever I eventually turned the thing back on. Still, I shoved that worry down deep because I knew I needed my phone to call my insurance company about the Jeep, whether there were messages on it or not.

Declan plugged it in and walked over to a door I hadn't been through yet.

"You ready?" he asked as he unlocked the chain lock on the back of the door and opened it, revealing another staircase beyond it.

"Yeah."

He gestured for me to go down the steps in front of him so he could lock his apartment behind him, and we both headed down into the surf shop I'd seen online.

When I got to the bottom of the stairs, a sudden thought struck me, and I asked, "If there's sand covering the road, how are we going to go check on your friends? Are we walking?"

Declan smirked. "You'll see."

I didn't read too much into that because I was still hung up on that smirk of his, but when I followed him through another door and down another flight of stairs into his two-car garage, Declan's smirk wasn't the only thing occupying my mind.

Big boy toys of all shapes and sizes were placed meticulously throughout the space.

A black, full-size Chevy truck was sitting on one side of the garage, sporting tires with tread as deep as my finger.

Two sick looking Harley Davidson motorcycles were perched up on weird-looking jack stands of some kind, and a jet ski was parked on its trailer beside the truck.

There was a four-wheeler that had four short white PVC pipes attached to the back of it in a row, and in each of them sat a fishing pole, reaching up to the sky, already hooked and ready to go at a moment's notice.

Over on one wall were a workbench and shelves, a giant toolbox, and enough power tools to satisfy even the handiest of handymen.

"Luckily, no water got in here, but when I move all these

sandbags and we open that garage door, sand from outside is gonna pour in. It happened the same way last time. I'm gonna have to shovel it out before we can leave so I can shut the door while we're gone, but it shouldn't take me too long," Declan said as my eyes finally found him again after my perusal of all the 'rides' he had out there.

It took me a second to wrap my mind around what he'd said, but everything became crystal clear as I finally saw all the sand-bags he was talking about.

He'd stacked them up against each of the garage doors to keep the water out, and judging by how dry the floor was, the tactic had worked pretty well.

However, I couldn't just stand there and watch him move all of them by himself, so when he started picking them up, carrying them to the backside of the garage, I followed suit and helped as best I could.

I may have only been able to lift one bag at a time while he carried at least three most trips, but pretty soon, we had them all moved, and I was only sweating a little bit.

"Alright, the moment of truth," he said as he walked over to press the button by the door, and I stood back, trying to catch my breath as the door lifted.

Sand, and I mean by the metric fuck-ton, stretched as far as I could see outside, and every bit of it that had been piled against the door fell inside instantly.

"Holy shit," I couldn't stop myself from saying.

I'd never seen anything like it... well, that's not true; it reminded me a lot of how snow acts in the winter up north, but in all my time on this earth, I'd never imagined sand could act the same way.

The sand was still wet and fell into the garage in little chunks, so at least it wasn't powdery and loose, but that also meant it was a hell of a lot heavier than it would've been if it were dry.

It took us a while, but eventually, we cleared a path for the garage door to shut behind us when we left, and by the time we were done, I was hot and sweaty all over, already longing for a nice, long nap, but those thoughts had to wait since Declan had places to go, and I wanted to go with him.

"We're takin' the four-wheeler. You ever been on one before?" he asked as he walked over to it and climbed on, eyeing me the whole time.

"No," I answered. "Don't you want to take the fishing poles out of it before we leave though?"

Declan looked confused before he asked, "Now, why would I do that? They're what we're gonna use to get lunch."

His smile was infectious, and despite the nervousness I felt and the surprise of deducing the fact that we were going to be fishing while we were out, I found myself smiling back at him as I climbed on behind him.

My hands found the bars beside me and grasped them tightly as Declan slowly drove the machine out of the garage and up the little two-foot-tall wall of sand outside. He pulled to a stop once we were fully out in the sun's rays, pressing a button on a remote I hadn't seen before, making the garage door shut behind us.

When it closed completely, he tucked the remote back in the little compartment in front of him and said, "You can hold onto those bars if you want, but you might end up falling off."

"Then what should I hold onto?" I asked as fear started to grip me.

Declan laughed but didn't ask for permission before he reached back and gently guided my hands to encircle his waist.

The feel of him between my legs and in my arms was doing some crazy things to my insides and girly parts, but all of that was nearly forgotten as the next words he spoke registered in my mind.

"Hold on tight; this ride might get a little squirrelly."

⁓

I was a melting pot of emotions, torn between the exhilaration I felt from riding on a four-wheeler for the first time and heartbreak at the damage I was seeing everywhere I looked.

Part of me wanted to laugh with joy at the wind flowing through my hair and how fun it was to ride over the compacted sand, while another part of me entirely was cringing hard at what we were riding past.

The second-row homes weren't nearly as badly damaged, but they'd still taken their fair share of the storm; there was no doubt about it.

One house on that row even had its deck collapse completely, but as I looked to the left, I realized it was because there were no houses on the beach side to block it from taking the full impact of the storm.

We were on the part of the island where the beach was on our left and houses were on our right, and I was glad Declan knew where he was going because there was no road to follow whatsoever.

Eventually though, we finally got to an area where the road was visible again. After a few minutes more, he pulled up to a second-row home that looked to be in pretty good shape despite the debris that was scattered about on the ground outside.

Before we could even get off the four-wheeler, a guy who looked to be in his late teens or early twenties stepped out the glass door above us, followed by a much older woman who was dragging an IV behind her.

"Hey Dec, how'd the shop do?" the guy asked, and I ducked my head, staring at the ground on impulse.

"Held up better than last time. Those sandbags were a good idea, kid," Declan said as he motioned for me to follow him.

"My boy's a smart one," I heard the woman say as we crested the stairs and stepped onto their deck.

Declan walked up to the woman, placed his hands on her shoulders, and kissed her cheek before he stepped back to look at her.

"How'd you guys fair?" he asked.

"Oh, we were fine, and you know it. Now, quit bein' rude, an' tell me who this pretty young thing is," she said as she gestured to me with a big smile on her face.

The young guy was staring at Declan and me, his eyes going back and forth between the two of us, but I tried to ignore it and the smirk that was plastered on his face.

"This is Kaliyah," Declan said. "She was rentin' the Stevens property, but when the windows started blowin' in, I let her come stay with me."

"Well, I just love your name, sweetie. I'm Beverly, but everyone 'round here calls me Moms or Mrs. Wallace, and this is my son, Nash. He works over at the surf shop with Declan. It's good to meet you."

I nodded, smiling back at her and Nash, eventually finding my voice a second or two later than was probably expected. "Thank you. It's good to meet both of you."

"Y'all come on inside and sit with me for a little bit."

'Moms' (because she wouldn't hear of me calling her Mrs. Wallace, even though she'd said it was an acceptable name) was a perfect blend of sweet and tough. She was the picture of southern hospitality too, even going so far as to offer each of us a glass of sweet tea to drink on her porch while they all talked about the storm and how long everyone thought it would be before the power would be turned back on.

The conversation never really flowed to me, and I was extremely thankful for it, not only because I was sure I'd dampen the mood with all the shit that had gone wrong in my life, but because I was having a good time just sitting there listening to them.

All of them had that southern accent I loved, and the way they were with each other just screamed that they were like family.

It was the first time since my parents died that I'd experienced that feeling again, and when it crept through me just from being around people who loved each other, I realized just how much I'd missed it.

There was a smile on my face the whole time, and I listened intently as they talked, made plans, and joked with each other.

When it was time to leave, Nash wanted to go back to the shop with us to help with any damages, but Declan told him it was both of their days off and that he didn't want either of them to spend it working, whether there was work to be done or not.

Nash didn't look too happy about Declan's call, but when Moms said, "Well, there's plenty you can do 'round here," with a smile, Nash's face fell. Still, he didn't complain.

When we were done with our teas, Declan said we had to go, and after saying goodbye, we got back on the four-wheeler, heading back toward the surf shop the way we'd come.

CHAPTER 10

DECLAN

J wanted to take Kaliyah fishing for our lunch, but I had to run back by my apartment to get my phone first.

I didn't want to miss any calls if I could help it, and I was pretty sure she needed hers too, judging by the look on her face when I told her what my plan was.

I'd taken the beach path rather than the road because debris was everywhere, and I hadn't felt like dodging it on the way back. There wasn't much beach left after the hurricane, but the tide was going out, and as it flowed out, there was more room to drive.

My stairs and walkway that used to pass over the dunes and out onto the beach were damaged beyond recognition, but since there were no more dunes left, I could go straight from the beach to my building without having to worry about them.

I ran in quickly and grabbed our phones from the solar charger I'd left on my back porch, powering mine on while I

made my way back to where Kaliyah was waiting, staring out at
the ocean.

She'd turned to face the wind so it wouldn't blow her hair in
her face, I assumed, and was leaning back on the bars of the
four-wheeler to soak up the sun when I came out, but my pace
slowed as I approached, drinking in the sight of her there.

Her shorts were short enough that if she bent just right,
spillage was bound to happen, but her shirt was loose and flowy,
covering her up way more than I would've liked. Those legs and
thighs of hers were on full display and glistening in the sunlight,
all the way down to her flip flops, and I almost had to punch
myself in the junk to get it to go back down after thinking about
those thighs wrapped around me for reasons other than just so
she wouldn't fall off the four-wheeler.

I handed her phone to her, and she turned it on while I
stuffed mine in my pocket to get back on the four-wheeler.
Before I could even sit down all the way, her phone started
dinging like crazy.

At first, I thought it was kind of funny, but after what
sounded like the millionth ding, I looked back over my shoulder
at her questioningly.

"I'm sorry. I guess this is what happens when you leave your
fiancé at the altar. I'll cut the ringer off," she said as she fiddled
with her phone, looking more anxious than she had all
morning.

"It's alright. We can wait to fish until you've handled all that
if you want?"

Her bright green eyes glanced up at me as she asked, "Are
you sure? I don't want to hold you up, and by the looks of
things, this could take a little bit."

"You know what? We can just fish from here. I mean, the
fishing isn't normally as good as my spot, but it'll get the job
done, and you can handle whatever it is you've got to do. How's
that sound?"

"Thank you. I'll just be over here," she said as she took her phone a short distance away and sat in the sand, looking at it with a worried expression painted across her features.

I tried to ignore her as I pulled my tackle box out and grabbed my fishing pole off the back of the four-wheeler, but I just couldn't keep my eyes from straying to her.

She kept putting her phone to her ear, pulling it back down, pressing a few buttons, and putting it back to her ear. Each time, the worry or sadness or whatever it was I was seeing on her face just seemed to get worse.

I baited my hook and cast out a line, pretending not to pay her any attention, but when I heard a little gasp from her a short time later, I couldn't help but look back.

She had tears running down her cheeks that she was wiping away almost as fast as they could form; however, her face wasn't sad at all.

I'd seen that expression many times in my life, and I knew what it meant.

She looked like she was ready to kill something... or someone.

I turned back to what I was supposed to be doing when she raised her head to glare death at the ocean in front of us, and a few minutes later, she came up beside me with her hands in her pockets.

She was obviously fuming, but she wasn't talking, and I didn't know how to break the silence without risking making things worse.

Turned out, I didn't need to.

"Are they biting?" she asked, and I could tell right away she didn't want to talk about whatever had been waiting for her on her phone.

I certainly wasn't gonna push her on it either, and right as she said that, I got a bite on my line.

"I guess so," I said as I started reeling it in, but what

surprised me was the way Kaliyah's eyes lit up when she knew I'd caught something.

I hadn't expected her to be the type, which just made me appreciate it even more, and when I saw the large flounder break the surface as I pulled it in, a laugh spilled from both of us at the same time.

"That thing is huge!" she said as I got it out of the water. "What is it?"

"It's a flounder, and it's big enough for us to keep and eat. Do you like flounder?"

Kaliyah nodded her head and said, "Yeah, I love it, actually."

"Alright, well, let's get this back up to the house, and I'll cook it for us."

She nodded happily and watched me take the hook from the fish's mouth like she was intrigued by what I was doing, but when I grabbed it by the mouth and thrust it toward her, saying, "Here, carry this so I can drive the four-wheeler back," her eyes got big and round with surprise.

"What?" she asked.

Immediately, I thought, 'Oh, here we go. That's the red flag I've been waiting to see.'

But when she shook her head some, as if to dislodge her initial thoughts, and reached her hand out to take the flounder, my assumptions had to do a double-take. Again, she surprised me, and as the day wore on, she never stopped.

A little bit later, when we were both full and happy, out of nowhere, she said, "I don't know if anyone should stay in that rental anymore with how bad it's messed up, so I think I should ask you if I can stay here until it's fixed, or my vacation is up in two weeks. If not, I completely understand, and I can try to find a way to get to a hotel or..."

"Yes," I said, cutting her off as soon as she started spouting any ideas that weren't staying with me. "You can stay here until whenever."

I said it without really thinking about it, but even once the words were out in the open, I couldn't deny the truth in them. I wanted Kaliyah with me for as long as I could get her to stay, no matter how hard that was to admit.

It was like as soon as the image of her driving away to go anywhere else slipped into my head, something in me bucked hard at the notion, and I didn't want to hear anything else about it.

Kaliyah looked surprised, but she smiled and thanked me anyway. I dismissed her thanks with a wave of my hand as I got up to go inside. "Don't worry about it," I said. "Just one person helping out another."

I just couldn't let her thank me when every reason I had for letting her stay was selfish and purely for my own benefit.

$\approx$

*P*retty soon, her phone started going off again and again, and even though it was on silent, I couldn't help but notice how her demeanor changed every time her screen lit up on the table.

Eventually, I couldn't not ask.

"Are you gonna face that, or just let it ring 'til it dies again?"

Picking it up and watching it ring with a disgusted look on her face, she asked, "Is throwing it into the ocean and never looking back an option? 'Cause I'd go for that over answering Cam right about now."

I smiled, but my concern for her prevented there being any real humor in it.

"I'm not gonna make you talk to him, but generally, waiting to handle things only makes them worse."

Her eyes cut up at me with an attitude, but she looked away quickly, sighed, and answered the phone as she got up from the barstool to go sit on the couch in the living room.

I knew I should've given her the privacy she needed, should've left what there was to do so she could have some space, but as I scrubbed the counter clean, again, I wasn't able to walk away or keep myself from listening intently to every word she said.

"Look, Cam," she said as soon as she answered the call. "I've made up my..." her words drifted off when she plopped down on the couch.

"No, I'm not coming back or telling you where I..."

It sounded like she was cut off again, and an anger I couldn't quite define or defend started seeping into me.

"Cam, I..."

"I don't care, you lying sack of shit! You..."

She was quiet for a minute, and even from where I was standing, I could hear him yelling at her.

Something wet spilled over my hand, and as I looked down at my hand, I saw I'd been squeezing the life out of the scrubbing sponge I'd been using to clean the counter. Huffing, I threw it into the sink and ripped off some paper towels to dry up the mess I'd made with more force than was probably necessary.

Kaliyah's head dropped into her hand in front of her as she tried to speak one more time, but Cam obviously didn't want to hear anything she had to say.

Instead of trying to fight him though, I saw resolve slip into her face as she pulled the phone away from her ear and disconnected the call in silence.

She stared at the phone for a second, and I saw when it lit back up again because he obviously wasn't through yelling at her, but instead of answering it, she placed it face down on the coffee table, got up, and came back over to the barstool she'd been sitting in before.

"Well, he seems like an asshole," I couldn't help but say, knowing I could've used a much harsher word to describe the guy I'd just heard, but I didn't want to upset Kaliyah any more than she already was.

Her laughter rang out through my apartment, and a smile formed on my face as I watched her.

"Well, that's an understatement."

"Do you wanna talk about it?" I asked as I grabbed two beers and came around to sit next to her.

She was looking at me like I was crazy as she asked, "Do you want to hear about it?"

Nodding, I opened her beer and set it in front of her before I opened my own. "It's not like we've got much else to do."

~

*A*n hour or so and five beers later, I was pacing through the living room while Kaliyah sat on the couch looking at me like I was the scary thing she needed to worry about, when that was the furthest thing from the truth... about as big of a lie as Cam's so-called love for Kaliyah.

I'd met men like him before, ones who could only feel like they mattered if they were literally destroying the people that loved them.

My stepfather had been the same way, and it had led to Mom becoming... whatever it was she became.

I couldn't understand why I felt so protective of Kaliyah so soon after meeting her, or why, when she told me about all the shit she'd been putting up with from Cam, it felt like my blood was boiling inside my veins.

I never lost my temper or worried unless there was a reason to, and since Kaliyah was states away from that asshole, I knew there was nothing to worry about, so long as she was with me, at least.

But even those thoughts didn't temper my anger.

If I was honest with myself, I'd admit that it was probably

unhealed shit from my childhood rearing its head again like it had a tendency to do sometimes, but I wasn't willing to go down that path... at least not while Kaliyah was around.

I just needed to calm down and see things rationally, but it seemed like the harder I tried, the more pissed off I got.

"Are you okay? I didn't mean to upset you or anything, if that's what's going on," Kaliyah said, a hesitant expression resting on her face, but all I could get out was a grunt until I got my shit together.

Yes, I was pacing, but my fists weren't balled, and I was schooling my expression so she wouldn't know just how angry I was.

Taking a deep breath, I finally sat back down because I knew I was freaking her out for a second there. When my eyes met hers again, I blew out the breath, trying to take comfort in the fact that she had left Cam and was here with me instead, no matter the circumstances that had brought her here.

It didn't stop thoughts of finding this Cam person and beating the fuck out of him for ever putting his hands on this woman, but it did calm me enough that I was able to get back into the conversation.

"I'm sorry," I said as I put my elbows on my knees and clasped my hands together in front of me. "I just needed a minute. I know I really just met you, but even hearing about a woman being put through something like that puts me on edge. I'm good now, though; you don't need to worry."

"I wouldn't have told you if I'd known it would upset you," she said, her eyes dipping to the floor in a way that was entirely too submissive for a woman like her.

Huffing out a breath, I said, "You know people get upset sometimes, right?"

I was being a smartass, and I knew it, but the way she smirked at me as she heard my words, showed she wasn't taking it personally.

"Yes." Her tone was all sass with a matching side-eye, a perfect example of the kind of attitude a woman like her should have, and when I saw it, I smiled at the challenge I saw in her eyes.

"I'm glad you told me," I said. "You might not be stayin' here long, but I would definitely like to get to know you while you're here, and what you've been through, as terrible as it is, it's still a part of you I want to know."

Her cheeks flushed, and her eyes sparkled before she dropped them to the floor again, but this time, she was smiling while she did it, and some part of me reveled over the fact that I had been the one to put that smile on her face.

CHAPTER 11

KALIYAH

The time I was spending with Declan was extremely new and out of my comfort zone, but it also seemed like every second I was with him was heightened in some way, like there was this intensity to him I'd never felt from anyone else before.

He had... presence, and not in an, 'Oh, look at me,' sort of way.

It was more like he didn't need to say anything, and my eyes would automatically be drawn to him, no matter where we were or what we were doing.

I was acutely aware of him... of where he was, what he was doing, what his demeanor was saying about how he felt, the way my cheeks flushed every time I felt his eyes on me, and how, when he was close to me for whatever reason, I had this over-whelming urge to get even closer to him.

The way he looked at me sometimes made my skin tingle, and the way he seemed to care without even really knowing me piqued a different and more intense kind of interest in him than was probably normal.

It might've been another sunshine and rainbows moment, where I was making a bigger deal out of things than I ought to, but there was no denying the fact that I was fascinated by Declan.

Fascinated, and comfortable enough to tell him all about Cam, which, even when they were alive, I'd never been open enough to tell my parents about.

Maybe it was because I was thoroughly outside of my relationship with Cam by that point - in my head at least - and hindsighting it.

Still, baring my soul like that and letting Declan know what I'd been through, what I was running from, shouldn't have been as easy as it had turned out to be.

I knew some part of me should've probably stepped in to protect myself, should've tucked those raw and painful memories of the years I'd spent with Cam away under lock and key until someone worthy came along, but no such consciousness or forethought ever came.

Opening up to him had felt like the most natural thing in the world, and surprising the hell out of me in response, Declan didn't shy away when he heard what I told him.

Not once did he say something like, 'You should've left a long time ago,' or 'How could you allow him to do those things to you?' - You know, all the stuff I'd been saying to and asking myself for the past six years.

I am my own worst critic.

But Declan proved he wasn't my critic at all in those moments.

If anything, he proved the opposite because he didn't comment on my behavior except to say I'd done the right thing by leaving Cam and that he was there for me if I needed to talk about it.

He even went so far as to offer up his couch for the foreseeable future until I could figure out what I would do when my vacation was up.

Which in and of itself, wasn't normal either.

People don't usually go around offering to open up their homes to someone they just met.

Combining all of that with his devilishly good looks and voice of sin… well, it was enough for me to entertain the idea of staying on Topsail past my two-week timeline, if for no other reason than so I'd have someone I might be able to call a friend in this shitshow of a world.

However, considering it was *all* I was willing to do after only knowing Declan and this town for all of two days.

I wasn't deciding anything yet, other than the fact that I was never going back to Cam - about that, I was sure and unwavering.

But before I got too lost in my own head, I pushed those thoughts aside, refusing to spend too much time worrying about my future when I had a whole two weeks to make a plan and a hot biker dude asking me to go swimming with him.

"I'd love to," I said after he asked, smiling because I hadn't told him I needed a distraction, yet he'd known just the same.

I changed into my bathing suit in the bathroom while he changed into his in his room, and when I stepped out, he was already waiting for me by the door with a couple of big beach towels slung over one of his heavily tattooed arms.

The sight of him in those swim trunks had heat swelling up inside my belly because of how dangerously low and loose they were sitting on his hips, showing off that v thing some guys have below his six pack.

When I was finally able to bring my eyes back up to his, I found him devouring my body in return, and suddenly the heat I was already feeling skyrocketed tenfold.

It was everything I could do to act normal and nonchalant

when I was more turned on in that moment by Declan's gaze alone than I'd ever been by Cam for any reason, but somehow, I was able to put on a straight face and walk over to him despite everything I was feeling.

He seemed to snap out of it too when I moved, and in short order, we were back out on the beach, laying our towels down and racing each other into the water like kids who'd been let loose with free rein in a candy store.

The water was warm and inviting, with waves building up slowly before they crashed onto the shore.

All the debris from the storm was further up the beach by the houses, and though Declan warned me about the possibility of finding some floating in the water, it was very low tide; as we got in the water, I could tell that at least where we were, there weren't any worrisome hazards floating around.

Honestly, it was as if it were an entirely different ocean than the one I'd seen breaking Declan's board the day before.

I was bobbing like a sitting duck on the incoming swells when I looked over to Declan and saw a gleam in his eyes.

Immediately, I knew he was coming for me, and a laugh escaped my throat as a small and sexy amount of fear crept through my system at the same time.

I tried to get away from him, but he was wicked fast in the water and caught me by my hips in no time.

Chuckling, he lifted me up, tossing me away from him farther than I would've thought he could, and a girly laugh-giggle sounded from my throat before I remembered I needed to hold my breath. As I splashed into the water a second later, another swell passed right over my head.

It was such a happy rush of excitement that in that moment, having fun with Declan, it wasn't the wedding day I was missing; there wasn't an abusive ex who'd cheated on me with my only friend lurking in the back of my mind; I wasn't completely alone in this life, and there certainly weren't make or break decisions that needed to be made.

There was just Declan and me, playing in the surf after a hurricane like we had no responsibilities in the world other than having fun and enjoying each other.

When I broke the surface again, I was laughing a little, savoring all the happy feelings coursing through me, but mostly, I just wanted revenge.

I set my sights on Declan with a plan already circulating in my brain, his eyes challenging me in a way I was all too excited to ignore.

I dove under the water and swam over to him, popping out right in front of him and reaching each of my hands out to his sides to tickle him.

There'd been no way for me to know whether he was ticklish or not before that moment, but I was hopeful nevertheless.

When my fingers dug into the flesh of his sides, the most hilarious, manly scream I'd ever heard in my life fell from his lips as he jerked out of my grasp, and I couldn't help how hard I laughed at the sound.

"Now you've fucked up," he said as he started after me with a predatory gleam in his eyes.

"But you attacked me first!" I screamed like I wasn't more than willing to shamelessly be his prey.

However, before he could really move toward me, we were both surprised by a man on a four-wheeler yelling out to us from the beach.

"Hey, Dec!"

Declan turned around, one hand resting on my hip sensually as he looked back at the newcomer.

"Sup, Dusty? You guys alright?" Declan yelled back as he started heading in, guiding me to come along with him.

"Yeah, we're good," Dusty said as we got closer to him. "Mama's house didn't have any real damage, and you've probably already seen that Roxy's apartment looks fine, other than all that sand."

I watched as Declan's eyes drifted up to the surf shop as he said, "Yeah, that's gonna take a bit to get cleared."

"I'm out looking for help though. The pier got fucked up in the storm, and a bunch of debris from it landed right at the meat market. They sent me to see if I could find some more able bodies to help with the cleanup, so here I am."

"Yeah, sure thing," Declan said, a new and determined set to his chin. "We'll go change real quick and meet you down there."

"Thanks, man. See ya in a bit," Dusty said before he drove off.

Declan looked down at me, the sun glinting off his blue eyes.

"I didn't even think to ask if you wanted to help. I'm sorry I just signed us both up for cleanup detail. You don't have to go if you don't want to."

A little taken back by the fact that he'd caught his own slight and apologized for it before I could even notice it myself, I shrugged, saying, "Thanks for noticing and apologizing, but really, I don't mind helping out at all." Then, trying to ease the mood some as we made our way back up to his apartment, I said, "Besides, the meat market seems like something people need right now."

Declan came to a full stop on the stairs as he laughed at that and looked back at me like I was clueless.

"What?" I asked. "Meat is important!"

Still smiling from his laughter, he said, "The 'meat market' isn't an actual store. It's what we call the spot by the pier where all the Marines from the base come to stand around, drink, and hit on anything that walks every weekend."

"Ah," I said as a laugh fell from me too.

Sobering some, he said, "Yeah, we like the fact that they buy their booze here and whatnot, but for me and some of the other locals, they can turn into a headache real quick. And you can bet your ass they won't be here to help clean up their spot either, whether the island is open or not."

"Hmm," was all I could say to that as images of half-clad drunken Marines flowed through my brain, and I made my way to go change again before we headed out to help with the cleanup a short time later.

~

*W*e took the four-wheeler down to where I'd first come onto the island into Surf City.

The pier that Dusty had been talking about was certainly messed up, and so were most of the houses and storefronts up that way too, almost as if the storm had hit this part of the island harder than it'd hit where Declan and I had been staying.

There were people out in it though, all helping out in one way or another as we pulled up.

Declan drove past a few of them and stopped by Dusty, where he was standing next to his four-wheeler, Nash, Roxy, and three other girls, pointing things out that needed to get done.

"Hey, you made it through the storm!" Roxy said as she spotted me, taking a step or two away from the group so she could look at me.

Immediately, heat swam up to soak my cheeks, but I pushed through how uncomfortable I was and smiled at her anyway. "Yeah. Luckily this guy is nuts," I said as I pointed to Declan with my thumb, "and doesn't mind rescuing people in the middle of a hurricane."

In hindsight, I can see how that might've been an attempt to focus the conversation over on Declan instead of me. Regardless of what my intentions had been though, all my words ended up doing was making me seem more approachable than I felt since everyone in the small group turned their eyes to me.

"Yeah, Dec's our resident psycho, for sure," a woman with short, dark hair said with a smile in Declan's direction as he and Dusty started walking away together.

"That's Mya," Roxy said, pointing to the woman who'd just spoken. "The short blonde is Bethany." She motioned to the girl that had been talking to Dusty when we pulled up, and I couldn't help but think she and Roxy could've been sisters with how alike they looked. "And this gorgeous vixen here is Kaylynne," Roxy said as she playfully poked a woman in the shoulder who looked a little older than the rest.

Kaylynne met me with a sincere and welcoming smile as she reached her hand out to shake mine. "And you are?"

Taking her hand lightly, I said, "I'm Kaliyah."

"Well, it's nice to meet you, though I wish it were under better circumstances."

"Are you helping us out with the cleanup?" Roxy asked, pulling my attention back to her.

It was then I noticed the box of big black trash bags she had in her hands.

"Yeah," I said, squinting in the sunlight. "I don't really know where to begin, but I'll help in any way I can."

A smile spread on Roxy's face while a calculating smirk showed on Mya's.

I took a trash bag when she handed one to me, and Roxy motioned to where Declan was standing with Dustin.

"My brother, Dusty, didn't listen and drove through the storm last night like a dumbass because he was so worried about everybody. He's trying to organize everything, so we're taking our marching orders from him. You can go ask him for something to do, or if you wanna hang with us girls, we're gonna be picking up as much debris as will fit in these bags from here down to the condos."

I thought about staying with Declan for a second, sticking with him because I felt safe with him, but then the image of me following him around like a lost puppy all day made me cringe hard on the inside, and I knew I couldn't do that if I had another choice.

I might not have known Roxy very well... or at all, really, but I did know I wasn't as nervous around her as I usually was with new people. She and the other girls were also giving off a super friendly vibe, even if they did look somewhat hesitant to bring me along with them.

"I'll go with you girls," I said, opening the bag she'd given me.

Each of us wound up standing about a foot away from each other, almost shoulder to shoulder on what beach was left, and began walking away from the pier in a line as we scoured the beach, picking up whatever we could as we got to it.

Roxy was on my right, oceanside, while Mya was on my left, followed by Kaylynne and Bethany.

It was quiet at first, and rather than allowing myself to over-think that fact or make anything of it, I focused most of my energy on the cleanup. Once we were out of earshot of any other volunteers, though, the girls around me started talking like I assumed they usually did.

"You know, this really isn't as bad as I thought it was gonna be," Bethany said from the end of the line. "Dad was so worried, but like, most everything is still okay, I think."

Judging by everything I'd seen, it looked pretty bad in my opinion, but I just accepted the fact that the people living here probably knew way more about those kinds of things than I did and tried to bury my concerns in the trash bag I was steadily filling the further we went.

"Your dad is supposed to worry like that," Roxy laughed, picking things up and stuffing them into her own trash bag. Looking at me conspiratorially, she said, "Her dad's the mayor."

"True," Bethany said, stepping over another board we couldn't put in our bags.

With that new bit of information, I found my eyes drifting

over to where Bethany was reaching down to pick up a small, seaweed-covered and unrecognizable plastic slab kind of thing. Bits and pieces of whatever it had been were everywhere, and we spent a good deal of time going through that section of the beach picking them all up. I tried not to let the squirminess I felt from the sliminess of the seaweed show on my face, but I would've been lying if I said it wasn't disgusting.

Bethany's blonde hair showed off dark brown roots as sprigs of brown leapt free of her ponytail to blow in her face from the breeze. She had on jean shorts, no shoes, and a plain dowdy sweatshirt, looking nothing like what I would've imagined a mayor's daughter would.

But if I'd learned anything from my time on the island so far, it was that no one seemed to act like I expected them to.

The man, woman, and bird from the beer and wine store had been the first to surprise me, but then Roxy had too because I knew I'd misjudged her when I first met her, and Declan had certainly turned out to be different from what I'd initially thought since he obviously wasn't just some big-headed biker guy.

"How'd all the rentals fare, Lynne?" Bethany asked a short time later after we got through the seaweed plastic.

Kaylynne sighed loudly. "They're all still intact from what I can tell, thank God. There's some damage, but nothing like there's been before. Just a few shingles and debris I'll have to clean up and fix."

"Oh, good," Bethany said with a sly smile. "I need my new place to be in good condition when I move in."

The girls laughed as Roxy said, "You know your dad isn't gonna let you move out until you're done with college, girl. Stop hassling Lynne all the time when you've still got like three years left."

Now that seems like something a Mayor father would do, I thought to myself with a small chuckle.

He might've been a farmer, rather than a mayor, but my own father had tried that same tactic the summer after I graduated high school, spouting out reason after reason why staying close to home would help my future, but I hadn't listened since my sights had been set on getting out of our small town with little regard for anything else.

"But I have so many plans," Bethany said, all whiny and dreamy-like. "Of white shag rugs, and boys sleeping on the couch, and red pots and pans, and boys drinking on a porch, and farmhouse tables... and laying on farmhouse tables with boys, and..."

"Oh, God," Roxy said with a smile. "Somebody stop her before I do."

Not a second went by before Mya took whatever small rubber piece of tubing was in her hand and chucked it at Bethany, who squealed in response as she ducked out of the way just in time.

There were smiles on everyone's faces, and I forgot myself entirely while I just enjoyed being around them.

"Let me know if you need any help, Lynne. It's not like the restaurant is gonna be open today anyway with the power being out," Mya said from beside me.

Everyone but Mya and me giggled at what she'd said, but I'd had no clue what they were laughing at.

I must have let the confusion show on my face, or Roxy was simply taking the lead on guiding me through this group of friends because, after one glance at me, she started to explain. "Mya is the head chef over at Island Thyme, and she gets all pissy when she can't work."

Huffing, Mya said, "It's not that *I* can't work, Rocks," and I saw when Roxy rolled her eyes at that. "*I* am perfectly capable of pulling together a dinner service on our generator's power. It's that Miles won't let me!"

"Miles owns the restaurant," Roxy said before she looked

past me to Mya. "Take the night for once. Have a drink. Enjoy the time off, you workaholic."

"I had a night off last night," Mya bit back bitterly, and the girls around me laughed again, pulling a smile to my lips as well.

"How 'bout this?" Kaylynne suggested after their laughter had eased some. "We'll meet back up at the restaurant later, and you can make dinner for all of us instead. Would that make you feel better?"

Everyone laughed again, but Mya's face was the picture of relief.

"Yes, it would actually," she said, which only drew more laughter from the lot of us. "Are we inviting the new girl?"

They all stopped walking and looked toward me at some unspoken cue, making what was starting to be a pretty nice time turn into something else entirely.

"Of course," Roxy said as she draped her arm around my shoulder. "It's not often we get someone around here who isn't afraid of getting dirty like the rest of us."

I assumed she was talking about how I was helping with the cleanup. The thought crawled through my mind, wondering who they'd met in the past that wouldn't have done what I had, but I dismissed it as an unavoidable smile broke out across my face, and I ducked my eyes to the sand at being included.

"Invite Declan when we get back, and I'll tell Dusty and Nash," Roxy said as everyone turned around to head back the way we'd come.

Apparently, the unspoken cue had had little to do with me and everything to do with the fact that we'd reached a large set of gray condos, which I'd deduced had been our stopping point, and I mentally slapped my forehead for thinking their stopping had had anything to do with me.

CHAPTER 12

KALIYAH

"How'd they get on the island?" Mya asked as she stared in contempt at a reporter and her cameraman who'd shown up while we'd been gone.

The female reporter was standing as close as she could get to the water without getting wet, her back angled toward the broken end of the pier as she prepped and primed her hair, though I could tell, even from how far away I was, that not a single hair was out of place.

Her cameraman was tall and lanky looking, his long limbs holding the camera down beside his leg while he talked to the reporter.

"I don't know," Roxy said. "But she probably trapped herself here on purpose so she could get a good shot of the damage today."

I could hear the resentment these girls seemed to have for the reporter in their voices, but their faces would've given it away whether they spoke or not.

"Yeah, I wouldn't put it past her," Bethany chimed in as we got back over to Declan, Nash, and Dusty.

They were heaving loose boards into a pile that a few other guys I didn't know were loading onto the back of a pickup truck in the parking lot at the beach access.

Declan paused what he was doing to eye me and the girls I was with when he saw me. "You make friends while you were gone?" There was a soft smile on his lips, and unless I was imagining things, there was also a hint of hopefulness to his tone as well.

"Yep," Roxy said as she threw her arm around me again. "We're quickly becoming besties. Even if she's only said like four words to us."

We all laughed at that, but mine was the only face tinted red as I giggled.

"That's great," he said as his eyes drifted past me and landed on the reporter behind me.

As soon as recognition dawned on his face, that small smile he'd been sporting disappeared entirely as he whipped around, showing me his back.

I didn't know if the others had caught Declan's movement or the reaction he'd had that I couldn't quite label as he moved, but I certainly had, and instantly, red flags and alarm bells started popping up in my brain.

I figured the reporter was probably an ex-girlfriend or something, someone who Declan obviously didn't want to be seen by, and who had also run afoul with the girls of the island for some reason.

I glanced questioningly at his back as he walked over to the parking lot in the middle of our conversation to get out of the reporter's line of sight.

I stood there not really knowing what I should do. It wasn't as if I'd expected his past to be squeaky clean, nor did I really have any reason to worry myself about his past in the first place.

However, as Roxy's arm left my shoulders and Mya put her hand there instead, my thoughts shifted from Declan's past back to relevant topics, like why these girls kept touching me as if that kind of thing was normal.

"Don't let it get to you," Mya said with a small knowing smile. "He hates being on camera or having his picture taken. It's just one of Dec's things."

"Was it written all over my face or something?" I couldn't help but ask as I tried to wrap my mind around what she'd said. But rather than taking comfort in Dec's weird trait or whatever because it meant the reporter wasn't someone I needed to worry about, my thoughts jumped to speculating about whether Mya was someone from Declan's past instead, since she seemed to be the one who kept spilling what she knew about him to me.

The girls all giggled some at my question, and Mya took her hand from my shoulder as she said, "Well, yeah. You're pretty easy to read."

"Good to know," I said. "I'm gonna be working on that from now on."

I was trying to lighten the mood some, and when they all giggled at me more, I felt like I'd been largely successful in that endeavor.

"Come on," Roxy said as we dropped our bags by the pile of wood, and she handed us new ones. "You can tell us about yourself, and we'll give you the inside scoop on Dec while we work on the other side of the pier."

In my head, I questioned how they knew I wanted to hear about Declan and why they were being so forthright with me when none of them knew anything about me, but I was also relieved that these girls seemed to be just as welcoming and open as everyone else I'd met on the island had been so far.

I wasn't used to having friends, and I certainly wasn't in a position to call any of these girls such a thing since I'd just met them... not to mention how far south my relationship with my last friend had flown only a couple of days ago.

However, as we walked, cleaned, and got to know each other, I found myself loving every minute I was spending with them.

Mya was really a hard ass from what I could tell, even though to me, she'd been nothing but nice so far. She'd been raised here but had gone to one of the most prestigious culinary schools in the country before she returned, throwing all that knowledge right back into the community she'd been raised by. She obviously loved her job, and from what the other girls said, she would quite literally go insane if she didn't have a way to cook for people on a daily basis.

Kaylynne was a rental agent for one of the last mom and pop agencies that still rented properties on the island. Apparently, most of the bigger named companies had been steadily putting the smaller ones out of business as the island's popularity grew. Since the owners were older and had poured their whole lives into that company, Kaylynne worked tirelessly to keep them afloat, even though it was getting harder and harder every year to do so.

I'd already learned that Bethany was the mayor's daughter, but she was also studying to be a nurse at the same college Nash was going to.

She worked part-time as a waitress at Island Thyme with Mya and had the hugest crush on Dusty, Roxy's brother, even though Mya said under no uncertain terms that he was entirely too old for her. He was 25 and ran the bar for Island Thyme, while Bethany was barely out of high school.

Surprisingly, Roxy stayed out of that particular part of the conversation, and I liked her that much more for it.

She wasn't shooting Bethany down for having eyes for her brother, but she also wasn't pushing her toward him either. She even let Mya talk a little shit about Dusty without doing much more than agreeing when Mya pointed out that Dusty wasn't one to settle for just one girl at a time, almost as if the news wasn't a shock to her at all.

It wasn't a shock to Bethany either, but I could see in her eyes that she still held out hope as she tossed something at Mya, saying, "Of course he wouldn't want to settle down with any of the tourists that come to the bar. I've just got to make him see that I'm a viable option, and things will turn around."

Even I rolled my eyes with everyone else at that, but we were all smiling while we did it, and there it was again, that sunshine and rainbows feeling, like everything was shaping up to be just what I needed.

I then proceeded to see myself exactly how I'd just imagined Bethany, as this naive and wonderstruck teenager, and threw all those thoughts out the proverbial window, self-preservation taking its place quickly.

It was technically still my wedding day, and all the shit I'd left back in Chicago was still going to be waiting for me when I woke up the next morning, whether these girls were my friends or not.

I had to keep reminding myself of that, or else I was afraid I'd fall too hard too quickly for everyone and everything on Topsail and be unable to see reason when shit inevitably hit the fan here too.

"So, tell us about you," Kaylynne said to me, pulling me out of my own head.

I took a deep breath because talking to these girls didn't seem nearly as easy as talking to Declan had been, even though I was fairly certain they wouldn't judge me either.

"Well, I grew up in Kentucky, went to college in Maryland to become a writer, and moved to Chicago about two years ago."

"Oh, man," Roxy exclaimed. "Have you written anything I might've read? I love to read just about anything."

Her face was brighter and more excited than it'd been

before, and a part of me hated disappointing her when she was obviously so hopeful.

"No," I said, covering the dropping of my head by picking up more seaweed-covered trash. "I haven't published anything yet, and honestly, I haven't even written in years."

I didn't need to look to see that Roxy's face had fallen, but when she spoke next, she surprised me. "Do you still want to be a writer?"

"Absolutely," the word fell from my mouth without thought, with a bit more passion than the moment called for.

Chuckling at me, she said, "Well, you'll just have to start now then."

The way she said that made it seem like it would be the easiest task in the world, like I could just sit down at my laptop and write out a best-seller in no time.

It was a glorious dream.

"Then, when you're done, you can send it to me, and I can give you my thoughts before you send it out into the world. I write stellar reviews if I do say so myself," she said with what looked like forced humility, and I started laughing at the face she was making.

"Alright," I said so that part of the conversation could end sooner. "Sounds like a plan."

Roxy seemed satisfied with that answer, then thought to herself for a moment before she said, "I didn't even ask how long you were staying," with a questioning tone to her voice.

It was yet another uncomfortable topic, and I couldn't help how my shoulders slumped some at the question.

"Right now, I've got plans to stay for two weeks, but I know I'm not going back to Chicago."

"Why not?" Bethany asked, and I knew my eyes widened as I glanced over at her.

She was actively avoiding looking at me so I could answer, and though I could appreciate her gesture, the thought of telling even more people about everything I had going on put pressure on my shoulders regardless.

I inflated my lungs and blew the breath out slowly, trying to figure out how to answer her question without saying too much.

Eventually, I went with, "I just can't."

It came out all sad sounding, even to my own ears, but surprisingly, none of the girls around me so much as flinched at what I'd said. They just continued what they were doing as if what I'd said was of no consequence to them.

Still, I could tell they were all mulling over my words, probably trying to figure out either how to move on to less touchy subjects or how to get me to spill more; I couldn't tell which.

After a few beats of silence that I couldn't stand, I went on, saying, "I'm gonna have to find somewhere else to live by the end of these two weeks, so I've been considering staying somewhere near here if I can figure out just how I'd go about doing that exactly."

Everyone stopped and looked at me again, but that time, I'd had enough of them doing that.

"You guys are gonna have to stop staring at me like that," I said with a smile. "It freaks me out when you all do it at the same time like this." I gestured to each of them, where they stood around me.

"That happens with us; you'll get used to it. But um, hello," Mya said. "Kaylynne rents out houses here and was just saying how many vacancies she's got to fill."

Immediately, fear and longing spread through me in equal doses as my mouth spoke of his own volition, "As nice as that sounds, there's probably no way I could afford any of the places here. I've got some savings, but I don't want to wipe all of it out just getting set up."

Roxy chuckled a sarcastic kind of giggle while Kaylynne

smiled softly at me, saying, "You'd be surprised how affordable some of the places here can be."

"Yeah. Girl, I work at a grocery store," Roxy said, leveling me with a look I couldn't quite name. "My apartment is right across the street from Dec's surf shop, and even though I don't make that much, I can still afford an ocean view. It might not be right on the beach, but it is affordable."

Quickly, I figured up what her salary might be like at Igan Grocery and compared that to the houses I'd seen around the surf shop. The two didn't compute. "But how, though?" I found myself asking as I stared at all of them in shock, nearly convincing myself that they were fucking with me.

Then another thought occurred to me, and I said, "Wait. There aren't any apartments around the surf shop, just a bunch of beach houses."

Mya smirked in a let-me-enlighten-you kind of way as she put her arm around my shoulder and turned me toward the houses lining the beach, our backs facing the ocean. "Tell me what you see," she said, and I couldn't help but feel like I was missing something important.

"Giant ass beach houses?" I asked.

"Yup," Mya said. "And do you think most of the rich ass people that own these houses live here full time?"

Immediately, I knew the answer to that question because the guy I'd been renting Sea Breeze Dream from obviously didn't live there. "No."

"Right. Most of the houses here are vacant for a good portion of the year, if not completely year-round."

I nodded, though I wasn't too sure what I was nodding about; I could've already guessed the info she was telling me.

"But what are rich people great at?" Mya asked though she didn't wait for an answer. "Getting richer. Even their playthings make them money, and the way some of them have done that here is by taking these 'giant-ass beach houses' and turning them into apartments or duplexes that they can then rent out all year long. Most landlords make enough in a single summer to maintain it through the slower months of winter, simply because this is a tourist destination."

Mya's smirk widened into a full-on smile as she made her point, taking her arm from my shoulders so she could look at me.

I glanced back up at the houses before me, trying to imagine them broken apart on the inside so more tenants could be squeezed inside one property, feeling like my knowledge of real estate and numbers was rudimentary at best.

"That's what's going on with the apartment I rent," Roxy said. "The lady is actually really sweet, and wanted to live here full time, but her parents needed her to help take care of them, so she had to move back to Virginia. For her, it was either sell and lose all she'd already invested or figure out a way to let it make her money so she could still afford the payments and insurance. She turned it into two apartments, one upstairs and one downstairs.

I rent the one downstairs because it was a little cheaper than the one upstairs, but really, there wasn't much of a difference. I just didn't want to lug groceries up a bunch of steps all the time."

We all giggled some at that as we got back to picking up more debris, and I could definitely understand the issue she wanted to avoid.

"Back where I lived in Chicago, the elevator stopped working for like a week, and let me tell you, I thoroughly hated life that week," I laughed out.

"I bet," Roxy said.

When the laughter had fallen away but smiles still remained all around, she said, "The upstairs apartment is still available. I'm not pushing you for staying or for renting it, but already I know you're cool enough that I should put it out there in case you do decide to take staying seriously. I know that doesn't handle your job situation, but hopefully it helps."

I smiled, but I couldn't string words together very well at that moment.

Suddenly, the empty 'life after Topsail' part of my unmade plan began to seem like I might not even need it. Hopeful thoughts skittered through my mind with images of living on Topsail full time... for the long haul. The more those thoughts solidified in my brain, the surer I felt about how my journey might play out.

Nothing was being decided just yet, but for the first time in six years, it seemed like I had a viable option that didn't include Cam, and no matter how I tried, I couldn't keep the happiness I felt from exploding inside my chest like a show of fireworks.

~

*L*ater that night, after stepping out of my second cold shower for the day and getting dressed, I opened the bathroom door to see Declan leaning up against the back of the couch with his legs crossed in front of him, the light from the battery-powered candles casting the perfect glow across his features.

He'd been looking down at the phone in his hands until I'd walked out, but as soon as he heard the door open, his eyes shot up to mine, and he slid his phone in his pocket.

His hair had been brushed, but I could tell he'd also run his hands through it a few times from the way it fell a little sideways on his head. The loose jeans he wore were dark and draped down his long figure perfectly, while his shirt lay against his form in such a way that it gave my eyes unfettered access to that trim waist of his.

He was drool-worthy, standing there like that, exuding a casual confidence that demanded to be savored and appreciated.

Considering how I found myself doing just that without question, I knew I was in trouble because my thoughts took a turn straight for the gutter.

However, as he stood and walked over to me, his eyes sliding lazily up and down my front one good time, it made me think his thoughts were traveling along the same paths as mine had, and that made my gutter-thoughts even more intense.

What was so surprising though, was that rather than feeling self-conscious or dropping my eyes to the floor under his gaze, like I'd become accustomed to with Cam whenever he'd shown some kind of desire for me, when Declan looked at me like that, I felt nothing but all the good things: flattered, empowered, sexy, desirable... wanted; the list could go on and on.

It was a set of feelings I hadn't felt in a long, long time, and as I lifted my chin slightly, I let myself savor the confidence his gaze afforded me.

It was like Declan brought out an entirely different side of me than Cam had.

I couldn't explain it, and I certainly didn't want to overanalyze it either.

I just wanted to bask in it, so when Declan offered me his elbow, I didn't hesitate to take it before he started leading me downstairs to the garage.

The girls had filled me in on what to expect at Island Thyme while we walked back with our second load of debris-filled trash bags earlier. They'd stressed the fact that though it was one of the classiest restaurants on the island, it also wasn't so upscale that you couldn't wear jeans or shorts.

Also, since we were likely to be the only people coming that night, there wasn't much of a need for more formal attire that the restaurant would've usually required.

I'd had a couple ideas for what I'd wear that might work with my flip-flops, but in the end, I chose a simple pair of jean shorts and a loose-fitting, dressy red tank top with silver, metal accents where the straps met the body of the shirt.

I hadn't bothered bringing any of my jewelry with me when I'd left Chicago, so I felt a bit underdressed knowing we were going out, but I tried not to worry about it.

Declan walked over to the weird-looking stands that were holding his bikes up and set about the task of pulling one of them down.

My heart fluttered inside my chest.

Apparently, we would be riding a motorcycle to meet up with everyone, and I'd never been on one in my life.

I was nervous, but mostly, I was just excited.

After opening the garage door with his remote, Declan walked over to his workbench, where he grabbed one of the three helmets that were sitting there and brought it over to me.

Without question or complaint, I took it and pulled it over my head, thankful I hadn't put too much effort into doing my hair. My fingers fumbled with the strap for a second as I tried to get it tighter, but warm, rough hands gently moved mine out of the way a second later.

"Let me," he said, his bright blue eyes heavy-lidded as he looked at me.

I couldn't tell what his look meant or what he was thinking; my only indicators that it was a good look being the slow build-up of tingles and heat that were growing in my belly as his deft fingers grazed the skin of my chin a few times.

When he was done, and the gigantic helmet was as secure on my head as it was going to get, his gaze lingered on mine for a moment longer than was necessary, and I could've drooled all too easily over that smirk he was wearing.

All too quickly though, he turned around and grabbed another one of the helmets from the workbench before he climbed on his bike, making it roar to life beneath him.

Even with the helmet dampening all the sounds around me,

it was still deafening, the noise from the engine bouncing off the walls of the garage to echo in my ears.

Adrenaline pumped through my veins as I stood there, honestly a bit fearful of what I was about to do, but when Declan turned his face to me and reached a hand out, my heart started racing, not in fear, but in something else entirely.

"Get on, and hold on tight," he said as I placed my hand in his so he could help me climb on.

I didn't know where to put any of my limbs, but seeming to anticipate that, Declan pointed to where I needed to place my feet, and once again guided my arms around his waist.

I wrapped my hands together in front of him, knowing I was squeezing harder than was really necessary, but in my defense, I was nervous as fuck.

Declan didn't seem to mind though, and after we'd gone up the precarious mountain of sand outside and he'd shut the garage door behind us, I felt his hand rub the back of mine for a second before he placed both his hands on the handlebars and took off.

A girlish kind of squeal tore through my throat as we started really moving, and a full-on smile threatened to split my face in two.

I felt Declan's laughter through the movement of his back in front of me, my memories of what he looked like when he laughed like that floating through my brain to make me smile even more.

When we came to where the roads were actually clear, our speed increased even more, and after chastising myself some, I forced my eyes open, refusing to miss out on any of what was happening.

There were no lights anywhere on the island that I could see but, as I gazed around me, I was surprised by how bright the moon shone, illuminating everything beneath it.

Yes, the houses were dark, but the light off the ocean on the other side of them made the water glisten dramatically. And the stars were so bright, the sky so clear, that if I'd had all the time in the world, I would've been able to count each and every one.

It was gorgeous. Gorgeous and mesmerizing. And somewhere along the way, I forgot myself and my fears completely as I relaxed into Declan's back while I took in everything I could see through the big helmet.

Eventually, we got to the restaurant, and as Declan cut the engine, the sudden quietness of the island overwhelmed my senses, seeming louder than the bike had been.

He climbed off, offering me his hand so I could climb off too. After taking his helmet off, he stuffed it into a bag on the side of the bike before reaching out to take mine.

Immediately, I got a little self-conscious about how my hair might look, taking a second to try and smooth it before he turned back around, but he caught my movements anyway.

"Leave it. You look amazing with your hair in a mess," he said before he turned around to head inside.

I tried to ignore how his statement made me feel, but it was completely impossible.

Island Thyme was a two-story building that sat right beside the intercoastal waterway, which separated the island from the mainland.

From the parking lot, I could even see that the restaurant had its own dock where people could drive up on boats to get to it, and something about that made me long for that kind of life. One where I could take a boat to get dinner; what a fabulous kind of life that would be.

The place looked like a beacon in the darkness as we approached the front door, standing out against the black backdrop because it was one of only a few places with a generator to power their lights.

The doors were big and heavy-looking, but Declan pulled

one of them open with ease as he allowed me to go ahead of him.

Inside, past the reception and waiting area, a cozy little restaurant was decorated to the nines in beach themed things. Rope nets hung from the walls, blue seat cushions adorned each and every booth and chair, and open flame candles sat lit on each table covered in a white tablecloth.

Declan didn't wait for someone to seat us like the sign said at the front entrance. Instead, he walked right through the beautiful dining room to head up the wooden staircase I hadn't seen from the front door.

The upstairs part of Island Thyme looked like a different place entirely, even though it had mostly the same features as were downstairs.

This section was obviously made with a younger, more excitable crowd in mind.

The whole place was basically a big balcony since three out of its four walls were actually railings where people could stand and see the ocean on one side and the intercoastal on the other. Multi-colored lights draped around the whole place, adding to the fun vibe it had going on.

There was a long bar that stretched from one end of the room to the other, and lights lit up the glass wall behind it, showering the alcohol shelved there in a bath of cool light.

Dusty was behind the bar, making several drinks at once, his hands moving with expertise as they poured everything without spilling a drop outside the six glasses in front of him.

Bethany, Kaylynne, Roxy, and Nash were posted up at one of the high wooden tables by the railing when we walked over, and when they saw us coming, they welcomed us warmly.

"Hey guys, come on over!" Roxy's signature smile brought one of my own out as I took the barstool next to her.

Beach music played somewhere in the background, loud

enough to dance to it if someone wanted to, but not so loud that it killed conversation either.

In what almost seemed like serendipity, Dusty brought over the tray of drinks he'd been making as Cheers (Drink to That) by Rihanna started playing through the speakers.

"Two virgin drinks for the neighborhood youngins," he said with a sarcastic smile as he passed Nash and Bethany their bright red drinks. They took them with smirks of their own without balking at him about calling their ages out.

Seeming to second guess himself, he looked right at me, his perfectly tousled brown hair falling in his eyes some as he asked, "You're over twenty-one, right?"

Nodding, I said, "You flatter me, but yeah, I'm twenty-four," before he nodded and sat one of the pretty blue drinks in front of me.

"Now, don't drink them yet," Dusty warned. "You know how Mya will get if we start without her."

"Too late," Nash said as he sat his empty glass down with a challenging smile in Dusty's direction.

"It's your ass on the line, bud, not mine," Dusty laughed as he handed out the rest of the drinks before setting his tray on an empty table and sitting down next to Bethany.

I could see the flush in her cheeks as she obviously reveled in the fact that he'd chosen the seat next to her rather than the other empty spot by Declan, and another covert smile played at my lips.

Bethany really was into Dusty, and from the way his eyes kept trying to meet hers, I had a sneaking suspicion he felt the same way about her.

Distracting me from my thoughts, Mya came through a swinging door at the other end of the bar with a gigantic tray of food resting on her shoulder.

"Can you please let me help?" Bethany asked in a whiny sort

of voice that I was growing used to, but Mya shut her down quickly.

"Nope," she said as laughter sounded around the table, and Mya headed back to the kitchen.

Once the door swung shut behind her, Bethany shot off her barstool and ran behind the bar, coming back with a stack full of plates and silverware, which she dished out in a hurry.

Then she started taking the large platters off the tray Mya had just set down and set them up down the table's center.

"Mya's gonna kick your ass, you know that, right, little one?" Dusty asked Bethany, causing her cheeks to redden even further.

She looked a little put out by his question but answered confidently a second later. "At least she won't have to set all this up by herself on top of kicking my ass."

She laughed at her own joke, right along with everyone else at the table as Mya came back through the door with yet another tray of food.

Bethany hurried back over to her seat and placed her hands on top of one another, putting on a good girl performance as she glanced at Mya with a knowing smile on her face.

"Girl, I swear." That was the only thing Mya said to Bethany, and I could tell she appreciated her help, even if she didn't want to admit it.

"Alright, ladies and gentlemen," Mya said after she got the rest of the platters set out on the table. "Tonight, for our appetizers, we have oysters, tiger prawns, and tuna crudo tossed in my secret glaze, and chilled mussels drizzled in a saffron marinade. For our entrees, we have my twice-cooked patata, made of sweet potato a la plancha, salsa macha, queso fresco, cilantro, with just a squeeze of lime, and some simple shrimp tacos. There are lobster rolls and crab dip as well."

She was standing at the end of the table in her white chef's coat as she described everything in front of us, and as my eyes drifted over each thing she listed, my mouth watered like crazy while my insides turned to mush.

I was nowhere near well-dressed enough for a place like this, and even though I'd been made to believe the restaurant was going to be a laid back and casual but still classy kind of place, the food before me blew all those thoughts out of the water.

The dishes looked like they could've won awards with how beautiful they were - so meticulously made I almost felt bad about them being eaten.

"You did not have to show out so hard for the new girl," Bethany said in accepting happiness as Mya rubbed her hands together in front of her in what looked like nervousness. "Now sit down and enjoy all your efforts."

"Of course, I did," Mya countered, even though she moved to take the last seat at the table on the other side of Declan. "First impressions are everything, and I never want someone's first impression of my food to be anything but my best."

I could sense an argument on the horizon, so despite how out of character it was for me, I said, "Consider my first impression of your food... absolutely blown away. I haven't even tasted it yet, and already my mouth is watering."

Mya smiled at me genuinely, and if I wasn't mistaken, a blush rose under her deeply tanned skin.

"Thank you. Let's hope it tastes as good as you think it looks," she said as she eyed her dishes with scrutiny.

Nearly everyone laughed at that, and as if on cue, everyone started reaching hands into the center of the table to grab this or that to fill their plates.

I had a little bit of everything, and when I say it was delicious, I'm not kidding.

Everyone around the table seemed to agree with me, and as the night wore on, I felt more and more at ease with this group, more so than I'd ever felt with any other group in the past, if I was being honest.

I learned a lot about each member while at the same time still not knowing them at all; such is the nature of a night out with new people. But by the time we were all ready to leave, I felt a tug on my heart as I thought about when I would see them again.

Already, no matter how hard I hadn't wanted them to, the people of this island had grown on me, and despite the logical side of me that screamed for me to take it easy and go about this slowly, by the end of the evening, I already knew I was hooked.

This place was magical. And the people here were what made it so. It was like I'd woken up from a nightmare to find the real world nowhere near as terrifying as my dreams, and as I rode back to Declan's place on the back of his motorcycle with my belly full, I started to really come to terms with the fact that I never wanted to leave.

CHAPTER 13

DECLAN

*Y*ou know how there are just some things in life that will always stick with you? Memories that shine in your mind like bullet points on a timeline?

Well, the sight of Kaliyah in Tristan's old helmet became one of those memories for me the moment I saw her standing there in it.

Her eyes had been big with worry or nerves or something, but that doe-eyed look affected me in ways I wasn't ready to accept, especially after her features softened at my touch.

I'd been doing my best to be a gentleman for her from the moment I told her I wasn't one after our game of Rat Trap.

There was just something about her that made me want to be what she needed, and because she responded way better to me when I was all nice and gentlemanly-like than she did when I was being an ass, I was willing to go out of my way to make her comfortable.

In reality, I wasn't doing anything that strictly went outside the range of my character; I was still being myself, even though I was being gentler and softer with her than I usually had a tendency to be.

I was still me, but I was being the me that Kaliyah brought out, rather than the sad and lonely one I usually was.

That night, after heading back to my apartment, we sat on the couch and stayed up ridiculously late talking about everything under the moon, and nothing at all at the same time.

Her laughter filled my living room - a sound it didn't hear too often - and later, when we headed to the bedroom because it was more comfortable than the couch, her laughter rang out in there as well.

We were play-fighting and bantering back and forth, neither one of us willing to call it quits or go to sleep, but when I saw the yawn Kaliyah tried to hide behind the back of her hand, I slid over to her slowly to drop my head in her lap.

Her back was resting up against the headboard, and though I could tell she was surprised by my movement at first, it was her turn to surprise me when I felt her fingers sliding in my hair to rub my scalp.

Neither one of us spoke about how close we were or what our bodies were doing; our conversation kept its same pace until my eyes were closing without my permission.

"Did you hear me?" I heard her ask, jolting me out of sleep a few seconds later.

Groaning some and burying my face in her thighs, I said, "No, I'm sorry. I fell asleep there for a second."

Her light-hearted giggle sounded around me again.

A few minutes later, her fingers still rubbing the top of my head, she said, "You're way too good for me, you know that?" in a subtle whisper she didn't think I would hear.

Despite my sleepiness, I mumbled, "You've got that backwards," as I playfully smacked her thigh before letting my hand settle where it landed.

Her fingers stilled in my hair, and I heard a small, audible gasp escape from her throat, but she didn't say anything else before sleep overtook me completely.

The next morning, I woke up with Kaliyah wrapped tightly in my arms again.

Her mouth was hanging open, her hair was all kinds of fucked up, and she was even snoring some.

She was absolutely gorgeous.

I laughed at her image quietly as I disentangled myself from her as gently as I could; I had to piss, but I didn't want to wake her like I had the previous morning.

Luckily, the power had been turned back on at some point during the night, and I took a long hot shower, thankful for it.

When I was done getting ready for the day, I checked in on Kaliyah, but she was still completely passed out, so I set about gathering all the electric candles I'd set up so I could get them out of the way.

The phone rang, but when it stopped a few seconds later, I knew Nash was downstairs, having opened the shop like usual.

Going about what I'd been doing before the phone started ringing, I tucked most of the candles away in the top of my closet before heading back for more when someone started banging on the door that led down to the surf shop.

I rushed over to answer it so whoever it was wouldn't wake Kaliyah, but all those thoughts vanished as I took in Nash's face.

"What is it? Is Moms okay?" I asked, pulling the kid in my apartment and closing the door behind him.

He looked worried, which for him, was never something you'd see on his face, ever. I couldn't get answers from him fast enough.

"No, she's fine," Nash said. "It's probably not that serious."

Taking in his demeanor, I had to disagree completely. "What's going on?" I asked, my voice clipped because I didn't know whether I needed to worry or not, and that always set me on edge.

"The shop just got a call," he said, seeming hesitant to tell me about whatever the call had been.

"Who was it?"

"I don't know," he said as his face pinched up like he was concerned I'd be mad or something. "They didn't say anything."

Immediately, my nerves settled, and in their place, confusion drifted in.

"So it was like a prank call? What's got you all worked up, bud? Just spit it out."

"I don't know, man," he said as he got up and started pacing. "All I heard was breathing, but the way it sounded, Dec..." his words stopped right as his feet did too, his eyes pleading with me as he searched for words to describe whatever it was he'd experienced.

"What?" I asked in confusion. "Like someone was just breathing into the phone? That doesn't make any sense."

"It wasn't like regular breathing, Dec. That's what I'm trying to tell you. It was..." He thought for a second. "Sinister."

I paused as a smile started spreading on my face in spite of how much I was trying not to let it happen.

"Oh, come on, man. I'm being serious," Nash said as a smile started spreading on his as well.

"Alright," I said, throwing my hands up. "The shop got a weird call. It's cool. Let's get some breakfast in you, and you'll feel better."

I turned around to head into the kitchen when I saw Kaliyah standing in the doorway to my bedroom with her eyes bugging out of her head. It was apparent she'd heard about the phone call, and as I took in her expression, I knew it had freaked her out.

"Don't worry," I said, knowing deep inside that I had every reason in the world to worry. "It's probably nothing."

143

"Are you sure?" she asked me before she turned her attention to Nash. "Could you tell anything about them? Like whether it was a guy or anything?"

I couldn't quite understand why she was asking such a thing, but Nash answered her quickly enough.

"Nah. It was just freaky soundin'."

"Y'all need to quit staying up so late," I said with a forced smile as I started pulling out bagels and cream cheese. "It was just a phone call."

Right then, the phone started ringing again, pulling each of us up short.

Steel in my veins, I readied myself to handle whoever was on the other end of the line as I picked it up.

"Smooth Rides Surf Shop," I said out of habit, my voice coming out more stern than it usually would.

"Hi, this is Mrs. Himby from Coastal Carolina Community College. Is Nash Wallace there?"

"Yes, he's here. One second," I said with a smile as I handed the phone over to Nash.

His face fell as he realized who was calling, and as I listened in on his conversation shamelessly with my arms crossed over my chest, I gathered he was confirming a testing time of some sort.

When he hung up a minute or so later, I couldn't stop myself. "You were just trying to get out of that test, weren't you?"

"No," Nash said, indignantly.

"Uh-huh," I said as I went about making the bagels again. "Sure. Whatever you say."

"I swear I wasn't trying to get out of anything," Nash said, even though he was smiling in my direction.

Kaliyah seemed to be trying to hide a smile too.

Instantly, I was thankful for that call, knowing it had gone a long way toward helping settle Kaliyah and Nash's worries.

In my gut, I knew something was wrong, but I wasn't willing to let fear grab ahold of the two people standing in the room with me; they were too innocent.

I'd take their concerns and make sure they were safe, so they wouldn't have to. And if it meant hiding the potential seriousness of the first call, so be it.

I wanted them to believe it was a prank call, even though the club flowed through my mind as the culprits the second I'd heard about it.

However, I'd prepared for this day - for the day when the club would come calling, and I had a plan.

I just needed to ensure Kaliyah and Nash stayed safe while I executed it.

~

"*Y*ou know what? Dammit, I think you have to go on a date with me," I said playfully to Kaliyah as I threw another bodyboard up to Nash, where he was setting them up in a new display.

Laughing as she handed me another one from the box we were unpacking, she said, "Oh, really? And why's that?"

Turning to face her fully and crowding her space some, I looked down at her as I said, "Because you want to."

My hands landed on each of hers, where they wrapped around the bodyboard she was holding. Her cheeks flushed bright red, but her eyes looked back at me in challenge.

"Who told you that?" she asked, her voice seductive and intoxicating.

Rubbing my thumbs over her knuckles with one hand and lifting my other to boop her nose quickly, I said, "Your face."

Giggling, she pushed the bodyboard into my chest harder than was necessary and I fake stumbled back before I handed it up to Nash without even looking at him.

"My face is a lying liar," she said as she reached back down into the box for another board.

"Oh, come on, Kali," Nash said, using his new nickname for her pleadingly. "Go on a date with him. What could it hurt?"

Kaliyah huffed with a smile as she placed her hands on her hips and stared up at Nash, leveling him with a bratty glare.

"Isn't it too soon for me to start dating? And really, how am I supposed to date him when he hasn't even outright asked me yet, huh? Sorry, but I don't go on dates until I'm actually asked to, and even then, only if the guy is really awesome."

Nash and I both laughed at how cute she was being.

"You want me to get all mushy for you?" I asked like a smartass as I took the board she'd grabbed from her hands and set it at our feet. "Fine."

I pulled both of her hands into mine and stared down deep into those green eyes of hers. "Kaliyah Bennett, would you do me the honor of going on a date with me?"

Still playing coy, even though I could tell I was getting to her, she said breathily, "What's in it for me if I do?"

A million answers to that question flowed through my mind right then, but I reined them all in.

I leaned down and put my mouth right up against her ear, letting my lips graze the delicate skin there. "You'll just have to agree and find out, now won't you?"

Standing back up, I met her challenging and lust-filled glare with one of my own, waiting for her to answer.

It was an excruciating few seconds, to say the least.

Sighing, she said, "Alright," so softly, I barely heard her.

"Excuse me? What?" I asked, squeezing her hands a little tighter. "I didn't hear you."

"I will go on a date with you," she said, her voice firm and unwavering like it should always be.

"Awwww," Nash said, breaking up the moment Kaliyah and I

were sharing, and after I let go of her hands, I thrust the board up at him harder than I needed to.

All of our laughter sounded through the shop at that, and it didn't stop for nearly the whole day.

Kaliyah fit in perfectly with Nash and me, her strong, silent type of work ethic merging perfectly with ours, and after we'd cleaned up everything the hurricane had left behind and closed down the shop for the day, I sent Nash home and Kaliyah upstairs to get ready for our date.

Once they were either gone or occupied, I pulled my phone out and dialed a number I knew by heart but hadn't called in two years.

It rang and rang, eventually going to Uncle Lyn's voicemail without him answering. As his voice played through the earpiece, I had a wave of emotions hit me all at once, and as the tone blared, telling me to leave a message, I couldn't get any words out.

Quickly, I hung up before I dropped my hands to the counter and my head to my chest as I closed my eyes.

I missed Uncle Lyn so much. Him, my brothers, and all the guys from the club.

I missed them so much it was hard to think straight, but as I heard the shower turn off upstairs, I snapped myself out of those thoughts and pushed the worries from my mind.

I could try to get in touch with him again the next day.

I had a date with a beautiful woman I didn't want to disappoint, and I needed to get ready for it instead of spending my time mourning my past.

~

I knew Mya would get upset if we went anywhere other than Island Thyme for our first date, and since it was still one of only a few places that had already opened back up after the hurricane, that's where Kaliyah and I went first.

Nash had spilled the beans to Mya shortly after Kaliyah had agreed to the date, and not too long after that, I'd gotten my own call from her where she basically said if I fucked things up with this girl, she'd kick my ass.

I might've been able to go toe to toe with many a man and hold my own, but Mya was not someone I wanted to cross.

And of course, Mya being Mya, she pulled out all the stops when we arrived.

We got the best booth in the restaurant - the one by the fire-place that was secluded from all the other tables - and we didn't even have to order because Mya had made 'something special' for us.

"Mya really didn't have to do all this," Kaliyah said to Bethany as she placed our crab and lobster-filled dishes in front of us.

Bethany chuckled a dark sort of laugh before she said, "I'll tell her you said that," and walked off, giving us some privacy.

"Now you've done it," I said with a smirk, watching as Kaliyah's face went red again.

"What? What'd I do?"

"You'll see," I said as I started digging into the badass meal in front of me.

Not a solid minute later, Mya came out of the kitchen and scooted into the booth beside Kaliyah.

"Bethany says you think I didn't need to do all this."

Seeming caught off guard and put on the spot, Kaliyah said, "Well, yeah," in a defensive and confused tone I found adorable.

Leveling Kaliyah with a smile as she rested her elbows on the table in front of her, she said, "I'm gonna clue you in, 'cause I think you're awesome."

In Kaliyah's defense, she didn't back down or rise to Mya's

attempts at baiting her, but instead sat there and waited for Mya to explain whatever it was she was going to go off about.

Honestly, there was no telling what it could be with that one.

"This guy here," she said as she pointed at me.

"Hey, I'm not in this," I said as I stuffed a bite of food in my mouth.

"Yes, you are. Shut up. Anyway," Mya said as I laughed at her. "This man has lived here for two years and has not once been out on a real date."

I huffed at her and put my fork down. "Thanks for throwing all my business out there."

Mya pinched her face and said, "You're welcome," like the smartass she was, and turned back to Kaliyah.

"Like I was saying, the second I heard Dec was taking you out, I had to get involved." Mya laughed some, and Kaliyah joined her.

"I'm glad you guys are gettin' off at my expense, but I promise it's not as bad as she's makin' it sound," I tried to cover up what was all entirely too true.

"He's basically the island's most eligible bachelor, but none of the girls here have ever struck a nerve with him like you have. So don't fuck it up, either one of you." Mya said threateningly to both of us, causing all of us to fall into laughter as she got back up.

"I'll see what I can do," Kaliyah said, smirking, and I glanced over at her, trying to ignore the promise hidden in her words.

Mya dropped both her hands flat on the table as she ducked her head. "Oh shit," she said, and instantly I knew a certain someone must have walked in the door.

Half-assed standing up as best I could in the booth, I looked over the wall that encased the booth to the front door, where I confirmed my suspicions.

Sitting back down and leveling Mya with a glare to get back at hers, I said, "Why don't you go ask Misty out already, huh?"

Then mocking a previous conversation we'd had, I said, "You're not gettin' any younger."

Mya slapped my shoulder in mock outrage, and I laughed hard at the face she was making.

"You watch your mouth," she said as she stood up straight and fiddled with her chef's coat, her eyes following Misty as she walked through the restaurant to take her seat. "I'll ask her when I'm good and ready."

Glancing around like she'd forgotten what she was supposed to be doing, she looked back down at Kaliyah and said, "I'm happy to do anything that'll make this dude happy too. He's got a heart of gold; this one does."

She started to walk away but turned right back a second later.

"Oh, and don't forget about the party on Bree's Island tomorrow. I'll strangle you both if you don't come." She slapped me on the arm again before she left to head back to the kitchen, and Kaliyah laughed, but all I could do was smile because I was definitely still embarrassed from what she'd told Kaliyah.

"I don't date tourists, which is who mostly comes here," I said by way of explanation, but Kaliyah waved a hand at me dismissively.

"You don't have to defend yourself to me. Your decisions tell me everything I need to know."

I was shocked by her admission because I could tell she was being truthful. It seemed like she was saying that, not simply in response to what I'd said, but as if it were just a general rule she was laying out there.

Her eyes met mine across the table, and her voice turned serious.

"I don't know what the future holds, but if this here," she motioned between the two of us, "is going to go anywhere significant, I'll go ahead and say it now: I don't want either of us to have to defend ourselves to one another. That only leads to lies and excuses for being who we are. We should be our truest selves with each other, and that should show us what we actually want.

You didn't want to date for two years; that's why you didn't. And that's perfectly fine. I'm not judging you, nor will I ever. If we have to defend our choices, I don't want it."

I was trying to grasp what was obviously very important to her, but I was having a hard time. "What do you mean?"

Sighing some, she said, "I just got out of a relationship where all I heard, all the time, every day, was lie after lie, and excuse after excuse. Cam was out there doing what he wanted to do, not being real or upfront with me about anything, and it drove me crazy. I don't want that shit anymore. I won't have it.

I don't know if this thing between us is even smart, given how sudden it is, but I don't want to have to defend my decisions, whatever they may be, and I don't want you to have to either.

If we want to start a committed relationship, we should just say it. If we don't, we should say that too. If we do start one, and one day you decide you want to sleep with other women, you need to tell me so I can pack up and move on. If we start one, and I start to feel like it's all happening too fast for me to be comfortable, I should be able to tell you that without repercussions."

She paused and looked at me with hope and sadness filling her eyes.

This girl was the realest woman I'd ever met in my life, and it was such a breath of fresh air; I literally blew out the breath I'd been holding as I relaxed under her gaze.

"I couldn't agree more," I said. "Life is too short to spend your days pretendin' to be somethin' you're not."

I wanted to spill everything I'd ever been right then, to drop everything that ever took place in my past at her feet to see what she'd do with it, but I held myself back because I didn't want to scare her off.

"We're still getting to know each other, and I know it feels like it's happenin' at the speed of sound, but as far as I know right now, somethin' with you is definitely what I want."

Her eyes lit up, and I couldn't help how my heart swelled at seeing it.

"I might not tell you everything about me right away, just like I'm sure you're not goin' to tell me everything about you right now either, but I'll go ahead and promise you I'll never lie to you. You've had enough of that already."

Tears started to shimmer in her eyes as they pooled there but didn't fall.

"Thank you. I'll promise not to lie to you either."

The look we shared over the table in that moment felt like it weighed a ton, and it took both of us a second or two to break out of it and get back to our food.

However, in no time at all, we fell right into that playful and fun back and forth we seemed to be so good at, and the heaviness of the conversation didn't come back up.

Later, for the second part of our date, I planned on taking Kaliyah for a drive on my bike.

She'd never ridden on a motorcycle before she'd met me, but every time I got her on that thing, I could tell her excitement level went through the roof, and I wanted her to have a longer experience than what I'd given her so far.

Heading off the island, I felt her relax into my back, and I sent my left hand to hers, where they were clasped together in front of me. Her thumb rubbed circles on my hand as we stopped at the light at the intersection of Highway 17 and Highway 50.

While we were waiting, I figured I'd warn her.

"I'm gonna stretch her legs, so you better hold on tight."

She didn't hesitate; she just squeezed me even tighter as the light turned green and I took off, hopeful the cops wouldn't be paying any attention to my speed that night.

The squeal she let out as we rounded the curves at top speed made me laugh and turned me on all at the same time.

She was having a blast, and I was what had caused it; I didn't think I'd ever get enough of that.

Soon though, after our ride was over and I parked the bike outside the garage because I didn't feel like putting it inside. I took her helmet and mine, placing them on the bike before I grabbed her hand and led her out onto the beach.

Kaliyah didn't ask questions, and she was fine with me leading, but she was soaking everything up as if it were her choice to do so, and something about that just spelled perfection to me.

When we got out onto the beach, the waves crashing a short distance away while the moon lit our faces, I slid one of my hands to each of her hips as I turned her to face me.

"You're kinda perfect, you know that?"

I was being truthful, but I was also trying to be sweet. However, a self-deprecating kind of giggle tore through her throat at my words, making it clear she didn't believe me at all.

I wasn't gonna stand for that shit though.

Reaching one hand out, I grabbed her lightly by the face, my hand cupping her chin just hard enough for her to look at me.

"You are."

I probably shouldn't have been so rough, but I wanted her to know how serious I was.

Her eyes swam with confusion and disbelief, but I saw them melting the longer I kept staring at her, and when I knew she'd finally accepted what I'd said, I loosened my grip and guided my lips to hers.

They were as soft as I'd imagined they would be, and when my tongue asked for entry, they parted sweetly, letting me finally get a taste of her.

In that moment, I was a goner; I was hers through and through.

I couldn't care less about anything else.

Kaliyah became my entire world right then, right there on that deserted beach in front of my shop.

I knew I would move mountains, break down heaven and earth for her if I had to, and I couldn't have been happier about it if I'd tried.

CHAPTER 14

DECLAN

*W*e didn't have sex that night, but we did have a
few pretty intense makeout sessions where it
was everything I could do to hold myself back and go at
Kaliyah's pace.

I wasn't getting a vibe that said she didn't want to; in fact,
the signs I was picking up screamed the opposite. However, it
was too soon after a very traumatic time in her life, and I didn't
want to rush into anything before I was sure she could handle it.

No matter what most people will try and tell you, sex always
comes with emotions when the people are in situations like the
one Kaliyah and I found ourselves in; there's no way around it.

You can't feel that intensely about someone and keep those
emotions at bay. Especially not when you add in the emotions
sex can bring to the table.

Don't get me wrong, I'd fucked without emotion before.

I'd hated it, but I'd done it.

The difference was, those girls hadn't had a hold on me like

Kaliyah did, and I knew as soon as we did have sex, how I felt about her would only increase.

I didn't know exactly how she felt about it, but that was my take away from the subject.

Instead, we played cards again and 'watched' Netflix. Really it was just playing in the background while Kaliyah and I made out, talked, and played around with each other.

Again, she slept in my bed that night, and I'd already decided I didn't want her sleeping anywhere else.

She didn't seem to mind either since she hugged my arm as she fell asleep.

The next day, everything was going pretty smoothly until we were nearing the end of the day.

We were all down in the shop, sitting around, talking while we waited for the customers outside to get done with their paddleboard rentals when the phone rang, and Nash answered it.

As soon as I looked at his face, I knew it was the same caller from the day before, and with a hefty dose of aggression, I took the phone from Nash's outstretched hand and spoke to the asshole on the other end.

"Who the fuck is this?"

The breathing stuttered for a second, but even what I heard of it let me know right away why it had freaked Nash out.

It was almost like the breathing was coming through some sort of device, like a voice scrambler, and immediately, I knew I was dealing with the club.

I was about to tell them to quit with the head games and just put the prez on so I could talk to him, but before I could say anything, the caller hung up.

I looked at the call history, but of course, the call came from a blocked number, and as I glanced back up with disappointment, I was met with two worried gazes staring back at me.

"Don't worry," I said. "I'll handle it."

"Who was it?" Nash asked, but I just shook my head at him.

"You don't think it's Cam, do you?" Kaliyah's worry had me second-guessing myself for a second.

"Do you think he'd do something like this?" I asked.

Kaliyah sighed dejectedly with a bitter laugh that held no humor in it. "There's no telling what he'll do. I mean, you've heard the voicemails, seen the texts. That man has lost his damn mind... even more than usual."

That was true. He'd been blowing her phone up all day, every day, with calls and texts. If I wasn't mistaken, he'd called or texted around two hundred times the day before, literally, but Kaliyah wouldn't let me do anything about it.

She'd just said he'd get tired after a while and silenced her phone.

She still told me what number he was at for the day because I'd asked her to keep me updated, which I appreciated, but it was still unnerving.

However, from what I'd seen and heard, all of his voicemails and texts had gone from screaming at her, to begging her to come back, so I didn't think he was the one calling the shop.

He seemed like he'd descended into sadness rather than anger, but the person who'd called the shop was definitely being driven by the latter emotion.

"I don't think it's Cam," I said, trying to ease her mind.

"Then who is it?" Nash asked again, his anger starting to show through. I knew it was just a front for the fear he felt because I knew him so well, but I couldn't deny the fact that he did have reason to worry, and he knew why.

Kaliyah didn't though, and I'd promised her I wouldn't lie to her.

Sighing, I looked straight at Nash.

"It's probably the club."

Nash's shoulders sank some as his face took on the look of a kicked puppy.

"So it's happening then," he said, sadness marring his voice.

"What? What's happening? What club?" Kaliyah asked, breaking my attention away from Nash for a second.

Nash looked at Kaliyah with sympathy in his eyes and then sent his gaze back to me in question.

I nodded at him, and he took the cue I was giving him, saying, "I'm gonna go check on the customers. Their time's up."

He got up and walked out the back of the shop as I turned to Kaliyah.

"I promised I'd never lie to you, and I'm not gonna break it by not copping up to this on day one," I started.

At first, for a split second, she looked scared, but no sooner had that registered in my brain than I saw her set her shoulders and lift her chin slightly as if she were physically readying herself for whatever it was I was about to throw at her.

The movement made me like her even more.

"Before I was born, my family helped start the Lost Savages Motorcycle Club out of Savannah, Georgia. My father, my Uncle Lyn, and their best friend, Ray, forged what's become one of the largest MC's in the south.

When I was really little, my dad had some heat on him, so he joined the military and took us with him when he got stationed down on Oahu.

He died in combat four years later."

I could tell none of this was making much sense to her as she listened to me, but to her credit, she didn't interrupt me or ask questions, which made getting through what I was about to say way more comfortable than it could've been.

"My mom, my brothers, and I had to move back to Savannah after that.

My uncle took us in and basically raised my brothers and me because my mom lost her fuckin' mind after my dad died.

She got remarried at one point, but that's not important.

My older brother, Gavin, my younger brother, Tristan, and I were raised in that club. It was all we knew."

Kaliyah was listening intently, but her face was an impassive one I couldn't read at all. It was nerve-racking, trying to keep talking when I couldn't tell how she was taking what I was telling her, but I pushed past all my reservations and just got it all out in the open.

"Well, you see, Gavin and me... we hated the military after Dad died. We were old enough to really feel the loss of him, but Tristan... I think he was just too young to understand how dangerous it was. He only saw that part of our lives before Dad died as being the happiest ones we ever knew, and ran with it.

He grew up idealizin' both Dad and the military. It was the only thing he wanted to do when he grew up, and no matter how hard Gavin and I tried to convince him otherwise, he was dead set on joinin' as soon as he turned eighteen.

So Gavin and me, we didn't patch in 'cause we knew if Tristan was goin' into the military, there was no way we were gonna let him go alone; that shit just wouldn't happen.

We went everywhere together, and Afghanistan was no different."

I paused for a second so I could get the words out, but Kaliyah didn't rush me.

"Tristan died while we were over there."

It felt like a ball was lodged in my throat, and the memory of Tristan coughing up blood and grunting in pain flashed through my mind, threatening to bring all those emotions right back up to the surface, but with everything I had in me, I pushed them down so I could finish telling Kaliyah what she needed to know.

"When we finally got back to Savannah, Gavin was spiralin'.

He'd been the oldest and had always put our safety on his shoulders, so he didn't know how to live without Tristan.

I didn't either... hell, I still don't, but Gavin...

He crumbled after that. You couldn't tell him shit. He'd drink himself into a stupor and fuck anything that walked, pass out in the middle of the street, and wake up the next day to start back over.

He was gonna kill himself, and there was nothin' I could do to make him stop."

I was lost in my own retelling of some of the worst months of my life, but Kaliyah sat through all of it without making a peep.

"I didn't know what else to do, so I called Uncle Lyn, and after a while, we got Gavin to start focusin' on the club instead of on missin' Tristan.

We both patched in and moved up the ranks faster than everyone else 'cause we'd been born and bred to lead the thing when we grew up.

Really, all the guys treated us like we were the long-lost prodigal sons returned.

I didn't much care for the hoopla, but I loved the fact that it helped get Gavin's life back on track.

Ray is the president, and my uncle is the VP, but they were both groomin' Gavin, Ray's son, Everette, and me to take over for them from the get.

So one night, they sent us all out on this run to meet up with the cartel."

I paused again to see if that word would make her go running out the back door, but she stayed firmly rooted to her spot as if it didn't faze her at all, so I continued.

Looking down as I remembered that night, I said it as quickly as I could so I could get past it.

"The deal went south for some dumbass reasons that aren't important, and the cartel wasn't playin'. Everette and Gavin both died that night, and honestly, I'm lucky I ended up livin' through it.

I woke up the next day in the hospital with a gunshot wound to my thigh that had nearly severed my artery."

She looked surprised at that, but I went on anyway.

"Everyone was losin' their minds, and nobody knew what to do.

There was only one prince left to take the throne, and it wasn't Ray's son.

Ray got it in his head that I needed to be held personally responsible for Everette's and Gavin's deaths, sayin' I should've died there with them.

I fuckin'…" my words died on my lips because it was so hard to talk about.

After a few deep breaths, I finally worked up the strength I needed and said, "I tried so fuckin' hard to keep them alive," but I couldn't look up from the counter while I said it because I didn't want Kaliyah to see the tears in my eyes.

"I would've died there with 'em if it weren't for Mac. We grew up together, and he was our best friend. He's been in the club from the day he turned eighteen.

It had been chaos that night, and I was firin' back, tryin' to keep pressure on their wounds, usin' myself to block more bullets from gettin' to 'em, but then Mac came bumrushin' through, tacklin' me to the ground before he started draggin' my ass back to the truck 'cause I couldn't fuckin' walk.

The cops were comin', and the cartel peeled outta there fast once they heard the sirens.

Then Mac wouldn't let me help him get Gavin's and Everette's bodies.

That fucker had to do it all himself, but by the time he got done loadin' 'em in the back, I'd already passed out from all the blood loss.

We tried tellin' Ray what'd happened, but he didn't want to hear it. Grief does some fucked up things to a person.

But the whole damn club divided ranks after that.

There were those that were loyal to my uncle and me, and those that were firmly on Ray's side.

But I'd had enough.

I couldn't fuckin' do it anymore.

I'd lost too many people.

Both my brothers were dead, Everette was dead, and Ray wanted me dead too.

So I left.

After I got the insurance money from Gavin's death, I added it to what we'd gotten from Tristan's that hadn't been touched yet, and I fuckin' left.

I came here, bought this place, and I've been here ever since, but I knew it would only be a matter of time before they found me."

Kaliyah's face was full of sympathy as I said, "I can't be sure, but I think the caller is someone with the club. The news crew that was here the other day, I know they got me on camera, and that news footage was broadcast all over.

I've always been cautious about that kinda thing, but I'm pretty sure that's what let 'em know where I was."

Kaliyah didn't say a word for a solid minute, just sat there and stared at me, and though I wanted to hurry up and find out what she thought about everything I'd said, I couldn't very well go rushing her when she hadn't rushed me.

She got up eventually, walked over to me, and wrapped me up in a hug I felt in my soul.

I hugged her right back, taking every bit of comfort she was offering up right then, letting it ease how terrible I was feeling.

Pulling away only far enough so she could look at me, she said, "We'll figure out who it is, and we're not gonna worry about it until we know for sure, okay?"

She'd flipped it on me.

I was supposed to be the one easing her mind, and there she was, putting my emotions in perspective.

"Okay," I said before I kissed her, losing myself in the woman that just continued to blow my mind.

CHAPTER 15

KALIYAH

I have no idea what most people would've done if they'd found themselves in my position; I've never been good at guessing what other people are going to do.

Every time I've tried, my assumptions have always fallen short; the actual outcome, no matter the circumstance, always ended up being something that never even crossed my mind.

I could've sat there and tried to guess what Declan was going to tell me as Nash walked out of the surf shop, but no amount of time in the world would've allowed me to come up with what actually came out of his mouth.

I guess I should've known a certain level of danger was going to come with Declan's territory since I was dealing with someone who was covered in tattoos, carried a pistol, and rode motorcycles and surfed during hurricanes, but I never thought, with how Declan acted, with how awesome his personality was, or with how many friends and close relationships he seemed to have, that he was basically living in hiding.

That was quite a shock to learn.

However, where other people might've run in the other direction for greener pastures, all I wanted to do was be there for him - to help him through whatever was coming, but to also take that pain he'd been living with and pull it into myself so he wouldn't have to feel it alone.

"Y'all have a good day," Nash called out before he closed the door to the surf shop behind him, snapping me out of my thoughts with a jolt of reality.

Declan's head had been laying on my chest, his arms wrapped around me, pulling me in tight to him as I ran my fingers through his soft hair, but when Nash walked in, Declan picked his head up reluctantly, shared a weighted glance with me, and rose from the stool he'd been sitting on.

"You're still here." Nash's smile was infectious as he made his way over to us.

Giggling a little, I said, "I think you guys will have to try a lot harder than that to get me to leave now."

Nash's face lit up at my words, but Declan's head whipped around to face me, an unasked question painted clearly across his features.

I still hadn't outright said I was planning on staying; in fact, I'd been dodging the subject whenever it came up because there'd been too much uncertainty floating around for me to make that call. However, I was done lying to myself.

I was in love with Topsail Island, everything on it, and every person I'd met here. So what if the worst happened and I ended up hating it? I could just pack up and find somewhere else if it came to that.

But deep down in my gut, I was pretty sure that wasn't going to happen.

No, I hadn't been here that long, and no, my life was nowhere near sorted out, but I figured Topsail was as good a place as any to make a fresh start.

"Yes, I'm staying."

I'd barely gotten the words out before Declan was swooping me up and spinning me around in a circle a couple of times, his and Nash's laughter sounding off the walls of the surf shop.

"You've made my day, woman," Declan said as he sat me back down on my feet.

"I'm not living on your couch though," I stopped my giggles to say sternly, putting my proverbial foot down.

I may have decided to stay on Topsail, and I may have been falling for Declan faster than I ever would've dreamed possible, but I wasn't going to be stupid with this second chance I was taking for myself.

"I haven't once made you sleep on the couch," Declan said like I'd wounded him.

Laughing, I said, "That may be the case, but I still need a place of my own. I need to talk to Kaylynne."

"Well, she'll probably be at the party out on Bree's Island. I'm sure you can talk to her there," Nash said, making his way around behind the counter.

Declan stood there for a minute, almost as if he were deep in thought, trying to decide something.

"What do you say to comin' with us, kid?"

Again, Nash's face lit up. He was just so easy to please or amuse that almost anything you said could make him smile. "You mean that? Seriously?" he asked, and I got the distinct impression this particular subject had been an issue for them before. "What about the shop?"

Declan dismissed Nash's worries with a single look.

"Okay, fine," Nash said, throwing his hands up in the air. "Don't look a gift horse in the mouth; got it. I'm gonna go grab some towels and call Moms to tell her."

He was already turning on his heel to run up to Declan's apartment, but he stopped mid-stride when Declan said, "Boy, don't go tell your mama! What the hell is wrong with you?"

We all laughed some more, and a short time later, I was climbing on Dusty's boat to head over to whatever Bree's Island turned out to be.

$\sim$

*C*oolers of alcohol were placed sporadically, where a bunch of people were gathering around a large bonfire. The island sat in the center of the intercoastal waterway, so though there were no waves, there was still plenty of calm water to swim in. Trees dotted the landscape, creating a comfy place to get out of the sun, and people had even gone so far as to set up more of those adorable little hammocks between a few of them.

Music was blaring through speakers I couldn't see, and everyone was clad in their bathing suits, already having a blast by the time we got there.

The girls of the island welcomed me like they had every time I'd met up with them, while Declan, Nash, and Dusty headed over to the grill to make burgers and hot dogs with a few other guys I hadn't met yet.

After tucking a beer into each one of my hands and grabbing two for herself, Roxy pulled me behind her and the rest of the girls as we made our way over to the hammocks.

Five of them were set up in a circular formation between the trees that surrounded a small fire pit, and each of us slung ourselves down on one before we cracked our beers open.

Bethany was drinking a Coke, but that didn't matter; I think that girl would have a good time no matter where she went or what she was doing.

The conversation was light-hearted and funny as we all talked and hung out, but soon the topic shifted over to whether I'd made up my mind about staying or not, and you would've thought I'd told them I'd won the lottery with how excited they got when I told them I'd be staying.

"Fuck yeah, more friends that actually live here!" Mya screamed as she threw her head back and her arms up in the air. "This is cause for celebration! I'm gonna get more beers." She clamored off, only stumbling a little as she walked.

"We might've pregamed a little too much," Roxy said, winking at me as she tipped her beer back with a devilish smile. "If you don't mind, I'm gonna need you to show me the places I can afford, Kaylynne."

"If I don't mind? Girl, you'll be saving my ass, not the other way around," she said with a dismissive smile in my direction. "What's your budget?"

Immediately I cringed on the inside and looked down at my beer as I considered all the factors. However, with the beer steadily feeding into my system, thinking about numbers was difficult.

"I've got some stashed away, but I'm gonna need that to live on too. I didn't really come with a plan, but I've been thinking I want to pay for a year upfront somewhere. That way I'll have time to figure out my job/author situation and see if that goes anywhere. If I have to cut that down to like six months or something so I can stay here though, I think I can make that work too."

"You just come by my place tomorrow, and I'll get you all set up with what'll work best for you," Kaylynne said. "We've got a lot of properties to choose from, so I'm sure there's something..."

"Yeah, there's something," Roxy interjected. "The apartment above mine!" Swiveling her head to me while her feet swung beneath her, she said, "I'd much rather have you as my neighbor than some rando that may or may not smell like pig's feet."

Laughing, I said, "I feel like there's a story there I'm missing," and immediately, everyone but Roxy groaned.

"Gah, don't get her started!" Bethany whined.

"Okay, look. Check this out..." Roxy's eyes got wider as she attempted to sit up straight, which was an impossible task in the hammock. She was all flailing limbs for a few seconds, and bouts of more laughter followed every movement she made.

"That's it. Imma head out," Bethany said as she climbed out of her hammock and made her way over to the guys while Roxy told me the horror story of the last place she'd lived.

Suffice it to say, the dude was gross. Roxy only stayed there for three days before she begged Kaylynne to find her somewhere else, and apparently, it had affected her so much, she'd told the story to all the girls 'at least twenty times' by Kaylynne's approximation.

I was dying laughing for what seemed like the rest of the day, and again, when it was time to leave, I just couldn't wait until the next time I would get to see everyone.

Nash had snuck quite a few beers by the looks of him when it was our group's turn for Dusty to take us back in the boat, and though Declan had a couple of choice words for Nash, he wasn't faring much better.

Honestly, the whole situation was just hilarious to me, and even though it had been a precarious trip back, with me driving the four-wheeler in the dark because they were too drunk to, it was still one of the most fun days I'd ever had in my life.

Nash and Declan were hanging off the back, trying to tell me how to drive the thing, drunk off their asses, which made me laugh so hard a few times I'd had to stop completely while I fell into hysterics. Which only made their chastisements worse, which only made me laugh harder.

I swear what should've only taken maybe ten minutes, tops, took a good thirty just to make it back to the shop.

When we finally got there, the boys argued over who would get to shower first, but while they were standing there arguing, I rushed into the bathroom and locked the door with an evil laugh they yelled at.

I took my sweet time, savoring the hot water as it poured over me. When I was done, I climbed into my comfiest pair of sweatpants and a tank top before towel drying my hair and throwing it up in a messy bun.

I was beyond trying to impress anyone, including Declan. The way I saw it, I might as well go ahead and show him what I could normally look like so there were no surprises down the line.

However, when I stepped out of the bathroom looking like that, I saw no disappointment on Declan's face.

Walking over to me, still in his black swim trunks that were riding dangerously low on his hips to show off his beautifully decorated skin, he towered over me, the lustful look in his eyes sending a steady current of electricity right through me.

Nash ran in the bathroom like he'd won a prize, but Declan's eyes didn't leave mine.

He raised one hand up to rub his thumb down my cheekbone sinfully.

"You look like the best kind of trouble."

My smile faltered at his words, and heat spread through me as I took him in, slowly pressing a hand to his firm, bare chest for the first time.

"You've got that backwards," I softly repeated his words from before.

The look on his face nearly killed me with how intense it was. As he kissed me again, more passionately than I'd ever been kissed in my life, my toes curled into the carpet, while any doubts I may have had about staying, disappeared altogether that very instant.

*T*he next morning, both Declan and Nash were hungover, and while I had a headache too, I didn't feel nearly as bad as they looked like they did.

Apparently, Nash was supposed to have gone home at some point, but since he'd crashed on Declan's couch that night, he'd woken up to a bunch of missed calls from Moms.

"She's pissed," Nash said as he leaned against the island, staring squinty-eyed at his phone.

"I'll take you home and talk to her, but we've got to get you cleaned up first, kid," Declan said, even though the same could've been said about him.

"Where do you keep your ibuprofen?" I asked with a smile as I forced them both to take a seat at the bar.

Declan looked at me like he was surprised I'd asked but answered me anyway, and after grabbing the bottle, I returned to the kitchen to make each of us a glass of water.

I dished out the pills and took two for myself so what I felt didn't worsen.

"Who's gonna run the shop while Moms chews us out?" Nash asked while I pulled out what I needed to make us some breakfast.

A little voice in my head told me it wasn't my house and that I shouldn't be going through, making myself so comfortable, but the way Declan smiled at me once he realized what I was doing silenced that voice completely.

"It'll just have to stay closed for now," Declan said, and Nash groaned as he put his head on the counter.

"We never close during the week in the summer," Nash said into the countertop, making me giggle some as I got the bacon going.

"I could watch it for you guys if you want me to. I mean, how long do you expect Moms to yell at you anyway?"

Nash picked his head up and shared a small smile with Declan. "There's no tellin.' It could be all day if the last time is anything to go by."

"Well, I might not have any clue what I'd be doing, but I can at least turn the 'open' sign on and count back change if I need to."

After a beat to consider his options, Declan agreed, and a short time later, after we'd eaten and Declan had walked me through the basic steps of renting out the stuff in the shop, they left, and I went back upstairs to make a cup of tea in my dad's mug since there were no customers yet.

When I was done, I strolled lazily down the stairs and took the tea out on the back deck.

It was around noon, and already the beach was filling up with people a little further down from where I was. However, no sooner had I sat down than the phone started ringing inside, and I'd had to rush through the store to get to it in time.

"Smooth Rides Surf Shop," I answered the phone, trying to sound like I knew what the hell I was doing, hoping I wouldn't have to answer any hard questions.

A second later, I heard the breathing, and instantly, panic and fear shot through my system.

The sound was unnerving, freaking me all the way out.

"So you're the biker's whore," the crackly robotic voice said, sliding ice through my veins.

"Excuse me?" I asked, dumbfounded and shaken. Nash had never said anything about the guy actually talking, and neither had Declan.

The voice breathed two more breaths, all slow and drawn out before he said, "Soon to be the biker's dead whore," and hung up.

I pulled the phone away from my ear and stared at it wide-eyed as my hands started shaking.

Someone who had their life together better than I did might have reacted better to the situation, but like I said, I'm not perfect, and sometimes I'm not the bravest.

That call had struck a chord of fear so deep-seated within me I didn't know what to do with myself as that someone's-watching-me feeling crept up my spine with a vengeance.

He might've been using some sort of voice scrambler, and I might not have had any way to prove my suspicions, but after hearing the voice, the fact that it might've been Cam would not leave my mind, and suddenly, every sound was a potential threat, every window and door, a potential access point, and every second that passed was a moment of borrowed time I didn't have to give away.

"That dinna sound like a good call," a man's voice sounded through the shop, startling the fuck out of me even further.

I hadn't seen him standing behind the aisle that ran down the center of the store when I'd rushed back inside to answer the phone, but as he spoke, he stepped around the corner so I could see him fully.

Dressed in black boots, jeans, a white t-shirt, and one of those leather vests bikers wear, the man tilted his head sideways as he stared me down and walked closer.

"Well, you look scared outta your wits, lass."

His accent was strange, like the southern one I was growing used to hearing from the people around here, but mixed with something older... Irish, maybe? I wasn't sure.

He looked to be in his fifties but still sported a full and dark, reddish-brown beard beneath ice blue eyes, which had crow's feet forming at the edges of them.

I stood up straighter and pushed all my fear back as best I could.

"Is there something I can help you with?"

I didn't want to admit how worked up I was, nor did I want

to over-analyze the situation and prejudge the man since I didn't know anything about him yet. He could've very well just been a customer in the surf shop who'd overheard the phone call, and I didn't want to scare off business by acting as hysterical as I felt on the inside.

"Fire veins," he said under his breath with a smile as he came up to the counter between us and rested his hands on its surface.

I would've backed up from his intimidating presence, but fear kept me rooted to my spot. However, I got the feeling by how the man smirked at me that he saw my rigidity as coming from a place of strength, rather than the weak parts of me that had really caused it. I wasn't going to argue about it.

"I'm lookin' for Declan Stone, lass. Have you seen him?"

Instantly, more fear spread through me because I had no idea how to answer the man. I didn't know whether he was friend or foe, or if I should cop to knowing Declan or lie about it, say I hadn't seen him or be truthful so the man might leave to look for Declan elsewhere.

However, after running each of those scenarios through my head as fast as possible, I knew I only had one option.

If this guy was out looking for Declan's blood, I certainly wasn't going to send him right where he could get it... not only Declan's but Nash's and Moms' as well.

"He's gone," I said, my voice coming out like I had balls of steel and an attitude with the man, like he was getting on my nerves. I'd hoped it would send the message that I wasn't too fond of him getting all up in my space, but apparently, I'd only caused him to have the opposite reaction.

Leaning even closer to me, he said, "I know that much, lass. What I don't know is where he's gone off to."

He stared at me for a second longer, and I knew he was assessing me, judging what he thought he could get out of me.

However, I stayed as still as possible, refusing to move even one muscle.

Then, backing up some as if what he was saying was of no consequence, he smiled as he added, "But dinna worry your pretty self about it jus' now. I'll take a seat and wait with you 'til he comes back."

CHAPTER 16

DECLAN

I'd barely made it halfway up the stairs at Nash's place when my phone buzzed in my pocket with a text from Kaliyah.

KALIYAH: Another phone call. Some Irish-sounding biker guy is here waiting for you.

My feet stopped moving altogether as it felt like my heart had stopped.

"What is it?" Nash asked, puzzled from the top of the stairs.

Sending a text back to her as quickly as my fingers could type it out, I didn't even bother responding to Nash as I turned on my heel and ran toward my bike.

ME: Stay where you are and try not to talk to him. There's a pistol under the counter. Use it if you have to. I'm on my way.

"Dec!" Nash yelled down as I started my bike up, but I didn't have time to explain my behavior. I didn't have time to break down the fact that as soon as I'd read Kaliyah's text, two different faces had floated through my mind, and I knew only one of them wouldn't outright kill Kaliyah if he thought she meant anything to me.

The whole way to the shop, it felt like I was moving in slow motion, like I couldn't get there fast enough, even though I was speeding as fast as I could go over top of all the sand that was still covering the streets.

However, as I finally pulled in a few minutes later, my fear began to vanish while my nervousness skyrocketed.

That was Uncle Lyn's bike parked outside. I'd been there the day he'd bought it, the same day I'd bought mine.

Parking next to Uncle Lyn's bike, I took my helmet off and inhaled a deep breath before I steadied my nerves enough to walk inside the shop.

I saw Kaliyah standing behind the counter with her arms crossed in front of her when I stepped through the door, and try as I might, I couldn't read her like I normally could. She was obviously putting up an impassive front to hide whatever emotions she was actually feeling, and right then, I couldn't have been prouder of her for it.

Uncle Lyn stood up as I rounded the corner, coming around the edge of the counter so we could face each other for the first time in two years.

His beard was longer than it'd been the last time I'd seen him, hanging a good two inches or so off his trim face, but everything else about him seemed exactly the same.

His chin-length hair was combed back like he'd always worn it, and the rings he never took off were still sitting on half of his fingers like I'd known they would be.

Our eyes met initially in what could have only been described as anger, but after a second, I saw the memories of our past in his eyes as they played away like a movie through my mind.

That anger I'd felt at first drifted away quickly into a sadness so strong it made tears threaten the backs of my eyelids, and a lump form in my throat.

It then morphed effortlessly into a rejoicing kind of happiness I felt in my bones, and I found both of us walking fast toward each other.

We wrapped one another up in a hug that had been way too long overdue, slapping each others' backs a few good times before we just stood there squeezing the fuck out of each other.

Taking one hand off my back so he could grab the back of my head, Uncle Lyn held my head there as he pulled away so he could stare into my face.

"God, I've missed ya, laddie."

"I've missed you too," I croaked out as we separated.

"Let me look at you." His face was all squinty-eyes and bearded smiles as he hit my biceps twice, laughing as he said, "Only gotten bigger, I see."

I reached out a hand to ruffle his hair because I knew he'd hate it and said, "And you've only gotten older."

We laughed for a moment more, but then reality sank into both of us at the same time.

I glanced over to see Kaliyah standing there with a bewildered and confused look on her face, sobering some so I could introduce them to each other.

"Kaliyah, this is my Uncle Lyn. Uncle Lyn, this is Kaliyah."

Uncle Lyn nodded at Kaliyah before he turned back to me. "You'd be proud, I think. The young lass wouldna say a word about where you'd gone, even with a beast like me askin.'"

I smiled at that. "Well, you must not be as scary as you think you are," I jested with him, pushing him in the arm one good time.

"Aye," he said as his eyes got bigger in self-assessment. "Maybe I'm losin' my edge." He glanced between Kaliyah and me for a second before saying, "I'll step outside and give you two a minute."

He turned to walk out onto the shop's back deck, and I waited until the door closed behind him before I stepped around the counter and wrapped Kaliyah up in my arms.

"I'm sorry. I didn't know he was coming, or I wouldn't have left."

"It's alright," she said into my chest. Stepping back, she looked up at me, and I could see the fear in her eyes as she talked. "Your uncle may not be here to murder anyone, but we still have a problem."

I listened to her tell me about the phone call, only barely containing the rage I felt growing inside my chest at someone, anyone, threatening Kaliyah.

The only reason that asshole, whoever he was, said anything was because she was a woman. That fucker hadn't said shit to Nash or me, and something about that just pissed me off even more.

I tried my best to put Kaliyah's mind at ease, telling her I was going to talk to my uncle about seeing if we could put a stop to it, but she was insistent on the fact that she didn't think the calls were from the club at all... that they were from Cam.

I would've been a fool to ignore her insight and opinion, so rather than continue to defend my thoughts about it by dismissing hers, I did my best to reassure her that even if that was the case, Cam was back in Chicago, and the only way he could reach her would be by phone anyway.

"If it is him, he's just still trying to control you. You can't let it get to you."

"But how would he know I'm with you?" Her voice had taken on this pleading sort of desperateness I hated hearing from her. "And he said I was going to be dead soon."

I knew nothing I said would put her mind at ease until I figured out who the caller was for sure and dealt with them. Hating to leave her sitting with her fear until that time came, I did the only thing I could do - I hugged her tightly, kissed her forehead, and walked out to talk with my uncle.

~

"*I* came to warn ya, laddie."

We were sitting in the adirondack chairs that sat in the shade at the back of the shop when Uncle Lyn spit that out.

"I've been coverin' for you for the last two years 'cause I knew you needed your time, but a few of the boys on Ray's side saw you on the news, helpin' with the clean up here, and it got back to Ray before I could stop it."

"What do you mean you've been coverin' for me?" My eyes were probably bugging out of my head at that point, but really, what he'd just said sent my head into a tailspin.

Smiling that knowing and sympathetic smile of his, Uncle Lyn reached over to lay a hand on my shoulder as he said, "You thought you were that good at coverin' your tracks on your own? Why, that's sweet, laddie. It really is."

His smartassness could go toe to toe with the best of them, but even though we smiled at his words, we sobered just as quickly a few seconds later.

He put his elbows on his knees, mirroring my own body language as he looked out at the waves. "After Gavin, God rest his restless soul, I knew you'd be leavin'.

You're just like your father in that way... never able to let the dead go quietly.

It hits you too hard... you feel it too deeply."

As much as I wanted to argue with the man, I knew I couldn't; he knew me entirely too well.

"I told 'em to let you leave, that you'd be back, and for a while, everyone was okay with that. They knew what you'd been through, and dinna want to rush you back if you weren't ready."

"What changed?" I asked, readying myself for whatever it was he was about to say.

"Ray's sick," he said, forcing an image of my old prez in his prime to flash through my mind. "Cancer."

I tried to equate the man I used to know with something like cancer, but Ray had always been the toughest, most brutal man I'd ever known, and the idea that someone like him could be even the least bit affected by something like a disease just didn't add up in my mind.

"So now everyone's vying for the top spots, gunnin' for my place too, and everyone's at each others' throats again. Some are wantin' to call you back, have you take my spot, while others think you deserve a traitor's death... it's not pretty, laddie, trust me."

Sighing, I ran my fingers through my hair.

"Do you have a plan? What do I need to do?"

Being in the club was a lifetime commitment, and I'd known that from the start. Even if I'd had a good two years to play lone wolf, I always knew that eventually, one day, I'd have to face what I'd left behind and seeing as how it was looking like things with the club were reaching a boiling point, I knew that time had finally come.

"I don't have so much of a plan right now as I've got some birds in the air."

Uncle Lyn had always been an incredible chess player, and he lived each day of his life like it was a move yet to be played - a move that had always been thought out way in advance. He was always thinking three, four, five steps ahead of what everyone else seemed to be thinking, and so far, from what I knew, it'd worked out well enough for him.

"I just came to warn you, and because I saw that you'd called."

"Yeah, we've been gettin' some weird calls here at the shop, and they've been scarin' the people I've got here. I was hopin' you'd be able to tell me if it was the club or not."

Uncle Lyn rubbed his hand down his beard as he thought for a second.

"I saw how that call affected that young lass you've got in there. She's a sweet one, by the way," Uncle Lyn said conspiratorially in my direction before he continued. "I don't know that they're comin' from the club, but I also don't know they're not. I'll look into it though and see what I can find out."

Standing because our visit with each other was obviously over, Uncle Lyn glanced around one good time while I rose to stand next to him.

Setting thick hands on each of my shoulders, he said, "It's been so good to see you, Decky."

I pulled him into another hug - one I had to have before he left my life again for who knew how long.

"Promise me you'll keep yourself and your people safe 'till I figure out somethin'," he said in my ear, but I couldn't do more than nod at him because of the lump that had reformed in my throat.

'Out of sight and out of mind,' had been playing a major role in my ability to move on with my life after leaving my old one behind, but it was like as soon as Uncle Lyn had shown up, not a single day had passed, and all the memories I had from back home assaulted me full-force.

Uncle Lyn slapped me one good time on the shoulder before he turned and walked away, going around the shop to get back to his bike. As soon as he turned the corner out of my line of sight, one of the tears that had been clamoring to fall from my eyes finally did.

I swiped it away quickly and got control of my emotions before I headed back inside the shop to reassure Kaliyah and call Nash so they would stop worrying.

However, my uncle's visit had only given me even more reason to be concerned, and I knew something was coming whether he was able to get in front of it or not.

I needed to be ready for when it came, and so did Kaliyah and Nash.

They were already too close to me; there was no way my old life wouldn't touch them when it came back to bite me in the ass. Hell, it seemed like it already had.

CHAPTER 17

KALIYAH

*W*hen Declan came back into the shop after talking with his uncle, he had every opportunity in the world to lie to me. He could've glossed over everything to ease my concerns, sugar-coated the threats we were facing or ignored them altogether, but he didn't do any of that, and it made me fall for him even harder.

He may not have been able to promise that everything was going to be okay, but he didn't lie. He was upfront, honest, and real with me, and after the past I'd had, I respected him more in that moment than I had any other man I'd ever known besides my father.

The club situation was far from handled and was probably going to blow up soon, but he and his uncle were going to do their best to ensure it didn't, and if it did, they were going to try and ensure it wouldn't affect me or any of the other people here.

He admitted that Cam could be a threat and that we needed

to treat him as such from that moment on, just in case it turned out to be him at the end.

Basically, Declan said, 'Yes, we've got some shit to deal with, but we're gonna face it together when it comes to get us,' and that was more reassuring and calming than any lie he could've told.

Nash showed up on his bicycle while we were talking on the back deck, looking like he was seconds away from crying. Seeing that happy kid's face so contorted in worry pulled at every single one of my heartstrings, but as soon as he saw us, relief flooded his face, and he dropped into one of the other chairs with an audible sigh.

"What the hell happened? Dec, you scared the fuck out of me." There was a sharp sliver of icy anger sliding through his words, and I saw it cut into Declan right in front of me.

"I'm sorry, kid," Declan said, his voice full of remorse.

He told Nash what all had happened, and though Nash still looked a little worried by the end of it, he also looked relieved because no harm had come to anyone while he'd been gone.

"Bring me with you next time," he said, insisting on being there for Declan if it were at all possible.

"That's not happenin' if I can prevent it, and you know it," Declan replied. The way he said that made it seem like there was no room for arguments, but Nash didn't care.

"What if you need backup? Man, that's what I'm here for!"

Smiling, Declan dropped a heavy hand on Nash's shoulder. "No, bud. You're here to earn a livin' while you go to school so you can make somethin' of yourself one day. I'm not lettin' you get wrapped up in this if I can help it, and you should let me give you that. This life isn't for you."

Nash's cheeks filled with a red tint as he snapped back, "And it is for her?!" He gestured over to me as he spoke words that might as well have been a slap in the face.

I had no idea whether he meant it wasn't safe for me either

or that I didn't belong with Declan, but either way, his words hurt, especially with how passionately he'd said them.

"Watch it, Nash," Declan warned.

"No, Dec! I'm not gonna sit at home and let you guys face all this by yourselves. I won't do it. There's no way the club's gonna come callin', and I'm not gonna be right here to help you."

It was a weird display of emotion from Nash. Though his voice held a great deal of conviction with every word he said, he also never rose to his feet, never raised his voice beyond a reasonable tone, the complete and utter respect and love he held for Declan keeping him remarkably centered given how passionate he felt about what he was saying.

Glancing down at the ground, Declan sighed before he looked back up at Nash.

"Alright, tell me then. What would you do if they showed up intendin' to kill me for bailin' on 'em, huh? You gonna try to save me by puttin' yourself in harm's way?"

Nash sat back like Declan had kicked his knees out from under him.

"What if they came and decided to hurt you or Kaliyah or Moms just to get back at me for hurtin' them? What would you do then?"

Declan's voice was calm and assertive. However, though I knew he was just trying to keep Nash out of harm's way, inadvertently, he was scaring me even more.

"Is that what's going to happen?" I couldn't stop myself from asking.

Declan's bright blue eyes shot up to mine like he'd just realized how his words could've affected me, and I could see the remorse he felt, but it did little to staunch my fear.

"Honestly, I don't know."

I knew he was being as truthful as possible, and though I was appreciative of his honesty, it didn't help much.

"Look," Nash said, pulling our attention to him. "None of us know what they're gonna do 'till they do it. That's always been the case. But I really think everything can go much better if we all stick together. Making me stay at the house when shit hits the fan only has the potential to make things worse. What if I could help? What if me being here is what keeps you and Kaliyah alive, Dec?"

Declan didn't answer him. Instead, he got up and started pacing at the other end of the deck. He ran one of his hands through his hair and blew out a long breath, but I didn't see whatever else he did because Nash was pulling me by the hand inside the shop.

"Come on. He needs a minute."

Following behind Nash, trusting he knew what he was talking about, I took a seat on the barstool by the counter where Declan's uncle had been sitting earlier while Nash walked around to the other side.

"I'm really glad you've decided to stay, but it couldn't have been worse timing," Nash said as he dropped his elbows down to the counter so he could lean on it.

"You say you're glad I'm here, but almost everything else you've said today has made me think you don't want me here. Is it that you don't want me with Declan?"

Nash sighed, and I could see realization seep across his features.

"Oh, no, Kali," he said pleadingly. "Don't take it like that. Please. I was just sayin' that if it's not safe for me here, then it certainly isn't safe enough for you. I've known this was comin' for a while, and I don't know... I've always just kinda figured I'd be here when the club showed up to take his blood. But the way he just left me at the house..."

It took me a second to understand what he was trying to say, but after turning his words over in my mind a few times, I thought I understood what he meant.

"I can understand how that must've felt."

"You can?"

"Yeah, you want to help him because you guys are like brothers, but he didn't even give you a chance to help today, even if nothing significant actually ended up happening."

Nash nodded and looked down at the counter between us.

"Do you see his side of it, though?" I asked hesitantly, hopeful I wouldn't make him angry again.

Nash sighed as he looked at me. "Maybe... I don't know. I mean, he's never outright said he wanted me here if somethin' happened, but with all the times he's taken me shootin', or taught me how to use a knife to defend myself, or explained the politics of the club, I just figured he was trainin' me to help him when the time came, you know? So when he didn't take me with him when he thought somethin' was goin' down today, it was just a shock."

Declan walked back in then, halting our conversation as he took a seat next to me, leaning his forearms on the counter as he looked at Nash.

"You're right, we don't know what the club is gonna do 'till they make their move.

We also don't know it's gonna come to that either.

We're all sittin' here, freakin' out, worryin' about somethin' that none of us have any control over.

Today, I didn't tell you what was happenin,' and I left you standin' there worryin.'

I know that had to suck, I can see that, but I need you to know that if there's any way I can keep you safe, that's the path I'm gonna choose every time.

It was safer to leave you at your house, and I didn't think I had time to explain what was goin' on before I left.

Next time, I might not get so lucky.

If they do decide to come after me, you might be here when that happens, and I'll be left with no other choice than to have you here while I face 'em.

So let's just leave it at that, alright?

If I have a chance to get you away, I will, and you'll go without question," he said before he turned his gaze to me. "Both of you."

Looking back at Nash, he said, "But if I end up not havin' another choice, you bein' here could mean more protection for Kaliyah and whoever else might be around.

If that's what ends up happenin', your job is not to help me, Nash; it's to get yourself, Kaliyah, Moms, any customers... to get everyone else away as quickly and as safely as possible. Do you understand?"

Nash seemed to revert right back into his happy demeanor at what Declan said, sending out a hand to shake his hand across the counter.

"Got it. I can do that."

"Let's hope it doesn't come to that, though."

~

A short while later, Declan and I were heading out to meet up with Kaylynne.

She'd called not too long after Declan and Nash's almost argument, saying she had some time on her hands if I wanted her to show me some rental properties.

I went over my budget with her over the phone, and excitedly, she'd said what I had would work out perfectly for a lot of the properties she had on her books, even with a one-year lease, paid upfront.

She met us outside the surf shop about twenty minutes later, climbing out of her little four-door Ford with her hair in a bun and a large coffee in her hands.

"Hey, guys," she said as Declan and I walked over to her. "I figured we could start here with the apartment above Roxy's since it's within your price range. Plus, I know Roxy would lose her mind if I didn't show it to you."

We all laughed a little before she said, "If it's not a good fit for you, that's perfectly fine though, and we can just go from there. Sound good?"

Her voice was chipper and excited, and there was a little bounce in her step as she walked with us across the street.

You wouldn't have been able to tell the house we were walking to was a duplex from just looking at it; it looked like your typical, everyday beach house.

However, as I got nearer, I could definitely see how the bottom part of the house, where the carport was on Sea Breeze Dream, looked decorated and lived in, while the floor above looked barren.

We bypassed Roxy's front door, climbed the stairs to the second floor, and after putting a code into the box on the door-knob, Kaylynne let us in.

"This one comes partially furnished, so you'll have to get a few things eventually, but it's move-in ready otherwise."

The front half of the apartment was open concept with a living room area off to my left and a dining area to my right. The living room didn't have any furniture besides a round wicker chair with a comfy looking blue pad laid on the inside, while in the dining room area, there was a cute little four-person wooden table and chair set.

As I walked through the space, the more furniture I saw, the less I knew I would end up having to spend, and the place just appealed to me even more.

The kitchen was off toward the back right side of the space, and it had a center island and a bar area as well. White shaker cabinets with light gray countertops were brightly lit by the pendant lighting that hung down over the bar, and there were stainless steel appliances.

There were two bedrooms with a small bathroom placed

between them down a hallway beside the kitchen, but I hardly even looked at them as I saw what lay beyond the back bedroom.

It took me all of about thirty seconds from the time I saw the cute little screened-in back porch that overlooked the intercoastal waterway for me to say, "I'll take it," without a second thought.

That back porch was remarkably similar to the one I'd fantasized about back in Chicago when I'd been leaving Cam, and though it wasn't an ocean view, somehow, the view of the intercoastal seemed so much better than what I'd imagined.

"Wow, seriously? You haven't seen any of the other properties yet," Kaylynne said with a giggle while Declan stayed as quiet as a statue.

I laughed as I took her back through the space, gushing my excitement. "Yes, I'm sure. Look, this one can be my bedroom since it's already set up to be one, and that one there can be my office for writing!" I walked into the smaller of the two bedrooms, pointing out the amount of light that came in through the window.

"I could hang some rope lights all around and put a desk right there in the corner!"

Kaylynne and Declan put up with my exuberance, and I was grateful for it because I couldn't exactly control it anyway.

The place was small, but it was perfect for me, and after I said as much, Kaylynne took us back to her rental office so I could pay for the place and sign all the paperwork.

Everything seemed to be going great, all my troubles forgotten as I signed paper after paper, imagining how I would make the apartment my own, when she ran my card, and it was declined.

Looking up from the paper I'd been signing, I asked, "It what, now?"

"It was declined. Are you sure about your funds?" Kaylynne asked, obviously uncomfortable having to ask such a question.

My mind was having a tough time trying to figure out what she'd just said because I knew I had double the year's rent on the apartment sitting in my bank account. There was no reason in the world why it shouldn't have gone through.

"I'm sure. Would you mind trying it again? I know what I have in there, and it is definitely enough to cover this."

Kaylynne said, "I ran it twice, babe. Do you want to maybe pay for half now? See if that works?"

It was not a solution I wanted to entertain, but swallowing my pride, I nodded.

However, after she tried that amount, it declined again, and my heart sank.

"Let me go call my bank," I said as fear and panic shot through me. "There's been some kind of mistake. I'll be right back."

Stepping outside the rental office, leaving Kaylynne and Declan behind, I ignored the now-usual, ridiculous amounts of missed calls, texts, and voicemails and put in a call straight to my bank.

"Hi, this is Kaliyah Bennett, and my card isn't working," I told the guy who finally got on the line to assist me.

I heard him put in my information, and after hearing his keyboard clanking a few more times, he said, "There's been a hold put on your account."

"A hold? Why?" I asked, my voice raising.

"It looks like the hold was requested by one of the account holders."

Instantly, I knew what had happened, and tears started welling up in my eyes.

"I'm the owner of the account, and I need to take the hold off."

The guy gave me some spiel about how it could be done but

that I would need to come into their branch to do it, and again, I felt like breaking down.

How the fuck was I supposed to afford a ticket to Chicago to sort everything out if all my funds were frozen? I tried explaining that I was states away, literally unable to afford anything without what was in that account, but it was of no use.

"I'm sorry, there's nothing I can do unless you come in."

Knowing I wasn't going to get anywhere by fighting a man who was only doing his job, I said, "Alright, I'll see what I can do," and hung up.

Dropping the phone to my side as the air flew out of my lungs, I looked around and saw nothing but Cam's face, mocking me in my mind. This was just like him. I'd known he would do something, but it'd never occurred to me that this is what he would've chosen.

Steadily, each way I was utterly fucked started flowing through my mind, and as each thought took shape, it seemed like more tears fell.

I'd just leaned my hands on the railing of the rental agency when Declan and Kaylynne stepped out.

Brushing my tears away as quickly as I could, I turned to face them, knowing I was going to have to explain what had happened, no matter how much I dreaded it.

"My ex put a hold on my account, and the only way for me to fix it is to go up there myself to have them lift it, but I don't know how I'm gonna do that when everything I have is in that account," the words spilled from me as more tears tried to leak out of my eyes.

"Cam did this?" Declan asked, but all I could do was nod since what I wanted to say was getting stuck in my throat.

"Well, Declan has already paid your first month's rent and security deposit, so at least you have somewhere to stay while you figure everything out," Kaylynne said.

I knew she was trying to ease my mind, but all she did was blow it.

"What?!" I asked before my gaze jerked over to Declan. "Why would you do that?"

More tears flowed from my eyes as Declan walked over to me, placing a hand on each of my biceps before he pulled me into a hug. My head landed on his welcoming chest, and it was everything I could do to keep myself from falling into full-on sobs.

"Don't cry, okay?" he asked. "I wanted to help."

"Thank you, but I can't pay you back. Not without..." I started to say, but Declan cut me off with a sshhhing sound and a slow-moving hand that slid down the back of my head.

"I'm gonna get us two tickets to Chicago for as soon as possible, and we can go get this all sorted together, alright?"

I pulled away from him and stared up at him, bewildered.

"No, I can't let you do that, Declan. You've already done too much," I said as I gestured over to the door Kaylynne had just walked through to give us some space.

Putting a hand on the bottom of my chin and lifting it, so I was facing him fully, he said, "I'll decide what's too much. Let me help you, please."

I could tell he really didn't want to ask, but the fact that he had melted me instantly, and honestly, what other choice did I have?

Sighing in acceptance, I said, "Fine, but I'm paying you back for all of this when I get things fixed at the bank."

He tried to wave a dismissive hand and look away from me, but I grabbed that hand, pulling his eyes back to mine.

"I will walk to Chicago before I go into this without you agreeing to let me pay you back. Don't test me."

His smile was infectious as he laughed at my words, but as he wrapped me up in his arms again, he said, "I don't doubt you for one second."

"I'm serious," I said into his chest with a half-assed attempt at slapping his arm, but all that did was make him chuckle to himself even more.

"Fine. You can pay me back when we get everything fixed, but you need to let me help all the way up until that point, okay?"

Nodding, I pulled away from Declan and wiped my eyes, breathing deeply to try to ease some of the anxiety I felt stiffening my chest.

"Now, let's go get your keys," he said, and at that, no matter what else was going on in our lives, a smile spread across my face that I simply could not prevent.

CHAPTER 18

KALIYAH

True to his word, Declan bought two flights to Chicago for the next day while I was moving the stuff I'd brought with me over to my new apartment. I set him up at my new kitchen table with my laptop and the directions to my bank at his insistence. By the time I'd brought everything over, he was sitting sideways in the chair, hands clasped together in front of him with one elbow on the table and one resting on the back of the chair.

"We leave first thing in the morning," he said as I dropped my duffels in the middle of my living room floor. "Are you sure you don't want to stay one more night at my place? It'll give you time to get sheets at least."

"There are four unopened comforter sets for that bed in the closet; I think I'm good there," I laughed out at his failing attempt to get me to stay another night with him.

Don't get me wrong, I didn't *not* want to sleep next to Declan again; I just didn't want to be any more of a burden than I was already turning out to be. Even if he was asking me to stay another night, I couldn't let myself do it - not with how much he'd already given me. To me, it would've just made me seem like a leech.

"But I have food at my place," he said as he got up and made his way over to me slowly, the sunlight from my big front windows falling all over him in glorious ways.

Giggling from his words and the nervousness he always caused in me, I said, "You make a good point. I'll eat with you, but I still want to spend my first night here. Speaking of which, that reminds me, I have food in the Stevens place I need to get. Oh, and wine too."

By this point, he was standing right in front of me, one of his hands placed lightly on each of my hips as his eyes stared down into mine, the sunlight shining through them, making them pop even more than they normally did.

"Oh, you mean the twelve boxes of frozen mac-n-cheese you threw at me?" he laughed out, and I couldn't help but laugh right back.

"Hey," I said, lightly slapping his arm again, "I didn't throw them at you! And don't hate on my mac-n-cheese addiction, alright? It's a relationship of love, and one not to be trifled with. I will straight up turn into a demon if I go too long without it."

Laughing even more at me, he said, "Note to self, always have mac-n-cheese for Kaliyah, or suffer the wrath of her demons. Got it.

If that's the case though, I know first-hand you haven't had any since you've been here. I think I'll have to rectify that tonight for dinner."

My cheeks blushed red while a smile tore across my face.

"I would very much appreciate that... my demons would too."

Leaning down with a smile, he kissed me, sending shivers down my spine.

It was short-lived and sweet, but I enjoyed every second of it nevertheless.

As he pulled away, he said, "I'll go get everything you left over at the Stevens place real quick. I don't want it falling over with you inside, trying to appease your mac-n-cheese demons."

I giggled some at that, but before I could thank him for being so valiant, he asked, "Speaking of, did you figure out what's happening with that Jeep?"

Nodding, I told him what the guy from the car rental agency told me when I'd called the day before.

"Yeah, they're gonna send somebody out to assess it, and they're even down to let me take another one for the length of time I was supposed to have it since I've already paid, but since I don't have a way to get to Jacksonville to pick it up, I told them I'd just get back with them on that because I didn't know what else to say."

Cupping my chin again tightly in that way I was getting used to, the way he liked to use to get my attention, he said, "All you need to do is ask around here, and somebody is bound to help. Especially me. If you need a ride to Jacksonville to get another car, I can take you."

His hold loosened on me, and I sent a hand of my own up to cup his chin in response, the same way he'd cupped mine. "You are already giving me too much. I'm not gonna go about asking for more."

Pulling away from me with a gigantic smile on his face, he motioned toward my new front door. "Alright, that's it. Go get on my bike. I've suddenly got some things to handle in Jacksonville. I don't want you in my hair while I handle them though, so I'm gonna drop you off at a car rental place, and you can just handle gettin' yourself back."

"Right now? You've got business in Jacksonville that must be handled right this very instant? What about the shop, Declan?" I asked like a smartass, matching his tone with my own, completely unable to hide how happy he was making me.

"You don't know my life, woman. Yes, I have urgent business in Jacksonville, and the kid can handle the shop while we're gone."

Coming over to me so he could start pushing me out my front door while I laughed and pretended like I didn't want to go, he said, "Go get that tight ass on my bike right now, before I tickle you and throw you over my shoulder to put you on it myself."

At that, I started running, squealing as his hands tickled my sides even though I was already moving in that direction.

And there it was again, yet another one of those sunshine and rainbows moments, where everything seemed as if it were falling into place.

Even with everything we'd already faced that day from our pasts and how much I knew we were still going to have to deal with, my heart was still light and happy, my soul hopeful and optimistic in spite of everything else.

～

*D*eclan's urgent business turned out to be eating at this amazing restaurant called Chicago, of all things.

"Yes, I urgently needed to eat here," he'd said as we pulled in for dinner a little while later.

I knew he was just making it up as he went along, so I wouldn't be able to say he'd been lying earlier when he'd promised me he wouldn't. Even though that was technically skirting the rules of our agreement not to lie to each other, I had to let him get away with it. His intentions were good, and I could see right through his lie from the beginning anyway.

I never could tell when Cam was lying or not, which over time was a terrible way to live - constantly questioning everything he said, even going so far at certain points to question myself simply because he was so good at it. There were quite a few times where he could have me questioning what I knew to be reality, and all that taught me was to not trust myself.

Really, I should've trusted my gut at every turn.

If I had, I might not have wound up in the situation I did, but that's neither here nor there. I couldn't change what had already happened; I could only learn from my mistakes and try not to make the same ones in the future.

So far, with every decision I'd made since coming to Topsail Island, I'd gone with my gut, letting intuition guide my choices, and as far as I could tell, it hadn't led me astray yet.

"I got us a hotel room in Chicago for tomorrow night since our flight back doesn't leave until the next day," Declan said before he stuffed a bite of gourmet ravioli in his mouth.

Nodding, I said, "Thank you. You really didn't need to do all this."

"Stop thanking me. It's done," he said with a smile before he took another bite of his food.

Thinking everything through, I knew I had to ask one more favor of Declan, so I sat my fork down, and looked over at him.

"You told me to ask if I needed anything, so I'm asking."

Taking in the seriousness of my tone, I saw him focus in on me as he too, put his fork down.

"I don't want to go back to Chicago at all, like ever, but since that's unavoidable because of Cam, I figured it's a perfect opportunity to wrap up my life there if I can.

The problem is that I don't want to see Cam, but I still need to get the rest of my things from his apartment.

While we're in Chicago, would you mind coming with me to pack up my stuff and ship it here to my new place? Maybe run interference with Cam if he tries to get in the way?"

Without hesitation, Declan said, "Of course. That won't be a problem at all."

I blew out the breath I'd begun to hold and relaxed my shoulders some. The possibility of seeing Cam again was unsettling enough; going alone though… that terrified me to no end.

I was no longer worried about the hold Cam had held over my heart because it had never returned after I'd read his texts, but that didn't make me stupid enough to go back there without a safety net of some kind.

I hated putting Declan in that position, asking him to basically be my bodyguard while I got my stuff out of Cam's place, but I really didn't feel like I had any other options. It was either ask Declan to come with me or never see my things again because there was no way I was going back there on my own.

"And don't feel bad about askin'," he said, causing confusion to sweep over me.

"I can see it written all over your face," he smiled, and I had to actively shift my features so he wouldn't be able to read me so well. "Like I said before, I want to help. Plus, while I was on your laptop, your email kept popping up with notifications in the corner, and I got a look at what he's been sending you.

I didn't mean to see 'em, but I saw 'em anyway.

No man should talk to anyone that way."

I could see his anger rising as he spoke about what he'd seen on my laptop.

"I'm not gonna go lookin' for trouble, but if he's there when we get there, I'm gonna have a talk with him."

Fear slid through me as I imagined Declan talking with Cam, and as hard as I tried to ignore the panicky feeling that gave me, I just couldn't.

"I don't want there to be any problems. I'm actually hoping we can go there, get my stuff, and leave while he's at work, so we'll never even see him."

"There won't be any problems, I promise," Declan said as if he truly believed that to be the truth. "If he's not there, that's fine. And if he is, I'm just goin' to have a nice, normal conversation with him, that's it."

When he put it like that, it didn't seem so bad.

I nodded, and we both got back to our meals, finishing them quickly so we could get to everything else we still had to do.

Not too long after that, the guy at the rental car agency suggested I choose the four-wheel-drive Chevy truck they had so I could combat the sand I was going to be driving over. I hadn't driven in sand other than when we were on the four-wheeler, and the truck seemed way too big for me, but I heeded his suggestion anyway, knowing it was my best option.

Declan followed me on his bike all the way back to my new apartment.

As I was getting out, he said he was going to check on Nash and help him close up but adamantly told me he wanted me to come over later for dinner. We set a time, long enough for me to take a shower and unpack a few things before he headed the other way, and I started up the stairs.

I wasn't halfway up them when Roxy pulled up next to my new rental truck, and it took her all of about five seconds to leap from her car and shout up to me, "Are we legit neighbors now?"

Laughing, I said, "Yep, you can't get rid of me now," and she took off up the stairs to come hug me.

I returned her hug as she gushed about all the movie nights and shopping dates we were going to go on, and though shopping had never really been my thing, I didn't kill her happy; I wanted a friend like Roxy in this new chapter of my life, and if that meant I had to go shopping every now and then, so be it.

She had a date that night that she had to get ready for with some guy she'd met in Wilmington at some point, but she wanted me to promise I'd hang out with her the next day. I told her I'd be in Chicago getting the rest of my things, but she didn't complain, and we switched our plans to the day I was getting back instead.

A short time later, right as the sun was setting, casting beautiful hues throughout the apartment, Dad's teacup was sitting in its new home, right next to the ones that came with the place, and Mom's scrapbook was lying in the center of my new-to-me dining room table.

My laptop and other writing things had been placed on the floor in what I planned to turn into my office, and all my clothes were hung up in the closet or folded up neatly and placed in the drawers of the dresser in my room.

The queen-sized mattress still had its plastic covering, showing it hadn't been used yet, and after ripping that off, I set about opening one of the bed-in-a-bag comforter sets that had been in the closet - the white one that had purple flowers embroidered on it.

Once all that was finished, I took my time setting up all my hygiene stuff where I wanted it in the bathroom and hopped in the shower. The water pressure was fantastic, beating my skin to a pulp while the heat melted away the tension that had been growing in my muscles all day.

I also took the time to finally dry and style my hair for the first time since I'd come to the island. Where naturally, my long brown hair would curl up with even the slightest bit of moisture, that night, it was silky smooth and as straight as a stick, and thoughts ran through my head about whether Declan would notice it or not.

I was just dotting my skin with smelly-good stuff when there was a knock at my door.

Instantly, my heart raced because, for some reason, Cam's face flashed through my mind, but I dismissed that irrational thought quickly as I leaned my head out of the bathroom and saw Declan standing on the other side of the glass door.

I waved him in as I started walking toward him, but I saw

confusion and then anger settle on his features as he stepped inside.

"You didn't lock your door?" he asked, pulling it shut behind him before he crossed his arms over his chest and stared down at me.

"No."

"Okay, we promised not to lie to each other, but I'm gonna need you to promise me something else too." His tone was all serious as he said, "Lock any damn door you go through."

"Any?" I asked, smirking back at him. "All doors, forever and always? Dec, I don't think I can do that. What if I'm at somebody else's house?"

"You know what I mean," he said, but I could tell I'd gotten him to lose some of his seriousness by the way he tried to hide his smile.

"I promise to lock my doors. How 'bout that?" I asked as I stepped over to him and wrapped my arms around his middle, letting my fingers spend a little too much time admiring the muscles he had back there.

His arms pulled me in closer as he said, "That works for me. Now, come on. Dinner's ready."

~

*D*eclan had gone all out, and I couldn't stop smiling as I ate the pork chops, green beans, and yes, macaroni and cheese he'd made. Don't even get me started on that cornbread; I almost died when I put it in my mouth and discovered it'd been cooked so perfectly it didn't even need butter to keep it from tasting dry.

I literally moaned as I savored that bite, and Declan's hand had squeezed my thigh as he heard the sound.

"What I wouldn't give to be what makes you make that

noise," he said, his voice all breathy and hot, seeping into and engulfing every one of my senses at once.

Being bolder than I'd ever been before, I slowly put my piece of cornbread down and turned to face him on the barstool, my knees falling to either side of him.

"Do you think you can?" I asked, hoping what I was suggesting was ringing clear to him.

Dropping his fork with a clatter as it hit his plate, he turned to me just as quickly as I'd turned to him and said, "Don't challenge me like that unless you're willing to let me prove myself to you."

My heart started racing a million miles a minute, and so many butterflies took flight in my stomach that it was hard to think straight, but I leveled him with a challenging stare anyway. I took my time, enunciating each word slowly, so the message was clear. "Do you think you can?"

The heat in his stare was nearly my undoing, but as his hands reached out and he picked me up without so much as a wince, I kept myself in check and wrapped my legs around him while he carried me to his bedroom.

His lips were on mine before we even made it there, and the passion I felt coming off of him in waves was driving me insane by the time he laid me on my back on his bed.

His hands swept through my hair and pulled my head back so he could send his hot mouth to my neck, and without think-ing, my hands grabbed onto his biceps for dear life.

He was making all the moves I'd only ever dreamed of expe-riencing in real life since Cam had been nothing but boring in that department during our time together, and as Declan's teeth sunk into my neck some, a moan finally escaped me that I couldn't prevent.

Declan growled into my neck, like actually fucking growled, and I nearly came apart, then and there.

However, not two seconds later, he was pulling back to hold

himself above me. "Told you I could make you moan like that." His face was all smiles and unresolved lust, but I was sure mine had descended into outraged confusion.

"Are you stopping?" I asked, my voice a bit whinier than I'd intended, but I was too far gone to really care by that point.

Declan's smile turned evil as he said, "Only if you want me to."

My heart melted at those words, while my girly parts sang about their happiness at the top of their lungs.

"I do not want you to stop, Declan," I said clearly, making sure I locked eyes with him while I said it, and instantly, his mouth fell back to mine as his body slid closer between my thighs.

We devoured each other for a short while longer before he was pulling back again, but this time, he was pulling me with him.

He kneeled at the foot of the bed where I sat and reached down to yank off the tank I'd been wearing, showing little regard for the garment; I couldn't have cared less about the tank top either at that moment as I sent my hands to take his shirt off as well.

As soon as his beautifully tattooed torso came into my line of sight, I didn't hold back from reaching out and running my hands down his skin, slowing to savor each peak and valley offered by the muscles underneath.

He sat there on his knees and let me explore him without a sound, but I could see that the more I touched him, the more heated his gaze grew, and all that did was add fuel to my already burning desire for him.

Sitting there in my bra and shorts with my legs spread before him, I ran my hands down the length of his sides, dipping my fingers beneath the waistband of his jeans ever so slightly as I got there. I moved slowly, my breath hitching in my throat as I saw how hard his erection was straining against his jeans, begging for freedom.

Carefully, I unbuttoned them and worked the zipper down over his hard length, telling my vagina to calm the fuck down some because she was practically panting in my thong, but the bitch didn't listen.

When I reached my hand inside his boxers and finally freed him, I felt the pooling sensation of my wetness increase tenfold as I took in the sight of him.

As if he couldn't stand the anticipation anymore, he stood quickly, dropped his jeans and boxers to the floor, and made his glorious way over to his nightstand. He pulled out a condom, ripping it open and sliding it on quickly as he made his way back to me.

Pulling me to my feet, he slid his hands down my sides like I'd done to him, and with much less finesse than I'd used, he pulled my shorts and thong down, shoving them to the floor like they'd done something to personally piss him off.

He then grabbed me by each of my hips and turned me around, reaching up to unlatch my bra not half a second later.

However, where he'd just been rushing through his movements, at that point, he slowed way down. I felt his body slide right up behind me as his face settled next to mine.

I could feel his gaze on my breasts as he slowly slid my bra straps down over my shoulders, ensuring the bra continued to cover my hardened nipples. When they were finally uncovered, I heard his intake of breath in my ear right before his teeth sank into that spot between my neck and my shoulder.

My legs wanted to crumble beneath me at the feel of his mouth on my skin, and as my head fell back to land against him, it was all I could do to just stand there and take what he was giving.

Reaching my hands back behind me to feel him, I barely

made contact with the skin of his thighs before he was turning me around to face him again.

As fast as lightning, he reached down to pick me up so he could toss me back on the bed as if I weighed nothing.

A giggle tore through my throat as I flew through the air, landing in the cocooning embrace of his bed a half-second later.

He crawled up me, taking his sweet ass time as his mouth and tongue trailed a path of heat and wetness from my ankle, up my calf, and over the sensitive part of my inner thigh.

My hands found themselves in his hair as his face hovered outside my entrance, looking for me to grant him permission for entry with a single look.

I couldn't speak I was so wrapped up in Declan, but my body knew what it wanted, and as I pushed his head so his mouth could descend on my folds, I saw the smirk on his face a millisecond before my whole world lit up with fireworks.

His tongue was a fucking beast, and as he sucked, licked, kissed, and teased me, I found my back arching off the bed under his expert attention.

"You taste so fuckin' good," he said, drawing my eyes from the ceiling back to his. I looked at him more closely, and even though I could only see half of his chiseled face, there was no denying how much he was absolutely relishing having his mouth on me.

I came right then as if I were putty in his hands, and he continued to work his magic on my most sensitive part as he let me ride out that high for as long as my body would let me.

"Fuck, that tasted amazing," he said when the aftershocks of my orgasm had worn off, my body threatening to do it all over again from his words alone.

Taking his sweet ass time all over again, his mouth forged another trail, but this time, it went up over my mound to my belly, where he lingered around my belly button before he continued up to my right breast.

Who fucking knew teeth on tits could feel so fucking good, huh?

I certainly didn't, not until Declan's were on mine at least, the sensation nearly tearing me apart from the inside out.

When he sent a finger to my folds at the same time, I came apart all over again, threading my hands through his hair so I could thank him by pulling his lips to mine.

I'd all but forgotten where his mouth had just been, but as soon as I tasted myself on his tongue, the eroticness of it all seeped into me, making me love every second I was getting of it even more.

I was so lost in pleasure, I hadn't even noticed he'd moved until I felt the tip of his erection slide down the top of my mound to rest right at my entrance eagerly.

My eyes rose to his, the blue of them shining brightly. His lips fell to mine at the same time he thrust himself inside me, one hand cupping my chin like he liked to do, so my eyes wouldn't veer from his.

He filled me more than I'd ever been filled in my life, and for a split second, I was genuinely concerned I might not be able to handle the size of him, but as he slowly started moving, what pain there had been eased away into the sweetest pleasure I could imagine.

His movements weren't gentle as he thrust into me over and over again, and his touch wasn't light where he held me to him, but his pace was absolutely punishing.

I soaked up everything he was doing greedily, knowing right then and there that I would never get enough of what he was doing, even if I had the rest of my life to feel it.

I screamed my pleasure into his neck, a full-on shudder racking my whole body as I came around him a short time later.

"Fuck, Kali," Declan groaned as he stilled inside me, reaching his own climax not long after I'd found mine.

We were both panting, sweat glistening off of each of us as

his forehead fell down on the pillow beside my head. He was still inside me, but as he rolled to his side and slid out of me, instantly, I missed the feel of him there, my vagina wantonly aching for more.

That girl was insatiable for Declan, it seemed. I couldn't blame her; I was the same way.

Sliding his hand up to cup my cheek, I lost myself in his eyes again as he said, "I don't think I'll ever get enough of you."

His tone was all serious and breathy, his eyes telling me he meant every word, and as I climbed on top of him, starting in on round two because, why the fuck not, I whispered down into his ear, "I don't think I will either."

CHAPTER 19

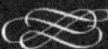

DECLAN

*W*e arrived in Chicago the next day a little before noon, and Kaliyah had been a bundle of frayed nerves the whole way. However, I figured the sooner she got things done, the better she would feel, so we didn't waste any time as we went straight from the airport to her bank.

It turned out to be surprisingly easy for them to lift the hold they'd had on her account, and for her to remove Cam's name from it as well. I think we were only in there for about twenty minutes total, making the whole we-need-you-to-come-in thing seem even more outrageous and ridiculous than it'd been when we'd first heard about it.

There was no reason why what she'd said in the bank couldn't have been said and verified over the phone, but red tape is red tape, and we all must suffer its bullshit sometimes.

We ate lunch at a Mexican food truck that was parked on the street between the bank and Kaliyah's old apartment, and she insisted on buying since I'd footed the bill for everything else.

I let her pay even though it went against every cell in my body because I knew it would make her feel better. However, despite the relief I knew she felt over having everything settled at her bank, her nervousness and anxiety only grew as we got closer to her old apartment.

I understand why she felt the way she did, but seeing her like that only reminded me of how fearful she was of Cam and how she'd come to fear him like that in the first place. By the time we finally got to her old apartment, I was seething on the inside, rage boiling just below the surface as she lifted her keys to the lock with shaky hands.

"The key's not working," she said a moment later, drawing my attention from focusing on how nervous she was.

Right as I was about to reach for the keys in her hands so I could give it a go, the door swung open, Cam's smug voice spilling out into the hallway as soon as the door started opening from the other side.

"I knew you'd come crawling..." his words died on his lips as he saw me standing there with Kaliyah.

"Who is this?" he asked, his voice purposefully pitched into a more proper way of speaking than the tone he'd been using as he opened the door.

If I wasn't mistaken, he didn't seem shocked to see me in the slightest.

My gut has never led me down the wrong path or let me misinterpret the different situations I've found myself in, so the way it seemed like Cam had already figured out who I was just didn't sit right with me. It threw up red flags like crazy in my mind, making me even more watchful than I'd been before... and that was saying something.

"I'm here to pack up the rest of my stuff. I didn't think you'd be home from work yet," Kaliyah's voice came out strong, and I was all the more proud of her for it.

She was standing up to him simply by not backing down.

Speaking to him like that, with a sneer on her face, was the perfect cherry on top.

"Then it's a good thing I've already boxed all of it up for you," Cam said, play-acting the definition of a gentleman. "Come on in." He swung the door open wide, putting his arm out as if we were long lost friends coming for a visit. "It's all over there in the corner waiting for you."

But I could see it in his eyes, the devil that lived within him; it matched the one I had living in me. But where mine would die to protect the people I loved, his kept him from being able to love anyone and drove him to hurt those that wound up loving him instead.

I could tell by the way his eyes followed us in calculation, the way they squinted when he thought we weren't looking, how he hovered with his hands twitching.

It set my ride or die, fight or flight response off, sending adrenaline pumping through my veins as I followed Kaliyah over to her boxes.

"They're taped up already," she said questioningly. "Are you sure you packed everything?"

With a smile that could've lived on the vilest of real-life demons, he said, "Of course, sweetie. Things may not have worked out between us, but I will do right by you. Even if you did leave me at the altar."

To Kaliyah's credit, she eyed him as if he had fish guts all over his shirt, but I was far from having my own emotions as reined in as hers were.

At that, I couldn't stomach it anymore.

I walked over to Cam while Kaliyah searched the apartment for anything he may have missed and placed a hand on the back of his neck, squeezing so he knew I wasn't playing around. "Let's give the woman some space and have a talk, shall we?"

Cam winced but tried to save face in front of Kaliyah, so he parked a forced smile on his face even though he still looked like he might shit his pants. He nodded readily enough and went where I was leading him without a fight.

To anyone looking on from the outside, they wouldn't have been able to tell just how much control I had over him at that moment, but believe me, he was mine right then.

I led him out into the hall, keeping my hand on the back of his neck until I closed the door behind us.

Once it was shut, he tried to jerk out of my grasp, saying, "What is wrong with you?" in this whiny voice that raked against my nerves, but I was having none of that as I released his neck and threw my arm around his shoulders, holding his frame tightly against mine with one arm.

He was looking down at the ground as I began to speak, knowing there was no way to get away from me, and I swear I felt a shudder run through him as my threat met his ears.

"Stop with the act," I said lowly, distinctly, so there would be no misunderstanding what I was saying.

"We all know who you really are. We both know the things you've done to that woman in there. You're the worst kind of scum this earth has; you can admit to that, right?"

He tried again to get out of my grasp, but all his movements did was make us face a different direction.

"Here's what's gonna happen. You're gonna go back in there and take a seat. You're not gonna say another word to her, do you understand me?"

Nodding because he knew I wasn't giving him any other option, he settled and dropped his gaze to the floor again.

"You're gonna quit bein' a little whiny ass bitch, and you're gonna stop calling her, texting her, emailing her, the whole nine. You're gonna stop tryin' to communicate with her, period. Do you understand?"

He nodded again, so I continued.

"If you try to contact her again, if you threaten her in any way, if anything happens to her because of you, I will kill you."

He bucked in my arms again, but it was a useless movement since I shifted him around in my grasp so he could look at me without me even really trying.

"Look me in my eyes."

He did, and I could see the fear in them.

"Do I look like I'm playin'?"

"No, you don't," he squeaked out, anger saturating his voice and his features at the same time.

"You won't be the first person I've killed, so don't test me, or it'll be the last thing you do. Do you understand me?"

He nodded, and I sent a brutal fist flying to his gut, catching him before he fell to the floor in pain a second later.

I stood him up, slapping him on the shoulder as I said, "Chin up. You're fine," before I opened the door and gestured for him to walk back inside.

The look he was glaring in my direction could've been described as nothing less than pure hatred, but he stood up straight anyway, squared his shoulders, and walked inside to his couch, sitting down like I'd told him to.

Kaliyah eyed us both with concern as we made our way back inside, but she didn't say anything, and soon thereafter, she started picking the boxes up so she could carry them out to the hallway.

I helped her move them, keeping a close eye on Cam the whole time, but within a few minutes, all the boxes were out in the hallway, and there was no longer a need for us to be there.

Right as I opened the door for Kaliyah, she turned to face Cam, where he was still sitting on the couch, fuming.

"Don't try to call me or text me again, Cam. We're over, and I'm not coming back. All it would take would be one simple phone call to have you put away for harassment, so if you were smart, you'd leave me alone."

Without saying anything more or even telling the fool goodbye, she walked out of the apartment and pressed the button for the elevator.

I kissed her neck as we waited for the doors to open so we could load it up with the boxes, and the smile she sent toward me had one finally breaking free from me as well.

In no time at all, we had all her stuff at the post office, ready to ship to her new address.

While Kaliyah was trying to pull her debit card out of her wallet, I handed my card over to the cashier quickly and told them to rush the boxes to her new place as fast as possible, ignoring it when Kaliyah tried to protest my paying for it.

She playfully slapped me in the shoulder again, but I just smiled down at her.

Kaliyah was as happy as I'd ever seen her that night, blossoming in front of me as stressor after stressor was lifted from her shoulders. She took me around to a couple of her favorite places before it got late, and we had to head to our hotel room.

The whole time, she reminded me of the sun, radiating light and happiness everywhere she went and finally giving the darkness within me the balance it needed in this life.

~

*O*nce we finally got back to Topsail, Kaliyah and I were both tired from our trip, wanting a nap or something to cure the fatigue of travel, but she had a 'writing date with her laptop,' as she put it, and I had to check on Nash and the shop.

We said our goodbyes, promising to meet up for dinner sometime later, and I walked across the street to the surf shop after I saw her go inside her new apartment, locking her door as it closed behind her.

Nash's eyes got a little bigger when he saw me, and right away, I knew something had happened while we'd been gone.

"What?" I asked, coming to stand on the other side of the counter from him.

He sighed like he was readying himself to talk to me. "Well, another one of those phone calls came in today. This time, the dude wasn't using that scrambler thing and said I needed to watch who I was hangin' with 'cause it might cost me, but I told him to fuck off and hung up."

"Alright," I said, throwing that bit of information in with what little else I knew about the caller, but as I stared at Nash a moment longer, I knew he wasn't finished. "What else?"

Looking like he was afraid to tell me, he started speaking fast. "Moms is fine; nothing bad happened to her, so you don't need to worry."

Immediately I saw red, my anger at the fact that Moms' name was even being mentioned in this conversation, setting me on edge.

"She was at the house when some guy pulled up on a bike earlier, revving his engine 'till she came out to see what was going on. The dude basically told her to keep me home and away from the shop.

She cussed him out, of course, but it made her angry, for sure.

She called me and told me about it, and I told her I would leave to check on her, but she didn't want to hear that. She said no gearhead was gonna come here threatening her son and that if I did show up when I was supposed to be workin', she'd skin me alive."

Nash smiled, and so did I as I imagined Moms doing just that, but at the same time, concern for her safety and Nash's tore through me like a branding iron to the chest.

"Alright, go on home then, and check on her; I'll close up today. But listen," I said as he started reaching for his bookbag, "text me and let me know what she says when you get there, or if you see anything out of the ordinary."

"Will do," Nash said as he came around to me.

"Dec, look, I know it seems like a big deal, but I don't think they'd actually do anything to Moms or me. They're just tryin' to scare us."

"And what makes you think that, huh?" I asked, my voice dripping with sarcasm.

The kid was smart, but he really had no idea what he was talking about when it came to the lengths the Lost Savages would go to. I'd been there, seen it, done it, and gotten the damn Christmas card.

"Because I don't think you realize how much you matter to them."

I had to do a double-take as I heard those insightful words come out of his mouth.

"And if they hurt the people you care about here, you'll never go back to them."

"Isn't that the point with offin' me, though? To make sure I pay for leavin' 'em and never go back?"

Nash smiled as he shifted his bookbag further up his shoulder. "Just try to remember you're their last prince, and that obviously means somethin'. If they really wanted you gone, they'd have done it by now. No matter what the prez or anyone else says, I'm right about that part, I'm sure."

I thought through his words for all of about five seconds before I dismissed everything he'd said and ruffled his hair. "Go on and get, and quit worryin' 'bout the club and me. Just make sure you and Moms stay safe."

Laughing some, he shrugged, and after I saw him get on his bicycle to head home, I locked the door behind him. Once everything was shut down in the shop for the night, I walked upstairs and tried to call Uncle Lyn.

I needed to see if he'd found anything out about the phone calls or heard about anyone planning to make a move on me or the people here, but he didn't answer.

Sitting on one of my barstools with my elbows on the countertop in front of me, my finger lingered over Mac's number, a tremendous weight of guilt spreading through me as I considered calling him.

I hadn't talked to my best friend since I left two years ago, and every day that had passed without some form of contact between us made it seem like I was spitting on everything we'd been through together, on the fact that he'd literally saved my life.

However, as Kaliyah's and everyone else here's faces slipped through my mind, I knew I didn't have any other choice.

I had to face Mac and my past, no matter how much I knew it was going to suck to do so. After swallowing down the last of my reservations, I pressed the call button, hoping like hell he'd answer and that he wouldn't hang up the second he knew it was me.

CHAPTER 20

KALIYAH

Declan seemed off when I went over to his place for dinner.

At first, I wasn't sure what to make of it, so I tried cheering him up by telling him how productive I'd been since we'd gotten back earlier.

"I've changed my phone number and my email address, and I have my bank stuff switching to one closer to here. I mean, the closest ones are still all the way in Wilmington or Jacksonville, but it's something, right?"

Looking up from his plate, he said, "Kaliyah, that's really awesome. Now, that fucker can't mess with you, even if he tries."

The happiness I felt from him was an improvement on how he'd been acting while he'd cooked, but it was still nowhere near how he usually seemed by any means.

"Is there something wrong?" I asked, leveling him with a

sympathetic stare, hoping he'd tell me whatever it was that was going on with him.

"I'm gonna be leavin' in the morning, and I'm not sure when I'll be gettin' back. It shouldn't take more than a day, but I don't know for sure yet," he said, his eyes locked on mine.

Trying to be as understanding and supportive as I could be while still getting him to spill whatever was going on, I said, "Okay. Can you tell me about where you're going or why?"

He sighed and stood from where he'd been sitting next to me, grabbing our empty plates and taking them with him to the sink, probably so he'd have something to do with his hands while he answered me.

"I talked to Mac today."

He was trying to hide it and was doing a damn good job of it too, but I'd heard the small crack in his voice that he tried to cover up. "Let's just say, my absence these past two years has been felt by everyone in the club... especially him."

"What'd he say?" I asked hesitantly.

I'd known they were best friends and that Mac had been the reason Declan had lived through what had killed his brother, but otherwise, I knew nothing of the man.

The fact that one conversation with him had thrown Declan's demeanor all out of whack implied he meant a great deal to Declan still, but it also meant their conversation probably hadn't gone as well as Declan would've liked.

"He was surprised to hear from me, that's for sure," Declan half-way chuckled before he continued. "But he didn't want to talk to me about the past at all and wouldn't hear any of my apologies. He just wanted to know why I was calling, and that was it. When I told him I needed info on the club because shit has gotten weird here, he told me everything he knew, but it wasn't a lot, and when he didn't have anything else to tell me, he had to go."

There were so many questions I wanted to ask right then.

Honestly, I wanted to interrogate him until I knew for sure whether the calls had been the club or not, but I knew that wasn't what Declan needed.

"Maybe if you start calling him again, you guys can work on fixing things with each other," I offered while Declan turned back around to face me from the other side of the kitchen island.

He put both of his hands on the countertop and looked down as he considered what I'd said. "Maybe that can work. It still sucks for right now, though."

"Did he seem angry or hurt?" I asked.

Declan's eyes rose to meet mine. "Both."

"Then hopefully, it'll play out how it did with you and your uncle. You guys looked like you were gonna rip each others' heads off when you first saw each other, but after a second, all that fell away because you both realized what really mattered."

Squinting and smirking at me, he said, "You caught all that, did you?"

I laughed a little to myself as I remembered worrying about what I was going to do if the two of them started fighting right there in the shop. "It wasn't that hard to read you guys."

Declan's chuckle met my ears a second later as he came around the counter and grabbed me by the hand so he could pull me over to his couch.

Once we were comfortable, he said, "All I really found out from Mac was what I'd already heard from Uncle Lyn - that loyalties in the club are divided, and since they don't know who's gonna take over once the prez can't ride anymore, things are fucked. It should be my uncle by rights, but apparently, some people don't want that."

I nodded my understanding, and Declan kept talking.

"When I got off the phone with Mac, Uncle Lyn called me back, saying he wants me to come down there and meet up with him."

Fear for Declan spread through me, feeling like liquid ice through my veins, but I kept my mouth shut and my face impassive.

"He says he can't leave Savannah right now, but that he'd make sure there was a clear path for me to come see him tomorrow so we can talk."

"What does he want to talk about?" I asked, my need to know that critical piece of information outweighing everything else.

Declan pulled me into his arms, and I rested my back up against his chest while he drew slow circles on my bicep with his thumb.

"I don't know for sure; he wouldn't tell me over the phone. But yeah, that's where I'm goin.'"

I nodded and thought to myself for a few minutes, trying to figure out exactly how I felt about the situation, and once I knew that, how I was going to handle it.

"I think I should go with you," I said.

The worry I felt about hearing him tell me 'no' was sending sweat to my palms and anxiety through my chest, but he didn't answer right away, so those sensations just kept building.

"I'm not sure that's the best idea," he said eventually, and I pulled away so I could look at him.

His face was somewhat pinched in concern, seeming almost like he didn't want to disappoint me, but I ignored it as I laid out my case.

"Okay, look. I know it doesn't seem like a good idea, but hear me out.

First, if you're by yourself, you're an easier target, and if I'm with you, they should at least think twice before they go after you.

Second, you're going to visit your uncle, so it's not like you're going straight into the lion's den or anything, right?" I thought to ask right as the words came out of my mouth.

"Not exactly, no," he said, smirking some.

"Right. And third, and probably most importantly, you came with me to handle Cam, and I want to be there to help you with your stuff if I can.

We don't know that there's going to be anything I can really help with yet, but I'd rather go and find out you didn't need my help, than be here, wishing I'd gone with you because you did and I wasn't there."

Declan reached a hand up to cup my face before he slid his lips over mine.

Pulling back for a second, he said, "Alright, you can come with me. But here's the deal, if at any point I tell you to get in the truck and leave, you have to promise me that you will go with no questions asked. That's the only way I can let you come."

Smiling, I nodded and sent my hand out to shake his. "It's a deal."

~

"*K*aliyah," Declan's voice roused me from sleep at some ungodly hour when the sun wasn't even up yet.

"Hey, come on, I wanna take you with me this morning."

I sat up slowly, only able to see a little because the bathroom light in my hallway was on, casting a glow into the space.

It could've been my sleep rattled mind, but I didn't understand what he meant; he'd already agreed to take me with him to Savannah.

"I thought we weren't leaving for at least another two hours," I said as I checked the time on my phone groggily.

"That's right, but today's a big day, and if we don't hurry, we're gonna miss it. Get up, and I'll show you."

"Miss what?" I asked as I dragged my ass out of bed with more anger than I really should have felt.

"You'll see."

He turned the light on, plunging me into light too bright for my sensitive eyes, and I threw a pillow at his head.

He laughed and threw it right back at me before I stomped over to my closet to find clothes to wear.

Grabbing me by the waist, he said, "Pajamas are perfectly fine for who we're gonna go see. Just grab your flip flops and your phone. Come on."

I thought about arguing with him hard, but in the end, I was just too sleepy to put up a fight, and I did as he said while he practically bounced he was so excited.

Once we were out the door, he grabbed my hand and led me across the street, past the surf shop, and out onto the beach.

"Once or twice a week, I do what's called a turtle walk."

By that point, I was about to lose my mind. "I swear if you get down on all fours and start crawling around like a turtle, I'm gonna slap you, and I won't even feel bad about it."

He laughed hard at me, but I was still grumpy and readying my hand just in case.

"Loggerhead sea turtles make their nests and lay their eggs here all summer long, and a few volunteers walk the beach every morning to see if any nests have been made during the night.

Well, about sixty days ago, when I was doing my search of this section of the beach, I found a brand-new nest and called it in."

I was trying to understand him as we walked further and further away from the shop, but honestly, the more he talked, the less I comprehended. "So we're out here to look for nests?" I asked.

"Not today, no," he said as he turned on the flashlight on his phone and pointed it at the ground ahead of us. "We're here to watch the baby turtles hatch and make their way out to the ocean."

My feet stopped as an excitement like I hadn't known in a while crept through my system. "Are you serious? Baby sea turtles!"

Pulling me along, chuckling some, he said, "Yes, look."

My gaze drifted to where his light was shining on the ground, and there in the sand were about twenty of the teensiest little baby sea turtles I'd ever seen in my life, just giving it their all as they tried to make it to the ocean.

"Oh my god!" I quietly screamed as Declan pulled me to my knees in the sand, a short distance away from the little path the turtles were forging through the sand.

He cut his light off once we were seated, and though I could still see the turtles some by the lights cast from the houses nearby, it was nowhere near as good of a show as it had been.

"I've got to turn off the light, so I don't draw attention to them."

"What do you mean?"

"Well, if the seagulls or whatever else that wants to eat these guys see them, they are far less likely to survive, and they already have the whole ocean goin' up against them."

"Couldn't we just swat the birds away or put the turtles in the ocean ourselves?"

Declan sighed and said, "I wish, but that's not what's best for 'em.

They need to find their own way to the ocean without our help so they can remember it when they have to come back later to make their own nests.

We can definitely swat at some flyin' sea rats if we want though."

I giggled at that, and for the next hour, we sat there and watched as turtle after turtle popped up out of the sand and made its adorable way to the ocean.

It was absolutely magical to watch, and I wanted nothing more than to just sit on that beach all day and watch them, but before long, we had to head back so we could get ready for our trip to Savannah.

I stopped on our way back then, struck by a realization: Declan was like the turtles. He may have crawled out of his nest and traversed an unknown world that wanted to eat him alive, but it was high time for him to go back and get his own nest straight. And I was just happy I was getting to go along for the ride.

Maybe I'll still get to swat at a few gulls at some point.

With that thought - and the mental image that went with it - I grinned and ran to catch up with Declan.

CHAPTER 21

DECLAN

*T*he almost five-hour drive in my truck to Savannah, Georgia, ended up feeling more like a road trip with a friend than the dreaded nightmare I'd originally thought it would be, and it was all because Kaliyah was with me.

Her random-ass playlist might as well have had multiple personality disorder because it went straight from old school gangsta rap, to new age indie ballads, to country love songs, to whatever the hell else she had on there.

That girl knew every word to every song, sang and rapped at the top of her lungs when she wasn't chatting me up or getting down on road snacks, and overacted every lyric that flowed through my speakers, keeping a smile on my face the whole damn time.

I had a feeling she was doing it on purpose to distract me from stressing over whatever my uncle had to tell me, and really, I appreciated the hell out of her for it.

Her window had been rolled halfway down for most of the

trip, and she'd been letting her hair blow carelessly in the breeze until we got close to my uncle's place. Once we got off the highway, she tried to rein it in so she could look 'presentable,' but she was having a hard go of it.

I told her he wouldn't care what her hair looked like, but she just rolled her eyes and kept fussing with it anyway.

My nerves kicked up a notch or five when we rolled into official Lost Savages territory, despite Kaliyah's best efforts.

There hadn't been a guarantee that anyone would remember and recognize my truck as I passed through, but I knew there was a genuine possibility that they could. Since Kaliyah was sitting in my passenger seat, I stayed on high alert and kept my eyes peeled the whole time, just in case.

However, true to his word, not a single issue popped up on our way to Uncle Lyn's house, even though we had to pass right by my old clubhouse to get there.

He lived a few miles from the clubhouse in a cabin that sat on a few acres of swampland. He'd always preferred his privacy, never staying at the clubhouse if he could help it, and through the years, him being in the swamp had proved to be pretty useful for the club in a lot of ways.

Honestly, that distance he always kept between himself and the club was why I thought he was able to keep himself in the best position with them.

Yes, he'd been their VP from the day my dad left for the military. Still, he'd hardly ever been there for all the dumbass drama that could unfold in a heartbeat at the clubhouse, wherein a single night, lives could be shattered entirely, and everything could go right back to normal the very next day.

I parked next to his bike and took a deep breath before we both got out of the truck.

"Alright," I said as we started walking up to his front door. "It shouldn't be an issue that you're here with me, but if it does come up and he wants to talk to me alone, you get in the truck and lock the doors, okay?"

Kaliyah glanced up at me with concern marking her face in the creases of her forehead, but she nodded at me anyway.

"There's a pistol in the glove box too. I don't think you'll need it, but I want you to be prepared just in case."

Again, she nodded to me without a word, and I knocked on Uncle Lyn's door, praying I was right and that she wouldn't have to worry about anything I'd just told her.

A few seconds later, Uncle Lyn opened the door in jeans and a black t-shirt with bare feet and a tin cup of coffee in his hand.

"I'm glad you both made it; come on in." He was smiling through his beard as we scooted past him into his living room.

It had been over two long years since I'd been here, but from the smell of the cedar wood paneling, to the banister by the stairs that still had mine and my brothers' scribblings on it, everything was exactly the same.

"Have a seat."

He made his way over to the chair that sat by the cold fireplace, setting his coffee cup on the ledge of it while Kaliyah and I sat down on his small couch.

"I see you've brought the lass with you. I assume this means you two are a thing?"

He caught me off guard with that question.

I glanced over to Kaliyah and her blushing smile for a second before I turned back to answer him.

"Yeah, you could say that."

"Well, I'm happy for ya, laddie," he said, smiling in my direction, but quickly, his features turned serious. "I'm assumin' that means you're okay with her hearin' all this, too, right? 'Cause I do have a real need to talk to you."

I nodded my head without hesitation, relieved he was leaving it up to me whether Kaliyah could hear what we were going to be talking about or not.

Others might've sent their woman away so they could talk shop, but I'd promised Kaliyah I wouldn't lie to her, and the best way to keep that promise was to have her by my side when things were happening.

"Aye," he said with a small smirk, "Okay, then. I'll get right into it."

I leaned forward and put my elbows on my knees as I listened while Kaliyah sat with her hands in her lap beside me.

"I did some diggin' 'round, like you asked," Uncle Lyn started. "And though you might've gotten a call or two from the guys that are still loyal to the prez, I don't think most of them were from us. So I'm bettin' you've got somebody else tryin' to fuck with you."

Again, I nodded as I looked over at the fireplace for a second, trying to piece together which calls had come from the club and which ones had come from someone else. I knew the most likely culprit would've been Cam, but I didn't know... nothing about him had screamed that he was crazy enough for something like that when I'd met him.

If anything, he acted like a little bitch, cowering when I put him in his place.

"Do you need help handlin' that, whoever it is?" Uncle Lyn asked, pulling me out of my internal speculation.

Looking back at him, I said, "I don't really know. Right now, there's been nothin' but annoying ass phone calls and empty threats, but I don't know who they're from or whether whoever it is, has plans to escalate or not."

Uncle Lyn looked contemplative for a second but then turned to me once the chess pieces had moved around in his brain some.

"Alright, laddie."

He shifted in his chair as he looked to Kaliyah. "Is there anyone in your life that could be causin' this?"

That man was more intuitive than most, that was for sure.

"Yeah, my ex," Kaliyah said.

Uncle Lyn thought that over and turned back to me. "Well, if it does end up escalatin,' all you need to do is call, and we'll help you handle it, whether it's the club or some pissed off ex. We'll keep you safe, you know that Decky."

I nodded, looking down because I knew he was telling the truth.

"The other thing I wanted to talk to you about is the Raging Heathens."

Looking up at him confused, I asked, "What about 'em? Gavin and I put 'em in their place a long ass time ago."

"Aye, you did, laddie," my uncle said. "But apparently, their memories aren't as long as ours. They've been tryin' to take over our hold on Wilmington since they got word Ray was sick."

"Have they lost their damn minds?" I asked, outrage settling in the pit of my stomach. "They didn't learn their lesson last time?"

Uncle Lyn's lips tightened as he breathed through his anger - the same anger that was spreading through me.

"I guess not," he said as he leveled a look at me. "It's why I'm wantin' to ask a favor of you."

I knew whatever he was going to ask for had to be important if he was asking me, so I listened intently, even if the thought of doing something for the club again sent a wave of unresolved emotions through me.

"Ray's been handlin' things up that way since Gavin and Everette passed, and well... let's just say he hasn't been runnin' as tight a ship as he needs to.

Now that everything is startin' to fall to me, it's been brought to my attention that we've been losin' or missin' shipments for a while now because the Heathens have been makin' side deals with some of Ray's guys, takin' shit that isn't theirs so they can make a name for themselves."

My mouth hung open.

"What? Who would do that? Everybody might be havin' trouble choosin' between you or Ray, but everybody's always been loyal to the club at least."

"Well, that's what I'm plannin' on findin' out while we're up there for the rally in Wilmington in a few days. And I'm gonna personally handle that whole situation with both the Heathens and whoever's turned traitor. But it's been a while since I've been up that way. You know the only times we even go through there is when we're pickin' up or droppin' off a shipment, so I'm bringin' a show of force with me to let them know we aren't the ones they wanna be messin' with."

"Alright," I said. "What do you need my help with?"

"I just need you to keep your ears open and let me know if you hear anything about the Heathens makin' moves anywhere. I know they're pretty active up your way."

Nodding, I said, "I can do that. They're constantly runnin' up and down Highway 17, goin' from Wilmington to Jacksonville, and they always like to stop by the island on their way. There's never been a group of more than like four or five though, so I've never thought too much about it, but I can definitely keep an ear out and let you know if I hear anything. No problem."

Really, it was a very small thing to ask of me, but something I knew would help him out a lot in the long run if I was able to gather any intel.

"Thanks, laddie," he said. "I'm hopin' I'll be able to bring you down..." his words cut off as we heard a car coming up his driveway.

Standing quickly, his face morphing into that angry impassive one he always wore when things didn't go his way, Uncle Lyn made his way over to the window and looked out through the blinds.

"Ray's here," he said, sending me a sympathetic look as a healthy dose of adrenaline dumped into my veins.

Standing as well, I reached a hand down to Kaliyah to pull

her to her feet. "You know how I said you might have to wait in the truck?"

She nodded at me, and I tried to ignore the fear I saw staring back at me in her eyes.

"Well, change that to the bathroom. Go in there and lock the door."

Then turning my attention back to Uncle Lyn for a second, I asked, "You still keep a piece in the medicine cabinet?"

"You know it, laddie," he answered back as he went to step out on the porch.

"There's a gun in the medicine cabinet. Don't open the door for anyone except for us, okay?"

Surprising me with the level of resolve I saw on her face, Kaliyah nodded wordlessly before she stepped into the bathroom I'd pointed out, closing the door tightly behind her.

I took a deep breath to get my wits about me just in time.

As I stood there, watching Ray walk in, his eyes landed right on me, and I knew I was about to get it; I just had to make sure whatever happened to me didn't reach Kaliyah in the bathroom.

~

"*L*yn," Ray said as he froze just inside the doorway with an oxygen tank trailing behind him. "You've got a traitor in your house."

Uncle Lyn stepped around Ray with an eye roll.

"You know damn well Decky isn't a traitor. He just needed time, is all."

Ray huffed out a bitter chuckle before he sat down where I'd been sitting a few minutes earlier, and I moved to lean up against the fireplace so I could keep an eye on the bathroom door.

Once he was settled in, Ray glanced up at me and asked, "So you stayin' or turnin' tail again?"

Crossing my arms over my chest to keep my anger in check, I glared right back at him. "You plannin' on offin' me if I stay?"

I had no intention of staying; I'd worked too hard to build up the life I'd made for myself in Topsail, but I hadn't been able to keep myself from taking his bait.

"Probably," Ray said nonchalantly as if we were talking about something inconsequential like golfing rather than him having me killed.

"About that," Uncle Lyn said as he sat back down in his chair. "Is all that really necessary, Ray? You know he dinna have anything to do with what happened to Everette and Gavin."

"May not have," Ray said as he sent his eyes up and down my frame with a look of disgust marring his features. "He's still a deserter, though, and I don't want that shit in my ranks. Better to off him instead."

Reaching into his vest, he pulled out his pistol and aimed it right at me with an I-couldn't-care-less look in his eyes.

"Woah there, ya blitherin' idiot," Uncle Lyn said as he stood up from his chair. "You'll not be murderin' my nephew in my own damn house. I don't care who you are."

Ray swerved the pistol in the air, so it was pointed at Uncle Lyn instead, and my heart jumped into my chest.

I hadn't moved from where I was standing, and once the gun was pointed at Uncle Lyn, he didn't move either.

"You gonna shoot your best friend, Ray? The guy who's been by your side from the beginning? Who's the real traitor here?" I asked, my arms still crossed over my chest.

The gun swiveled back to me, and I breathed out an inaudible sigh through my nose now that the danger was off Uncle Lyn again.

"You've been gone for years, boy. Don't you question..." Ray descended into a coughing fit that shook his entire frame, his hold on the gun loosening so severely he nearly dropped the damn thing.

Uncle Lyn and I shared a barely perceptible glance with each other before we both sprang into motion.

He grabbed the gun while I jumped over the couch and reached back over to grab Ray, holding him tightly in a choke-hold from behind so he couldn't move, but not so hard that he couldn't breathe.

"That's the last straw, you old fucker," Uncle Lyn said as he walked over to a drawer in his kitchen. He came back a few seconds later with a rope dangling from his hands.

Ray was cussing up a storm as we moved him and tied him to a chair, but in almost no time at all, he was secured and unable to do anything about it.

Breathing heavily from the fight Ray had put up, Uncle Lyn put the pistol up on the mantel and turned to me.

"You get the lass and head on back now. I'll call Mac, and we'll handle all this."

Patting him on the back, I asked, "Are you sure? Do you think you can get the club to agree to handle him?"

Nodding while he looked back at a gagged Ray, he said, "I might've been mistaken when I talked to you before, lad. When I was diggin' I figured out that most of the boys have been wantin' to vote Ray out for a while. Once they hear he pulled a gun on me, I'm sure that'll be all they need to hear. You just worry about what we talked about, and I'll handle Ray."

We gave each other a hug before I stepped over to the bathroom, letting Kaliyah know it was time for us to go.

She stepped out hesitantly but made her way through the house with her head held high. It wasn't until we were opening the door that Ray said something through the gag in his mouth, but when I looked back in question, Ray fell into another bout of coughs, and I dismissed whatever it was he'd said, confident Uncle Lyn would take care of it.

CHAPTER 22

KALIYAH

I could've sworn Ray had mumbled something about a biker's whore as we were leaving but, like Declan had said when I'd told him about it in the truck on the way back, Ray wasn't going to be a problem anymore if his Uncle Lyn had anything to say about it.

That set my mind at ease some, but not entirely.

I knew from Declan's talk with his uncle that someone from the club had made a call or two, and as soon as I thought I heard Ray say those words, I'd figured those calls had come from him.

However, that didn't dismiss all the other calls that had come through to the shop, and something inside me was just screaming that the rest of them had to have come from Cam.

Still, since we hadn't heard about more calls since we'd come back from Chicago, I'd also figured Declan's talk with Cam had done the trick.

I wasn't taking any chances though, so I'd changed my

number and email address, and with all of those tactics working in unison, things were starting to look up.

When we finally made it back late that night, we were both exhausted and, after taking a bit to savor each other again, we fell asleep together in my new bed like it was just normal for us to sleep together now.

The next morning, as Declan was leaving to go to the shop, he stepped outside and said, "Hey, all your stuff's out here."

Sure enough, when I stepped out the door with him, all of the boxes we'd shipped from Chicago were sitting pretty by my front door. He helped me carry them inside, and I thanked him for his help before I shooed him away so he could get to work.

"I've got boxes to unpack," I said before he leaned down and kissed me goodbye, only looking back once as he made his way over to the shop.

I made another cup of tea in my dad's mug and stared at the boxes, trying to get the motivation I needed to start unpacking them. However, all it took was one thought about the rest of my mom's scrapbooks to have me whipping out a knife from the drawer so I could open them.

The first box held nothing but all those clothes I'd left behind.

Figuring I'd go ahead and get a trash pile going, I moved everything from that box into an empty trash bag, then broke the box down and laid it over by the door to carry out later.

The next box was the same thing, so I repeated the process and moved on to the next one.

The third box held all the manuscripts that I'd written in college and a few other miscellaneous things that would be placed in my office. I took it all in there and left it by the wall since I didn't have a desk or shelves to tuck everything away in, and went back out to the living room.

Everything was in as good a condition as it'd been when I'd

left it in Chicago, up until I got to the box that held the three other albums my mom had made.

As soon as I opened that box, tears rose up to cloud my vision, and I felt like I'd been stabbed in the gut

"No, no, no," I said, my voice shaking as my hands froze above the box because I could hardly bring myself to touch what I saw.

Placed haphazardly inside, the covers she'd made had been ripped from their bindings, and the pages that had once lined them and been so pristine were now torn apart with black sharpie ink covering every scrap.

Almost as if Cam had sat there, scribbling and defacing every picture in them before deciding that still wasn't quite enough pain to cause me, then set about shredding them too without an ounce of remorse.

It was just like Cam to do something like that, and as I fell into heaving sobs over the box before me, I couldn't help but hate myself for leaving them behind for him to fuck with in the first place.

I should've known the bastard would do something like this, especially with how readily he'd given me the boxes while we were in Chicago.

Suddenly, there was a knock at my door, and it was all I could do to stand up and walk away from the box to answer it.

Wiping the tears from my eyes, even while my heart was throbbing inside my chest, I opened the door to find Roxy standing there with concern written all over her face.

"I don't mean to pry, but I can hear you downstairs. What's wrong?" she asked, but I couldn't get any words out as another sob tore through my throat, and my head fell into my hands.

Immediately, she pulled me into her arms, trying to comfort me by rubbing her hand down the back of my head.

"Girl, what is it?" she asked, her voice sounding more worried than she had at first.

I didn't want her thinking anyone or anything beyond my own sentimental feelings were hurt, so I pulled away long enough to point at the box.

Roxy went digging inside it, pulling all my memories out and laying them beside her in color-coded piles gently while I somehow found the words to explain.

She listened intently as I talked, her own anger seeping out onto her face as she moved. When she'd finally gotten to the bottom, and everything had been sorted out as best she could without having seen the albums before they were ruined, she pulled out a little white envelope that she handed right over to me.

Taking it from her hesitantly, I opened it and read it slowly as fear started welling up inside my chest.

My dearest, sweet whore Kaliyah,

It pains me greatly to learn you've been slumming it with biker scum since you left me at the altar, but I meant what I said in those emails and texts I sent.

I WILL HAVE YOU, and there's nothing you or your little distraction of a boyfriend will be able to do to stop me. I know you're only with him because you're missing me.

You've belonged to me from the day I first laid eyes on you. You seem to have forgotten all that, but I'll remind you, it's okay. I'll forgive you. This... this hiccup we're going through won't be the end of us. I'll make everything right again, so don't you worry.

I'll be there soon.

Until then, I remain your most adoring fiancé,

Camdyn Fletcher

~

"So the dude is fucking nuts," Roxy said as she dropped her hands to her lap, having just read the letter I'd handed over to her.

"Absofuckinglutely."

She sighed and thought to herself for a minute before she eyed me warily. "Do you think he'll make good on what he's sayin' here?"

I shrugged.

"I have no idea. I know he's batshit crazy sometimes, but I figured he would've moved on to one of his other women by now and left me alone.

It doesn't make any sense.

If I meant so much to him, why the hell did he treat me like he did or cheat on me in the first place? I really just can't wrap my head around that part.

That's what makes me think he might not actually be serious or do any of the things he's said - because how he treated me doesn't add up with what he's been saying, you know? But then again, what if he tries?"

Roxy nodded before she started placing everything back in the box gently.

"I need a drink, and so do you. Plus, if this is all you have," she said as she gestured around my apartment, "you're in desperate need of a shopping trip, and because of Kaylynne, I know you've got the money to get what you need.

I say we put all this aside, for now, go grab the girls for an emergency shopping date, make a plan to handle your psycho ex, and get shitfaced by the end of the day. How does that sound?"

My laughter fell out of me as I asked, "What do you mean if this is all I have?"

Without missing a beat, Roxy said, "Girl, you don't even have a couch! I'm not gonna be spendin' half my time here, havin' nothin' but those hard-ass dining room chairs to sit on. Nuh-uh. No, ma'am."

She was exactly what I'd needed at that moment, and I couldn't have turned her down if I'd tried.

The next thing I knew, I was riding in Mya's big four-door pickup truck, singing along with Alanis Morrisette as she blared out the speakers.

Mya was driving all of us but Bethany down to Wilmington because apparently, they had the best furniture and decor stores. Bethany had been in school in Jacksonville, so she hadn't been able to make it, but that hadn't stopped the rest of these girls from rallying together for me in the slightest.

From the moment Roxy had called Mya, it was like the well-oiled machine of the girls of Topsail had started up, and making me feel better had been their ultimate goal. Well, that and getting furniture we all could enjoy in my new apartment.

And it just made me love them even more for it.

The general consensus on Cam was that he was simply a nutjob who had no intention of following through on his threat to come get me.

Mya had said, "He's just mad and blowin' smoke up your ass. He wants to get a rise out of you, and since all his other methods of tryin' to call you haven't worked, that's what he resorted to."

"Yeah, especially since he had to have written it before you guys showed up there and Dec talked to him," Roxy added on. "Dusty never wants to have a personal talkin' to from Dec again because last time, he scared the hell out of him."

She descended into hysterics after that, saying, "You guys remember when..." until I had at least three embarrassing stories of all the guys on the island, Declan included, and I was smiling so much my cheeks hurt.

While we were gone, I spent an almost sickening amount of money on all the things I needed to turn my apartment into a home, but I couldn't find it in myself to really care that much since I was the one making all the final decisions.

The couch, desk, bookshelf, and other furniture I bought were going to be delivered in a few days' time. Everything else, we just piled into the bed of Mya's truck as we went from one store to the next, barely pausing at all between them.

We didn't drink while we were gone, but by the time we were done, and it was time for Mya to head into Island Thyme to prepare for their dinner service, we'd made plans to have a celebratory girls' night the next day because Roxy, Mya, Bethany, and Kaylynne would be off work that night.

Roxy helped me bring everything upstairs, but then she had to go too because the other chick she worked with at Igan Grocery had called in sick.

We said our goodbyes, and even though I had to face the dreaded box and everything else once I got home, it was a lot easier to deal with after the carefree and fun day I'd had.

I was going about my apartment, setting up everything I'd bought, when Declan knocked on my door a short while later.

"You ready to eat?" he asked, and as soon as he said that, my belly growled loudly enough for him to hear it. Laughing, he said, "I'll take that as a 'yes,'" and I went with him back over to his place for dinner.

"I need you to tell me how much I owe you so I can pay you back," I said, handing him things while he started cooking.

He gave me a look that could only be described as 'get out of here with that,' but I wasn't backing down.

"If you don't tell me, I'm just gonna put a ridiculous amount in an envelope and tuck it in your mailbox."

Smiling, he said, "Fine, I'll tell you, but I'm not takin' it back. I'll give it to the cleanup efforts at the north end of the island if you insist on payin' me back, but I really don't need it.

I put back everything I'd need while I was in all the way with the club. When I added in the insurance payouts from Tristan and Gavin to my savings too, well, let's just say I'm not hurtin', and helpin' you out didn't hurt me either."

Eventually, we agreed that I'd just send the money to the cleanup efforts. Even though I thought Declan was being stubborn in that regard, I was also immensely grateful because talking money with him was drastically different than talking about it with Cam had ever been.

Changing the subject as he sat down next to me with two plates of food in his hands, he said, "I'm sorry if all that shit with my uncle and Ray scared you. I probably should've apologized for it already, but I hadn't thought about it before now because I was still tryin' to wrap my mind around everything."

He slid one of the plates over to me, and I dug right in after I said, "I was only scared for a little bit, but it seems like your uncle has things under control now, so I don't think either of us needs to worry about Ray at least."

Thoughts of Cam's letter fluttered through my mind, but I forgot them entirely when Declan turned to look at me, his face all kinds of serious. "I don't want to lie to you, but I also don't want you to lie to me. That's the deal, right?"

My belly filled with butterflies and nerves when he spoke to me like that, but I answered with a head nod readily enough.

"Be honest, do you mind being involved with me, knowing about my ties to the club?"

I swallowed the bite of chicken I still had in my mouth and regarded him as seriously as he was regarding me. "You could be running that thing, and I'd still want to be with you."

Obviously taken back some by my words, he asked, "Are you sure? Why would you be okay with that? It can get dangerous."

Putting my fork down, I turned to him so I could face him fully.

"Yes, I'm sure. The club was a part of you long before I came along, and even though you haven't been involved with them as much over the last couple of years, I'm also smart enough to know that with a club like that, you never really get out and stay out.

From the moment you told me about them and your history

with them, I knew I would stay with you whether you were all the way in or all the way out.

The dark side of you is the right kind of dark for me.

It doesn't hurt me like Cam's did; it protects me like only you will, and I don't think I'll ever get enough of it... whether it comes with club strings attached or not."

His lips fell on mine in a relieved and punishing kiss that I felt in my soul, and as I let him pull me into his lap, we completely forgot about the rest of our food for a while.

I straddled his hips where he sat on the barstool, and right away, I could feel his bulge pressing teasingly against me right where I wanted him.

His hands slid under my shirt and up my back as I kissed him, while one of my hands wrapped around the back of his neck, and the other threaded itself in his hair.

Declan unhooked my bra in one simple sweeping motion and sent both of his hands to rest on the sides of my ribcage.

He lifted me off of him, making me want to pout instantly because the movement had broken our kiss, but I kept my bottom lip in check since as soon as we were standing, he ripped my tank top and bra off aggressively.

He must have had something against me wearing shirts since he always ripped them off like that, but every time I found myself bared before his hungry gaze, my shirts became the furthest thing from my mind.

I sent my hands out to take his black t-shirt off as well, but he beat me to it, tearing it off just as fast as he'd taken off mine, so I let my hands fall to his waist instead as my eyes drifted down his front, taking in that v thing I would never get tired of looking at.

Heat was pooling within me, and the anticipation I felt made me shiver as my hands moved over the skin of his torso. When he grabbed the hair and pulled, leaning my head back so my eyes would lock onto his, I nearly fell apart with need, desire flooding my system so thickly I was surprised my knees didn't buckle beneath me.

His other hand came up to cup my chin as his lips met mine again. As he kissed me, he walked me backward while I worked on unbuttoning his jeans, and soon, my ass bumped up against the side of the couch's armrest.

Letting me go, he took a step back and said, "Take those off," as he pointed to my shorts.

Something about him telling me what to do set my insides on fire, making me feel way more glorious than I usually felt, and at his words, something strange came over me.

Playing coy and innocent, I put my thumbs in the waistband of my shorts and asked, "You mean these?" as I pushed them to the floor, making sure I left my thong in place.

I kicked my shorts over to his feet, lapping up that lust-filled gaze of his, and then made the same motion with the sides of my thong as I asked, "Or these?"

Coming over to me quickly before I could start taking my thong off, he leaned down and whispered in my ear, "Those can stay on," right before he turned me around and bent me over the side of the couch, smacking my right asscheek hard as fuck.

A little yelp spilled out of me at the same time as my legs squeezed together, as if their movement would stop the open floodgates of sensation I felt between my thighs; dumbass legs, nothing was stopping all that.

The sting of the slap was soothed away a second later as Declan's rough hand slid over the spot in smooth circles.

His fingers drifted over to where my thong was sitting, and in one deft motion, he moved them over to the side, exposing me to him in every way before his fingers slid tantalizingly over my folds.

A moan filled the air, and I was pretty sure it had come from me, but I couldn't focus on that because all I could think about was how good Declan's hand was making me feel.

He started out slow at first, but he didn't make me wait too long before he was working me into a frenzy at a speed my body just couldn't comprehend, and sooner than even I would've expected, I was coming apart altogether, right there in his hand.

Leaning down to pull my head back by my hair again at an angle that would allow me to see him, he whispered in my ear, "Good girl," and proceeded to put those very same fingers that had just been inside me, in his mouth.

I felt like a fucking goddess in that moment, and even as he walked away to take his jeans off and roll on a condom, I didn't move, knowing I was in the position I wanted him to take me in when he came back. I hadn't felt him in this position before, and my vagina was practically begging for Declan to fill her up from behind.

A few seconds later, he slid behind me and, without hesitating at all, thrust inside me slowly as one of his hands grabbed each of my hips.

A moan fell from both of us at the same time, and I basked under the sound of it.

Declan was incredible in so many ways; he was both sensitive and rough around the edges, a good guy with a troubled past, a bad boy who truly did have a heart of gold, and as he ravaged me, right there on the side of his couch, I knew I loved him.

I never said I was perfect, and I knew that might not have been the best time to make such a decision, but here's the thing...

It wasn't a decision at all.

It was the easiest and most natural thing on the planet to love Declan, and I didn't regret it one bit.

I didn't regret it as he held me in his arms to fall asleep that night, or when I woke up the next morning to find him drooling on my pillow, or when we kissed each other goodbye by his back door.

Even when we stepped outside to find decapitated animals on each of our doorsteps, I never regretted loving Declan; he was the smooth current in the wake of all the trouble that was following us, my safe haven from the storm that had been our lives before we'd met each other. I knew if we could just find a way to get our pasts settled, we had a good chance at finding that epic kind of love I'd always dreamed of.

CHAPTER 23

DECLAN

"Yeah, I got one on my porch this morning too," Nash said as he pulled up on his bicycle. "I'm just glad Moms didn't see it; she woulda lost her mind."

Kaliyah and I were standing outside the shop after I'd gotten the animals that had been left on our doorsteps wrapped up.

I would've thought seeing one of the neighborhood cats and a random mouse in that state would've had Kaliyah freaking out, but instead, she'd pulled down that mask of impassivity that I was growing accustomed to seeing on her.

It seemed like she did that whenever she was feeling a whole lot and didn't want anyone else around to know about it.

I couldn't begrudge her that if it kept her calm, but I did want to know how she felt, so I'd kept her with me all morning in an attempt to break her out of that headspace, hoping she'd either let me in and tell me what she was thinking, or calm down enough so that it wouldn't matter.

"I'm sorry, Nash," Kaliyah said, her voice betraying the amount of sympathy she held for him.

"What are you apologizin' for? You didn't do it, did you?" Nash asked even though he already knew the answer to that.

Kaliyah just wasn't capable of real violence, I didn't think. Sure, she could protect herself if she had to, but it takes one sick fuck to kill an innocent animal, and a sick fuck, Kaliyah is not.

"No, I just... it sucks is all, and what does someone say about something like this?"

Nash kicked out the kickstand on his bike and walked over to Kaliyah, throwing an arm around her shoulders. "You don't have to say anything. We all know it sucks, and we all know there's nothing we can say that'll make it any better."

"You guys go on and head inside; I'll be right behind you," I said, trying to prevent Kaliyah from watching me dispose of the animals.

They didn't argue, and when I got inside the shop, they were both leaning up against the counter, talking easily with each other as if they were old friends.

"There is no way you actually think Star Wars could beat The Lord of The Rings head-to-head," Kaliyah said with all the conviction and judgment in the world.

Nash stood back like he'd been wounded. "Woman, you can't even compare the two!" he laughed out, making a smile form on both Kaliyah's face and mine.

"Sorry to break it to ya, kid, but she's right," I said. "Star Wars isn't even in the same league as The Lord of The Rings."

"Not you too," Nash said, and for the next few hours or so, we distracted ourselves from our gruesome finds as best we could with topics from movies to favorite past times and everything in between.

There were quite a few customers heading in and out of the shop as the day wore on, and Kaliyah didn't mind handling the front counter while Nash and I set up a few customers with their rentals and gave a few surfing lessons.

I was dead set on paying her for her time, but she didn't know it yet.

Nash and I were just putting up the last of the kayaks that had been rented for the day when Kaliyah came out back looking as white as a sheet with a manilla folder in her hands.

"Declan," she said as she handed me the folder and the pictures that had obviously been inside it.

Looking through them, I could see someone had a peeping Tom fetish because Kaliyah and I were front and center in the pictures in my hands, going at it beside the couch in my living room. There were also pictures of our faces when we saw the dead animals that morning.

"Where'd you get this?" I asked, my tone harsher than I wanted it to be, but I couldn't help the level of rage I felt from seeping out into my voice.

Kaliyah ran a hand through her hair as she said, "I went to the bathroom 'cause I had to pee, and when I came back, it was just lying there on the counter with my name on it."

I turned the envelope over, and sure enough, her name was printed on a shipping label, attached to the front.

"There wasn't anyone in the shop when I went to the bathroom, and no one was in there when I came back out later."

Nash stole a peak over my shoulder but looked away quickly, his fists balling at his sides a second later.

"Declan, look at the angle. Whoever it was had to have been standing in the Stevens place I'd been renting."

I'd known that from the second I saw the first picture, but hearing it said out loud, acknowledging how close this guy had gotten to us, was hard to swallow.

Shoving the pictures back in the envelope, I grabbed Kaliyah by the hand and told Nash to come with us as we went back inside the shop.

Nash and I locked all the doors and checked every nook and cranny in the building before I felt comfortable enough to stop and have a conversation, but even with all that, I still felt like I was being watched, and it didn't sit right with me at fucking all.

"From now on, I don't want you going anywhere without Nash or me, okay?" I asked, but Kaliyah balked immediately.

"What? No," she said, "I'm not gonna live in fear of some perv. I just got my life back, Declan."

Running a hand through my hair as I blew a breath out of my nose, I tried to keep my temper in check.

"I don't want to scare you, but whoever's doin' all this is definitely escalating, and until I know for sure that it's Cam or the club and deal with it, I can't have you in any more danger than you already are." I was trying to plead my case, but I ended up just making Kaliyah worry even more.

"What do you mean you don't know if it's Cam or the club? It's obviously Cam because your uncle is handling the club, right?"

Sighing, I said, "He's handlin' Ray. The rest of the club is a different story. There are still those who are loyal as fuck to Ray and who will probably go to great lengths to make sure he stays in power, whether his health is failing or not."

"But what would they have to gain by doing all this?" she asked, gesturing to the envelope on the counter between us, making a solid point.

I'd already worked out the answer to that question though.

"The guys who are in Ray's corner can't make a move without a vote from the club. They're tryin' to bait me into doin' somethin' stupid just so they'll have a justifiable reason to call a vote for puttin' my head on a choppin' block."

"So we still don't know who's doing this?" she said under her breath as she scrubbed her hands down her face.

Nash spoke up, saying, "Kali, I know it's not ideal, but I really think Dec's plan is a good one. Whether it's Cam or the club, I think the real reason they haven't outright gone after you yet is that you've had someone around you most of the time."

She looked over at Nash, her face contorted into a mixture of both understanding and fear before she glanced between the two of us as she spoke.

"I'm supposed to have a girls' night tonight, and I know I probably sound like a whiny, ungrateful bitch for using that as an excuse on this, but I mean... It's girls' night, and I really want to go.

Plus, when will it end, huh? What's it gonna be next time? I'll have to have one of you with me when I go to the grocery store to buy tampons? Or wake you up in the middle of the night because I want to make a late-night taco run?

I can't stop living my life or ask you to give up yours so you can watch me.

I won't do it."

As much as it sucked, Kaliyah did have a point. It wasn't one I liked at all, but it was still a valid point regardless.

"Alright, we won't hover over you," I said as I stood up. "But I'm givin' you this to protect yourself, and I'm not takin' 'no' for an answer."

Handing her the small caliber pistol from under the counter, I locked eyes with her as she nodded her acceptance of what I'd said and checked to see if the weapon was loaded.

"That's a solid compromise," she said as she tucked the gun in the back of her shorts and pulled her shirt down over it to hide it.

It wasn't the best option, but it did make me feel somewhat better as she left a short time later to get ready for girls' night.

Nash and I both watched her walk across the street and go inside her apartment, neither one of us willing to walk away until we knew she was safely inside.

I'd told her I wouldn't hover, but if I stayed there watching her like a hawk like I wanted to, I knew that's exactly what I was gonna end up doing. So instead, I turned to Nash and said, "The Raging Heathens are due to be stoppin' in tonight down at the Jollyroger, and I've got a few questions to ask 'em… what do you say to blowin' off a little steam?" And at hearing those words, Nash couldn't have been more relieved or excited.

CHAPTER 24

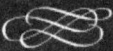

KALIYAH

*H*onestly, girls' night couldn't have come at a better time. With everything that had happened lately, I felt like I was being suffocated by either Declan's past or mine... both if I thought about things logically.

I desperately longed to escape the stress of it all, even if it was only for one night out with the girls.

Don't get me wrong, I knew I loved Declan and my new life here, and I already knew I wouldn't trade it for anything, but between the trip to Savannah to see Declan's uncle, the calls, the dead animals on our doorsteps, the pictures of Declan and me that were obviously taken by someone who'd been less than twenty or so feet away, and all the stuff Declan had told me about Ray's followers in the club, stuff had been piling up so much that, at times, it had been hard to even think through.

I went back home to my apartment, knowing Declan and Nash were watching me until I stepped inside, but I couldn't find it in me to be mad at them for it.

Even if they ended up following me around like lost puppies with a grudge to settle for the foreseeable future, I wouldn't have been able to be angry with them.

Though they both disagreed with me about whether I should have a bodyguard or not, they hadn't forced me to comply with their wishes, and in some backwards ass way, that made me okay with them watching me closer than they usually did.

However, after I'd gotten dressed in a cute little black skirt and a loose flowy tank I could hide the pistol under, I knew as soon as I stepped outside to knock on Roxy's door that Declan and Nash weren't there anymore.

I had no idea where they'd gone, but as I stood there in the dark, wondering why the hell Roxy didn't have a front porch light, I started to wonder if I'd made the right decision.

I felt exposed in their absence, a prickling sensation traveling down my spine as my hand twitched at my side, readying to grab the pistol if I ended up needing it.

Soon though, my worries were cast away as Roxy opened the door with a curling iron still in her hair, holding the plug she'd obviously just taken out of the wall.

"Girl, I know I said I wouldn't be long when I texted you, but damn if my hair isn't being a straight-up bitch tonight."

"You want some help 'til the Uber gets here?" I asked with a laugh as I stepped into an exact replica of my apartment upstairs.

"Please," she pleaded with me, bending her knees some as she said it, making me laugh even harder as I closed the door, being sure to lock it behind me.

With both of us working on it, we had her blonde hair in some semblance of a style that looked pretty cute within a few minutes, and by the time the car honked its horn outside, she was just putting her shoes on by the front door.

No sooner had we stepped out of her apartment than Mya

and Bethany started fighting over who got to yell out the back window at us to hurry our asses up.

Smiles were shared all around, and laughter filled the space inside the Uber, causing even our stoic driver to crack a smile eventually - a feat Bethany practically drooled over as she sat next to him. As the night wore on, and drink after drink made its way into my system, the smiles and laughter just kept coming, seeming like there was no end in sight.

At some point during the night, we made our way to a second bar where Dusty was bartending, and I asked, "How many places do you bartend at, anyway?"

His laughter had Bethany sitting her chin on her hand to stare at him as he answered. "Just here and Island Thyme. You guys haven't been lettin' her drink, have you?" He was pointing at Bethany, but even with our drunkenness, we weren't that far gone.

"Of course not!" Mya said a bit too loudly, even for the bar we were standing in, but then Bethany broke into the conversation, surprising all of us.

"I might've stolen a drink or two from behind the bar when CJ wasn't looking," she said as her face pinched up with the admission.

Instantly, five voices yelled, "Bethany!" in outrage at the same time.

It was like we'd all rehearsed it, but all the good it ended up doing was sending another round of giggles through all of us.

All of us except for Dusty, of course.

He leaned across the bar and placed his hand over Bethany's, killing off her laughter instantly as he leveled her with a glare even I could feel from where I was sitting.

I couldn't hear what he'd said, but I could read Bethany's reaction fairly well.

Her cheeks got all kinds of flushed, and her smile was sweet and genuine before he said something else, and she ripped her hand out from under his, all of her features turning angry in an instant.

"I'm not a child anymore, Dusty, so fuck off trying to babysit me. I'll do what I want."

She got up then, slinging her hair over her shoulder as she made her way to the bathroom.

"Uh oh," Roxy said, hopping down from her stool to follow after her.

Mya sent a seething glare at Dusty, where he was standing there looking confused before she grabbed Kaylynne's and my arms, pulling us to the bathroom as well.

It was your usual, run of the mill, drunk and love-struck, angry teenager talk, spilling out of Bethany as I walked in, but after all of us did what we could to boost Bethany's confidence back up, within a few minutes, we were all walking out of there like we owned the place, heading to an area away from the bar, but still, of course, within sight of the bar.

The dance floor was right beside us, and though there weren't that many people in the bar that night, there were a few guys that looked like Marines, eyeing all of us up from across the room.

Bethany jumped right on that bandwagon, making damn sure Dusty was getting an eyeful of her having fun with some other guy, and though I wanted to laugh, I couldn't because the expression on Dusty's face looked like she'd just punched him in the gut.

I was about to get up and join her for the distraction I knew dancing would bring, but then I remembered the pistol at my back and thought better of it.

More and more drinks kept coming our way, but I never pulled out my debit card once. I think Mya had bought the first round, but after that, I had no idea who was buying, and it didn't occur to me to mind until later.

When I was this close to not being able to see straight, I

knew I was getting close to becoming full-on Blackout Drunk Me, and I realized I hadn't set up any precautions other than the gun that was hiding in the back of my skirt.

The thought actually sobered me up some. I let the girls know I was reaching my limit, proud of myself for admitting it when a massive part of me really didn't want to.

However, where Cassie would've complained or something, all the girls I was with took me at my word. They ordered an Uber right then, every single one of them willing to call it a night simply because I was, and well...

That made Sad Drunk Me come out to play hard.

I cried the whole damn way back to my apartment despite the girls' attempts to make me stop.

Granted, they were laughing their asses off at me at the same time, and I shared in many of those laughs with tears on my face, but regardless, Sad Drunk Me was there to stay, it seemed.

Roxy and I got out of the Uber and waved goodbye as they peeled off down the street, but before we could turn around to head inside, Declan was walking across the street to meet us.

It was dark, but I knew it was him for sure when he asked, "Did you have fun tonight?"

A tiny sob spilled from me as I replied, no matter how hard I tried to keep it from happening. "Yes, it was so much fun."

Chuckling some, he said, "Then why are you crying?"

"I think she's just at that point, Dec. If you've got her, I'm goin' to bed," Roxy said as she fluffed my hair like a doting mama, and when Declan nodded, I watched her go inside, sniffling and wiping at my face the whole time.

"Are you a drunk crier?" he asked as he started guiding me up to my apartment.

"Apparently," I said as I tried to remember where I'd put my other flip flop, getting sad all over again as I remembered pulling it off for some reason in the Uber.

However, as I pulled my keys out, I saw it hanging from my hand, and I got all kinds of happy about it.

"There you are!" I said as I lifted it up to show Declan proudly, but when I looked past my flip flop to see his face, I nearly dropped it as I took in the shiner he had on his left eye.

"Oh my God, what happened to you?" I asked as he took my keys and opened the door for me.

"It's nothing really," he said as he led me inside, but I stopped dead in my tracks as I stared him down.

He must have noticed the change because he looked back at me like he was worried as I said, "Do not lie to me."

I saw him deflate at that, and even though it was taking everything I had in me to keep my composure as he maneuvered me into the bedroom, I wasn't letting up until I knew what had happened to him.

"You remember how Uncle Lyn asked me to check on the Raging Heathens?" he asked as I pulled out the gun and laid it on the bed so I could change.

His eyes followed my movements, a subtle smirk playing at his lips as I nodded, and he continued.

"Well, I had to go do that."

Try as I might, composure had to go fuck itself because my dinner was coming up whether I liked it or not. Luckily, my apartment was small enough that I made it to the toilet just in time.

Declan followed me in there with guts of steel, holding my hair back without me even having to ask him to, making even more tears fill my eyes than were already there before.

"You're the sweetest, you know that?" I asked between bouts of my stomach heaving.

He chuckled some. "Only for you, woman."

His words made me smile at the throne before me, and when I finally felt like I could pull my head away from it, I lay on the cold tile floor, letting him rub his hands over the side of my head.

"What happened with the other MC?" I asked with my eyes closed.

"Well, everything started out fine," he began, and I listened as hard as I could, paying as close attention as I could muster in my inebriated state. "They've definitely been takin' shipments from the Savages, but it wasn't 'till one of them tried to recruit Nash that I lost it."

Sitting up and regretting it two seconds later, I asked, "They what? What do they want with Nash?"

Declan saw the wooziness hit me and eased me back down to the floor.

"He's a smart, loyal kid, and he's built like a brick shithouse. What's there not to want for any MC?"

I nodded, though I'd nearly forgotten what I was nodding for.

"So how'd you get the black eye?"

"Okay, so," he started, and I knew it was going to be a good story instantly. "The sergeant at arms for the Heathens was there, and that's who I'd been talkin' to. He didn't know I was with the Savages, and with how much he'd had to drink, he was looser with information than a guy in his position should ever be.

Anyway, well, he was tellin' me all about how these Savages had made a dumbass deal with them when one of the other Heathens took a likin' to Nash. I was tryin' to pay attention to what the sergeant was sayin', but somethin' 'bout how the guy was sizin' Nash up just didn't sit right with me.

So, I go over there, still bein' all friendly and whatnot, but when the guy told Nash he'd let him prospect, I jumped in, tellin' Nash it was time to go.

Well, that guy didn't take too kindly to me 'orderin'' Nash

around, and tried to grab the kid by the shoulder so he wouldn't leave.

Nash turned around and decked him just like I'd taught him, and we had to fight our way out of there, but we tore off, laughin' the whole way 'cause there were like six of them and only two of us, and we still beat the hell out of 'em."

His laughter echoed around me in the bathroom, and I found myself smiling, even as concern drifted through me too.

"I got a black…"

But that was all I heard before I blacked out.

~

*T*he next morning, I woke up in my bed with a splitting headache.

I reached out for Declan, but he wasn't there, and as the frown took shape on my face, I was kind of glad he wasn't seeing it.

When I threw my legs off the bed with quite a bit of effort, on my nightstand was a bottle of ibuprofen and a glass of orange juice.

Smiling like a madwoman at the thought of getting relief from the headache I had and from the thoughtfulness of the gesture, I popped some in my mouth and inhaled the whole drink because my throat was so dry.

I needed more, so I slowly got up and made my way to the kitchen.

On the counter, there was a note, and after refilling my glass, I opened it up, smiling.

Good morning Kaliyah,

I hope you slept well. I don't know if you saw it, but I left you some medicine and orange juice by your bed.

I also set up your office for you while you were sleeping.

You mentioned you haven't written in years, and I just think that's a travesty. No, I don't know how good or bad of a writer you are, but I do know that if you want to write, you should.

I don't know if you remember, but last night you were telling me about how you lost yourself in your relationship with Cam, and really, you 'bout broke my heart, woman.

I want to be with you, but I also want you to have your own adventures, pursuits, and passions, and if that comes out as writing, then dammit, you better write.

I never want you to lose yourself again. Not for me or anyone else.

Well, that's all I really had to say, and I don't really know how to end this now.

I'll be over at the shop if you need me.

Love,

Declan

*T*ears were streaming down my face as I walked through my apartment and opened the door to my office, nearly crumbling when I saw that even with no desk, Declan had made the space almost exactly how I'd wanted it.

The rope lights I'd bought while I'd been out with the girls were strung up, casting the space in a cool blue light. One of the comforter sets that had been here when I moved in had been opened and spread across the floor with the accent pillows thrown in for good measure. In the center of the blanket on the floor, my laptop was plugged up, sitting there with my stack of sticky notes and pens.

Even my books and manuscripts had been stacked up neatly against the wall since there was still no bookcase, but as I looked at the space, I seriously considered telling the stores to keep the furniture because I loved Declan's gift so much.

As fast as I could, I ran to my room to grab my phone.

I had to thank Declan as soon as I could, and as he answered, I fell into more tears, gushing over what he'd done.

CHAPTER 25

DECLAN

J'd nearly forgotten about having to take Nash to Jacksonville for the test he had to take that afternoon, but once he reminded me, I called Kaliyah to let her know where we were going and closed the shop early.

She'd been in the middle of writing something, and she'd seemed a bit distracted, but I didn't mind. If that was what made her happy, I could occupy myself while she let that part of herself out.

The night before, she'd been rambling about her life before she met me as I tucked her into bed and tried to get her to fall asleep, but once she finally did, everything she'd said played through my mind on repeat, and I couldn't get myself to wind down.

The shit she'd given up for Cam could've been put on a list a mile long, while that selfish bastard hadn't given up anything for her. Not that relationships needed a blood sacrifice from both parties to work, but any sacrifices made should damn well be appreciated by the other person, at the very least.

"Alright, I'm ready," Nash said, pulling me from my thoughts as he grabbed his stuff from behind the counter.

I closed up the shop as he climbed in my truck, grabbing out the notes he needed to study before I'd even pulled out of the garage.

"You mind quizin' me on these on the way?" he asked as we rode through Snead's Ferry. "I'm tryin' to do it on my own, but it's just not workin.'"

"Yeah, hand 'em over," I said as I reached across the cab to take the notebook paper he was handing me.

The kid wanted to have a career in the medical field, like a physician's assistant or paramedic or something. Since he hadn't made up his mind yet about which one he wanted to put all his time into becoming, he was kind of going through his classes all willy nilly.

Granted, I knew they were going to help him no matter which path he ended up choosing, but at times I thought he was packing more on than he needed to and stressing himself out more than was necessary.

I quizzed him on the way, and by the time we got there, he seemed pretty confident as he got out.

For the better part of an hour, I sat there scrolling through social media to pass the time. I'd thought about texting Kaliyah, but I knew she was finally writing, so I didn't want to interrupt her just because I was bored.

However, as soon as Nash was done, he came out with a larger than normal smile on his face.

"You think you passed?" I asked as I put the truck in drive, trying to figure out what had gotten the kid to smile like that.

"What? Oh, yeah. I'm not worried about it."

I was about to ask him what I was wondering, but he beat me to it.

"So you know that blonde girl I was tellin' you about? The one who cussed me out my first day here?"

"The one I said probably had daddy issues?" I asked with a smirk.

Nash laughed as he remembered that conversation. "Yeah, that one."

"What about her?"

Sending his nose in the air and cocking his head to the side, he said, "She winked at me in the hall today."

Laughter fell from me as I drove us home. "Awe. Boy, you're 'bout as hopeless as I am."

His face got all red as he laughed with me and began that incessant talking thing he liked to do for the rest of the drive. Again, I didn't mind though.

Once we got back on the island, I had to stop by Igan Grocery to pick up a few things... feeding three meals a day to two or sometimes, three different people had a way of dwindling anybody's supplies.

We got out at Igan Grocery and made our way inside, saying 'hello' to Roxy behind the counter before we started loading up the cart with everything I might need for the next few days. Nash added a few things he knew he wanted to snack on while he was at the shop, but I insisted on paying for them like always so he could keep growing that little nest egg he had going.

He didn't like it much, but that was why I almost always brought him with me when I went to get groceries - so I knew he wasn't spending that money himself.

I was pretty sure he'd caught onto my tactic after a while, but by that point, I figured he'd gotten used to it.

Roxy was ringing everything up for me when I heard a bunch of motorcycles pulling up outside, and immediately, I knew something was up.

So did Nash, given that he walked away to look out the glass at the front of the store.

"Dec," he said, everything he was thinking coming across through that one word by his tone alone.

"Roxy, can you put all this behind the counter for me, and I'll come back in to get it?" I asked after I paid for everything.

She looked worried but agreed and did as I asked.

"You stay here," I said to Nash, but he just huffed and followed me outside anyway.

Eight Heathens had parked around my truck in the parking lot, and once I saw them, I knew what this was.

It was revenge for last night.

"Can I help you with somethin?'" I asked, subtly loosening myself up for the fight I knew was coming.

The guy who'd tried to recruit Nash the night before stepped out of the group to face us. "Yeah, there's a couple of pussies walkin' 'round here somewhere that need to be taught a lesson."

Laughing, I said, "Yeah, I know. I'm looking right at 'em."

They definitely caught my humor, but they didn't think it was funny.

I hated being jumped, but it was the price I'd signed up to pay the second I'd decided to go rogue, and this was just me dealing with those consequences.

Nash, however, didn't need this shit. I mean, he'd just gotten winked at by a girl he liked after acing a test that was probably hard as fuck.

However, that didn't stop him from having my back or me from having his.

We might've taken more hits than we inflicted, but we definitely got our own licks in, and we were both still standing when the cops showed up.

The Heathens drove off as soon as they'd heard the cops coming, but Nash and I waited for them patiently as I checked Nash out to make sure he was okay.

He had a broken nose and a few other cuts and scrapes, same as me, but otherwise, we were both fine.

My phone started ringing in my pocket as the first policeman got out of his car and walked over to us. It was Kaliyah, and apparently, Roxy had called her the second shit started going sideways for us.

I definitely needed to have a talk with Roxy for getting Kaliyah all riled up, but that would have to wait.

"Don't come down here. I promise we're alright," I said after Kaliyah told me she was about to head our way. "We've got to talk to the cops, and I don't want you involved in all this. I'll let you know as soon as we get back though, okay?"

She wasn't too happy about it, but I got her to agree to stay at her apartment until we got done giving our statements to the police.

It was a long, drawn-out process, but by the end of it, Nash and I were free to go. I grabbed my groceries from inside the store, promising Roxy I'd have a talk with her soon, and started heading back to the surf shop about an hour after I'd talked to Kaliyah.

I wanted nothing more than a shower and to lay in the bed with her while my wounds healed, but as life goes, of course, that's just not what ended up happening.

CHAPTER 26

KALIYAH

I was going outside of my mind with worry.

Roxy had called to warn me about what I'd be facing whenever Declan got back, but she didn't know me well enough yet to know that I wasn't the type of person who could just sit idly by, waiting for him if I thought there was any chance I could help in any way.

Everything had already gone down by the time she'd called me, and immediately, I rang Declan to see if he was okay and to tell him I was on my way, but he'd told me to stay at home, so I didn't get involved.

I didn't want to listen, but I did it anyway because he seemed so adamant.

As the minutes ticked by, I found myself pacing through my living room, waiting to see his truck pull up across the street so I could go check him and Nash out for myself.

No matter how many times he told me he was okay, I was never going to believe him until I saw it with my own eyes.

I wanted to do something to help, so rather than pace a hole through the floor, I started making some chicken-flavored ramen because it was the closest thing to chicken noodle soup I had in my cabinets at the time.

If I left it watery and steamy, it was basically the same thing, so that was my plan to distract myself until they pulled up a short time later.

I saw both Nash and Declan go up into Declan's apartment through my glass front door and sighed with relief as I went back to the kitchen to grab the ramen because neither one of them looked like they were limping at all.

I'd just taken the last step off the staircase to my apartment, planning to cross the street, when I heard an engine rev up.

Startled, I looked to my right in just enough time to jump back out of the way, so the big truck didn't take me clean out.

I fell over sideways, dumping the hot liquid all over myself in the process, but I couldn't care less since I was just thankful to be alive right then.

However, as I saw the truck turning around and doubling back because he'd missed his target the first go-round, I found myself sprinting as fast as I could up to Declan's apartment, flying through his door as panic seized me.

Declan came rushing down the stairs to see what was wrong, and I hardly had any time to tell him what had happened before he was stepping around me and running outside with Nash right behind him.

"No!" I screamed. "He'll just try to run you over too!"

But it was too late; the guys were already outside, jumping in Declan's truck as they attempted to follow the asshole who'd tried to run me over as he sped away. I was left standing there, pissed off, scared, worried, and covered in noodles without much more to do than twiddle my damn thumbs in the air.

~

*T*hey showed up a little while later after having lost sight of the truck on some backroad they told me the name of, but I'd forgotten it the second I'd heard it.

"Did you get a look at who was driving?" Declan asked, his anger so evident it was almost palpable, but I was still pissed he hadn't listened to me and stayed inside earlier.

"Oh, now you wanna ask questions?" I nearly screamed, I was so angry.

Looking at me in surprise, he said, "Well, yeah. What else do you expect me to do? Sit here and not do anything about somebody trying to run you over?"

"Yes!" I yelled. "Making sure I was okay should've been your top priority, not getting revenge for something that didn't even happen to you!"

"Kali," Nash said in a way that I knew was his attempt at calming me down, but my nerves were too frayed to see reason or compassion.

"You're just as much at fault for this as he is," I said, pointing at Nash before I turned my gaze back to Declan. "If you must know, I'm fucking positive it was Cam. The windows might've been tinted, but I'd know that fucking sneer anywhere."

Declan and Nash shared a disbelieving look with one another, and instantly, even more anger settled in my stomach. "You don't believe me?!"

"It's not that we don't believe you, Kali," Nash rushed to say. "It's just that Cam should be all the way up in Chicago. If he'd come all the way down here, don't you think he would've tried to talk to you to get you back, rather than try to run you over?"

I couldn't believe what I was hearing. I knew damn well who'd I'd seen in that truck, and whether they wanted to listen to me or not, that fact wasn't changing. However, I was too far beyond anger at that point to be anything other than spiteful.

"Oh, I don't know what could've clued me in that running me over would be exactly the kind of thing Cam would do, Nash," I said like a smartass.

"Maybe it was all the years we spent together where I was his favorite punching bag. Or maybe it was in those text messages he sent me, saying he would find me eventually. Or it was the scary-as-fuck letter he left in the box with my mom's ripped up photo albums, basically spelling out the fact that he's a complete fucking psycho! Oh! I know! It's the fact that I saw him with my own damn eyes!"

"What letter?" Declan asked immediately, making my eyes drift back to his as I remembered that I hadn't told him about it yet.

Sighing and running my hands through my hair to relieve some of the stress and anxiety I was feeling, I said, "Cam left me a letter. It's next door if you want to read it."

"Nash, stay here and lock the doors. We'll be back," Declan ordered, leading the way for me to take him back over to my apartment.

As I went to cross the street, I hesitated, panic dumping adrenaline into my system as a very rational fear of being run over flashed through my mind.

"It's okay. I'm not gonna let anything happen to you," Declan said, none of his anger from earlier, present in his voice anymore.

That alone deflated my own anger tremendously.

After leading him up to my apartment and handing him the note from Cam I'd put in my kitchen drawer, I hopped up on the counter while he read it.

He dropped it on the counter next to me as he slid in between my legs and wrapped his arms around me.

Parts of his face were starting to swell, and I couldn't sit there without doing something about it. I pushed him back, got down, grabbed a frozen bag of peas, hopped back up where I'd been, and pulled him by the shirt back over to me.

As he started speaking, I put the bag up against his face and held it there, daring him with my eyes to tell me to stop.

"You don't have to do this," he said, indicating the bag I was holding.

"And you didn't have to go chasing that truck down, but here we are."

He smiled at me, forcing a smile to my own lips as he said, "If you really think it was Cam, then I'll trust you."

I deflated even more, instantly.

"Thank you."

"But if that's the case, I can't stress enough how much I want either Nash or me to be with you at all times."

I couldn't ignore the pleading tone in his voice any more than I could turn him down because of it. "Alright," I relented.

Declan sighed, dropping his chin to his chest for a second before he lifted his head back up to look at me.

"Thank you. I know it's not the best solution, but at least we'll be doing what we can. The thought of anyone hurting you, especially that piece of shit…" his words trailed off for a second. "I just can't lose you. I love you, Kaliyah."

My heart turned to sappy mush at those words, and without hesitation, I said, "I love you too, Declan."

Immediately, the sweetest kiss I'd ever felt in my life took up every part of my heart and mind, leaving no space for anything else. There was no Cam, club, fights, or anything as I lost myself to Declan's touch in the best way.

I reached up and ran my hand over the side of his face where I wasn't holding the peas, and he winced as he pulled back some.

"Oh, sorry," I said as I looked at him, tasting copper on my tongue. I glanced down and saw the corner of his mouth was bleeding, and I half-assed slapped his shoulder again. "Why the hell are you kissing me if your lip's busted?"

He just laughed at me for a second before he said, "Fuck this lip; if I want to kiss you, and you're willin' to kiss me back, that shit ain't stoppin' me."

I laughed and dropped my head to his shoulder, reveling in all the happy feelings I felt sweeping through me.

"What do you say to takin' another road trip?" he asked, and I pulled my head back up to look at him. "It'll confuse Cam, give the Heathens time to calm down, and us a chance to get away for a little bit."

What he was suggesting sounded like a dream at that point, so I nodded adamantly. "That sounds like a great plan. Where do you want to go?"

"The outer banks?"

Smiling because that had been one of my other top destinations if I couldn't figure out how to make honeymooning on Topsail work out, I agreed, and within almost no time, we were both packed and ready to go.

We'd thrown my bag in the back of Declan's truck before we climbed the stairs to his apartment so he could get packed, and once he was, he gave marching orders to Nash.

"I'm gonna drive you home, but don't worry about openin' the shop tomorrow, alright? Take a day like we are. Those ribs of yours probably need some time to heal, I'd think."

Nash nodded but didn't look too happy about not working the next day.

"Keep an eye on Moms too. With the club business not being settled yet, the Heathens, and Cam, there's no tellin' who might try to get to us through her," Declan said, and again, Nash just nodded.

After we dropped him off, and Declan went up to apologize to Moms about Nash and him getting in a fight both the night before and that day, we peeled out of their driveway and started heading up the coastline.

I knew we weren't going that far and that we weren't planning on being gone that long, but I was so glad to be leaving without anyone knowing where we were going that I settled back in my seat, smiling to myself as relief washed over me.

CHAPTER 27

DECLAN

The drive up to Nags Head took about three and a half hours, but it was three and a half hours of hangout time with Kaliyah, so I thought it was time well spent. There was hardly any traffic because it was so late, and our conversation didn't slow down until we got to the hotel, and I went inside to check us in.

After coming back out, parking, and grabbing our bags, we went up to our room, which had a balcony overlooking the ocean, and a whirlpool tub I planned on soaking my wounds in at some point while we were there.

Like a moth to a flame, Kaliyah walked out on the balcony to have a look at the view, and once I put our bags away in the closet, I stepped outside to join her.

I walked right up behind her, pinning her there with my hands on the railing on either side of her as I sent my nose to her neck to breathe her in.

She leaned her head back on my shoulder, her eyes closing

as she relaxed back into me. "This is so nice, Declan. Thank you."

I didn't answer her because I was so distracted by her neck. Sending a hand up to brush her hair out of the way, I kissed her there gently, but it just wasn't enough to satisfy the intense need I was feeling for her right then.

Kissing, licking, and sucking on her neck had her moaning right next to my ear, making my hard-on grow even harder, but once she sent her hand back into my hair and I bit down on that part between her neck and her shoulder, and she pulled, I 'bout lost it.

I couldn't wait to have her for even a second longer, and since it was dark outside and no one could see us where we were on the top floor, I pushed her shorts and thong down without hesitation and unbuttoned my jeans.

Reaching around with my hand to tease her, her breath already coming out in short little pants that were driving me crazy, she was already wet for me.

She leaned over some, putting the bottom of her ribs up against the railing, giving me better access as she stuck that tight little ass out perfectly.

I was seconds away from sliding into her when I had to stop, putting my head on her back in disappointment with myself.

"I don't have a condom," I admitted, my dick feeling like it might fall off if I didn't get it inside her asap.

Looking back over her shoulder at me, she said, "Fuucck-kk," in the most adorable little panting whine voice I'd ever heard.

"I'm clean and could pull out in time if I wanted to, but I know spilling inside you would be too hard not to do, and I don't have that kind of willpower."

She thought for a second, and as I'd just begun to accept my fate, I felt her hand come up between us to grab all of me.

"Why would it be hard not to cum in me?" she asked sinfully, her voice and the motion of her hand making me unapologetically loose-lipped.

I reached back around with my hand, determined to please her like she was pleasing me, and whispered in her ear, "You have no idea how much I want to be bound to you forever, to spill my seed deep inside you and claim you as my own. I want it so fucking bad I could cum just thinking about having you that way."

Without missing a beat, she turned her head toward me and said, "Then do it," making my breath stutter in my chest. "I want all that too, just as much as you."

There was no denying the seriousness I heard in her lust-filled voice.

Her hand was still curling up in my hair, her eyes begging me to fulfill both of our fantasies at once, and without taking my eyes from hers, I slid all the way inside her.

Our moans mingled, and I stilled for a second, savoring the feel of her because it was the most glorious feeling in the world to take her with no barrier keeping us apart.

I sent my hand up to grab her by the throat as I started moving at a desperate pace, keeping my head right up beside hers as I pounded into her, her pleasure-filled moans spilling out quietly into the air surrounding us.

"You're mine now, just as much as I'm yours," I whispered in her ear as the rocking of her body made her ear pull my bottom lip down some.

"Uh-huh," she moaned, but that wasn't good enough for me.

"Say it," I commanded, knowing she knew what I meant.

"I'm yours, and you're mine," she said right as she found her own release, and I followed soon thereafter, finding my own not two seconds later.

I came deep inside, holding her tightly to me until every last drop had spilled within her, and I couldn't, even for a second, find it in me to regret my decision to do so.

Carefully sliding out of her, hoping none would drip out, I reached down and pulled her shorts and thong back up, letting her button them herself as I righted my own clothes. However, as soon as I looked back up into her eyes, we both got the memo that neither one of us was done, and within seconds, we were back at it, wrapped in each others' arms all over again, devouring one another as we made our way back into the hotel room.

We didn't emerge for the rest of that night, or even most of the next day.

The hotel had room service, so we stayed naked the entire time, lost in each other unless we were sleeping, showering, or eating.

My soul had never felt so right with the world; my heart had never felt so fucking full before; I really thought it might burst inside me. And I knew it was all happening because of Kaliyah.

Nothing else seemed to matter while I was with her, and as we settled in for another night in each other's arms, I thought very seriously about not even answering my phone when it rang, but once I saw it was Nash, I knew I had to answer.

"Dec! The shop's on fire!" he screamed through the phone, making my heart freeze up inside my chest.

CHAPTER 28

KALIYAH

*N*ash had yelled so loud through the phone, I'd heard every word he said before Declan sat up, his face going as pale as a sheet.

Fear and panic were nearly overwhelming me, and since I didn't know what else to do with myself, I started laying out our clothes on the bed and packing up while Declan screamed at Nash through the phone to get out of there.

Apparently, that's when the line went dead because Declan looked like his head was about to explode.

I got dressed and kept packing, guiding him to get dressed too, even while he kept trying to call Nash back.

He didn't answer though, and I could see the sheer terror he felt as I looked in his eyes.

Once he was dressed, I grabbed our bags and the keys to his truck, pulling him along with me as he tried calling anyone else he could think of that might be able to help.

"Fuck, I don't know if he called the fire department," Declan said as we made it out to his truck, and I climbed in the driver's seat without asking.

Within seconds, I had my navigation pulled up on my phone and took off, driving faster than was both legal or safe, but I didn't care at that moment, and neither did Declan.

He called and reported the fire, making sure to tell them Nash might still be inside, hung up, and immediately started calling everyone else again.

Dusty ended up being the only person who wasn't working at the time, and as soon as he heard what was going on, Declan said he was going to go over to the shop to look for Nash.

The fear never settled out as I flew down the highway. If anything, it only seemed to get worse the longer we went without hearing anything from anyone.

We were a little over halfway there when Declan spoke into the silence.

"If I lose that kid too..." He didn't finish his sentence as worried tears broke the surface of my eyes to fall down my face.

I couldn't let my emotions get the better of me though. Declan was in no state to drive, and we had to get there as fast as that truck would get us there, so I pushed all my feelings aside and just drove.

About ten minutes later, Dusty finally called Declan back.

While they spoke, I couldn't tell what was being said, and it was driving me insane, not knowing if Nash was okay or not, but Declan filled me in after he hung up.

"We're headin' to the hospital in Wilmington, not the shop.

Nash was layin' on the ground, coughin' like crazy, with burn marks all over him when the firemen and Dusty showed up at the same time. They put him in an ambulance, but the closest hospital is in Wilmington."

I'd started changing the destination in my phone from the second I knew we were going somewhere else, but once that was done, it added a whole other hour to our drive.

"Did they say whether Nash is going to be okay or not?" I asked, unable to not voice that question.

Declan's eyes met mine in the glow cast down on us by the passing street lights, and said, "Dusty didn't know."

A few seconds later, he added, "He said the firemen got the fire out at the shop, but there's been a whole lot of damage."

"I'm so sorry, Declan."

I didn't know what else to say, and neither one of us knew what to do with ourselves as we just kept driving to the hospital, but at some point, when we were getting closer, Declan slid over next to me to hug me as best he could while I was driving.

"Thank you for doing all that back there and helping us get going. I didn't even need to ask, and you were already moving."

I didn't want to be thanked for doing something so small and insignificant, so I just brushed my hand over his thigh until we finally pulled into the parking lot of the emergency room.

Dusty was already standing there when we walked up, waiting to guide us up to Nash's room.

"He's got third-degree burns all over one side of his torso and down his right arm, but otherwise, they think he's gonna be fine. They're already talkin' 'bout skin grafts and stuff outside my wheelhouse, but they've given him some pain medication, and he's awake right now if you wanna talk to him."

Declan looked at Dusty like he'd lost his mind and said, "Of fucking course I want to see him."

He was snappy, but I couldn't be mad at him for it. Hell, if Declan hadn't said something first, I was going to; we were both just right on the edges of losing our shit completely.

As soon as we stepped into the room and saw Nash's smiling face, Declan came to a full stop and just stared at him for a second. Moms was sitting next to Nash in one of the two chairs in the room, but when she saw Declan, she rose to her feet to walk over to him, pulling her IV behind her.

"He's gonna be okay, Dec. It's alright," she said before she left

Declan and me in the room with Nash, pulling Dusty along with her.

"Hey, Dec," Nash said, obviously trying to be cheerful. "You look like shit."

Nash's words snapped Declan out of his frozen state, and without missing a beat, he said, "Well, that's all your fault, now isn't it?"

Nash laughed, but I could tell the movements caused him pain under all the bandages that decorated his right side.

Sobering as we both took a seat, Declan asked, "What happened?"

Nash sighed before he answered, and I could tell he wasn't looking forward to this part. "I don't know. I really wish I did, but I don't.

I know you told me not to go into work today, but I just got this feelin' like somethin' wasn't right, so I went down there to check on it. Before I even got there, I thought I could see the smoke in the sky, but I wasn't sure what it was because it was gettin' dark.

By the time I got there on my bike, the flames were already coming out the windows downstairs, and that's when I called you."

"Why didn't you call the fire department first? And if you weren't inside, how the hell did you wind up burned?" Declan asked.

Nash's face pinched up like he was expecting some kind of blow to follow what he said next.

"I ran inside?" He said it almost like a question, ignoring the first question Declan had asked, but even I could tell he was just stalling.

Declan sighed and ran a hand down his face. "Spit it out, kid."

"I went in to get your and your brothers' stuff off the wall."

Startling the hell out of me, Declan stood up fast, looking

down at Nash as if he didn't know who he was right then. "Why the fuck would you do somethin' so dumb as that, Nash? You could've died!"

Smiling despite Declan, Nash said, "I saved all of it. It's all over there on the counter. I made 'em bring 'em with me in the ambulance."

Sitting down with a huff that made it look like all the air had left his lungs, Declan just stared at Nash for a few beats.

"You're gonna get yourself killed one day, you know that, right?"

Nash laughed, but a second later, his face turned serious as he said, "There was a bike parked across the street when I got there though, and if I've heard you right about what he looked like, the guy sittin' on it was your old prez, Ray."

~

We stayed in the room with Nash until the hospital staff kicked us out. Declan grabbed the things Nash had saved and drove us back to Topsail, discussing this plan he had going in his head the whole way.

Apparently, the motorcycle rally his uncle had been talking about was going on, right there in Wilmington, so nearly the whole Lost Savages MC was less than an hour's drive from the shop.

The way he saw it, his best bet was to call a meeting... I think he called it 'church,' but that's not important. He wanted to get everyone together and 'handle this shit once and for all.'

He wanted to find out who was doing what, where, and when.

He wanted names, and he wanted them right then.

He wanted to confirm or deny who was making the phone calls, taking the pictures, killing the animals, trying to kill 'his people,' and everything else that had been going on.

Because once everything happened with Nash and the fire, there was no telling Declan that Cam had to have been responsible for at least some of it; he wouldn't hear it.

He was convinced that every bit of it had been the club and that the only way to ever get it to stop was to call a meet.

I had a bad feeling about it, but once Declan saw his shop in person for the first time, I knew there would be no changing his mind until he talked to the club.

"I need you to stay here while I go handle this," he told me, handing me the same pistol he'd given me a few days before. "Keep your doors locked. If you want to be extra careful, try to make it seem like you're not even here. I'll be back as soon as I can."

I nodded, accepting that this was just a part of who Declan was, watching as he sent out the text to the club, calling a meet in Wilmington before he climbed on his Harley and took off.

I tried not to worry, I did, but that was a useless endeavor; I was going to be a wreck until I knew Declan was safe, no matter what I did.

～

*T*ime was passing by excruciatingly slowly as I waited for an update or something. It had already been past one in the morning when Declan left, and though he hadn't seemed to think that would be an issue with the club, I certainly had a problem with it.

Not only was I battling exhaustion already, just from all we'd done and been through, but now I had to add being sleepy and being worried out of my mind to the list too.

He called to tell me everyone would be there for the meet, but the anxiety I was feeling didn't ease up one bit with the news.

"Do they seem upset at all?" I asked him, trying to get a read on what the situation was going to be like for him, but he kind of grunted in response before he actually answered me.

"It's tough to tell with this lot; they're always riled up over somethin.'"

It was a non-answer, and I couldn't help but think he was just trying to prepare me for the likelihood that things might not go his way.

"Where is the meet?"

"Down at Carolina Beach," he said, but that seemed like all the information he had time to give me. "I've gotta go, babe, everybody's starting to get here."

I felt like crying, I was so overcome by this panicky and fear-laced worry, spreading out to take over all of me.

"I'll call you when I'm done. I love you," he said, and tears spilled down my cheeks.

"I love you too," I said, hoping he'd heard me before he ended the call right after I'd said it.

I pulled the phone away from my ear and stared at it, imagining the million different ways this meet could go wrong. I tried to imagine just how many ways it could go right too, forcing myself to remain as optimistic as possible, but it wasn't doing much good.

Standing up and sliding my phone in my pocket, I started pacing again in my living room, not knowing what else to do.

Without any better ideas, I tried to distract myself as much as possible by climbing into the shower, and once I realized how long the hair on my legs was, I decided to just say 'fuck it,' and take a full-on bath so I could handle all of my bodily issues.

By the time I was done, my phone still hadn't rung, so I got dressed in some pajamas that could easily be worn out if I ended up needing to leave in a hurry.

I brushed out my hair and did any other hygienic thing I could think of to pass the time while I waited, even going so far as to pull out my tweezers to begin plucking at my eyebrows.

However, when I'd done everything I felt like I could do, I walked out into my living room again as this feeling like something was going terribly wrong started creeping up through my senses.

It was weird because I hadn't felt it until I was back in my living room, but I dismissed the feeling soon thereafter and set about making myself a cup of tea in the kitchen to calm my nerves.

I'd thought it'd been long enough for them to have come to some kind of decision, so without overthinking it, I tried calling Declan, but it went straight to voicemail.

Right as I was about to leave a message and had mixed the tea with the perfect amount of sugar, something pushed my head down, smashing my face into the countertop from behind, breaking my nose on impact, and shattering my dad's teacup all across the kitchen floor.

Note to Future Me: never ignore a feeling like that, ever again.

CHAPTER 29

DECLAN

*I*t had been a long ass time since I'd worn my cut, and even though it had gone through hell and was covered in soot and ash from the fire, I could still see the club's name, logo, and charter on the back, and my old SGT AT ARMS patch on the front.

Gavin's wasn't in as good of a shape as mine was, but in its defense, his did have bullet holes in it.

It might've seemed like I had a flare for the dramatic side of life as I waited in the shadows until almost everyone had gone inside, but I didn't care.

This wasn't a full-on club meeting where everyone attended; it was just a meeting of the executive officers... basically, those that had a vote. The enforcer, road captain, and prospects were there too, but not to make decisions; they were just there to make sure everything went smoothly.

Those who stayed outside set up a perimeter around the building, so they had eyes everywhere, and once I'd talked to

Kaliyah and told her I loved her, I put my phone on silent and started stepping out of the shadows.

As soon as the prospects saw me, they shut the hell up with whatever it was they'd been talking about and showed me all the respect in the world - probably because my relationship with the club was so tumultuous that they had no idea whether to praise my return or snub me.

They opened the door to the warehouse the Lost Savages used to store shipments, and I walked inside with my head held high, carrying Gavin's cut in my hand.

The office where I knew we were going to be meeting was at the back of the warehouse, and sure enough, there was the enforcer and road captain, standing outside that door looking like bearded bouncers at a nightclub.

As soon as they saw me, their ceremonial bullshit took over, and they squared their shoulders, crossed their arms over their chests like they were supposed to, and nodded at me as they let me pass.

"Good luck, Dec," Ethan said under his breath as I walked by him.

"Yeah, good luck," Holden said, but I ignored them both since my mind was focused on dealing with what I had lying in front of me that I needed to tackle.

Slinging the door open with all the rage I felt, I walked into the meeting, taking in every person seated around the table as I walked to the end of it, throwing Gavin's cut on the table before I removed mine and threw that one down as well.

The smell of smoke, fire, and leather filled the small room, and I really fucking hoped they smelled it, every single one of them.

"Here I am," I said as I slapped my chest with both hands before I sent my arms out wide. Dropping them to my sides, I said, "Do what you want with me, but you will leave Kaliyah and Nash out of this. You'll leave all my people out of this. If you want my head on a fucking spike, take it. I don't want it."

It took me a second to realize that Uncle Lyn was sitting in the prez's seat, while Mac had taken the VP spot Uncle Lyn had always occupied. Kinley was wearing a new-looking sergeant at arms patch, while Tito was in the same secretary patch he'd always been in, and some kid whose name I couldn't recall right off the bat sat in the treasurer's spot.

It was a whole new line-up from the one I'd left behind, and as I took a look around, a little bit of hope started spreading through me because it seemed like most of the people in that room had always been loyal to Uncle Lyn and me.

However, as Kinley spoke, some of that hope I felt started seeping away fast.

"The nerve you must have, walkin' in here after so long with my rank across your chest, and then disrespectin' the cuts by throwin' 'em down like that?"

I wasn't there to play games though, and as much as I loved Kinley like a brother, I wasn't leaving unless I got the assurances I needed or they carried me out in a body bag.

"The nerve you guys must have to let Ray go so he could try to burn my life down and kill the people I love," I snapped right back, unable to control the snarl on my face.

"We didn't let Ray go, Decky," Uncle Lyn said, bringing my eyes to his. "The two guys that were supposed to be watchin' him let him go, but they've already been dealt with." He paused for a second before he continued. "What happened?"

"Ray set my shop on fire, nearly killin' the kid that works for me." I could barely get the words out through all the hate I was feeling right then, but as concerned gazes drifted around the room, I started to feel a bit better because it told me they had no idea that was going to happen.

"Sorry, Dec," Tito said, the Spanish lilt to his voice seeping into even those few words. "Ray has been even crazier than usual now that he's lost the club and been stripped of his patches."

"You stripped a founder's patches?" I couldn't help but ask.

Laughing, Uncle Lyn said, "We're not above the laws of the club, laddie; no one is."

"Speakin' of," Mac spoke up for the first time, and I tried to ignore all the guilt in my chest as he looked at me. "That means you aren't immune to them either."

Nodding as I glanced down at the ground, I picked my head back up and reset my feet as I squared my shoulders, "That's right, and I accept my fate, whatever that may be. I left you guys high and dry and had no intention of comin' back."

Mac slammed his fist down on the table in front of him as he leveled me with a pain-filled glare. "Dammit, Dec. Don't you understand?"

"Understand what?"

"When Gavin died, and you left, it was like we lost both of you!"

That lump formed back up in my throat again, but I wouldn't disrespect Mac and lower my eyes while he was being so real with me. He deserved every bit of my attention.

"You realize that, right? I could kill you for puttin' this club through that... for puttin' me through that."

He flew out of his chair and stormed over to me, sending a fucking haymaker at my face, but I didn't raise a fist to fight back against him. I deserved at least that much, and I knew it. I just straightened myself up and stared right back at my best friend, ready to take whatever else he needed to send my way.

His hazel eyes met mine as his face pinched up, tears forming in his eyes as he sent his arms around me. "I fuckin' missed you, Dec," he said into my shoulder as I hugged him right back, having a hard ass time holding my own emotions back as they swept through me like a tidal wave.

"I missed you too, brother," I barely got out past the lump that was still lodged firmly inside my throat.

We stayed that way until we both got ourselves in check, and as we pulled away from each other and Mac went to go sit back down, both of us wiped the tears from our eyes, and no one in the room dared to say a damn thing about it.

"Tito?" Uncle Lyn said, nodding toward the Savages' secretary.

"I'm putting forth a motion to strip Declan Stone of his sergeant at arms patch."

Shocked, I looked around the table at Kinley, who smirked as he said, "All in favor?"

A round of 'Aye's' sounded around the room, and I nodded, looking down at the floor as I tried to process what I'd just lost.

Then I heard Kinley start speaking again, so I looked back up to accept my fate.

"Motion passed. I put forward a motion to start a new charter on Topsail Island, with Declan Stone acting as Founder and President."

My eyes grew big as I took in all the knowing smiles that sat around the table in front of me, letting my gaze fall lastly on Uncle Lyn's.

"All in favor?" he was barely able to ask before another resounding round of 'Aye's' filled the space around me, each of the men getting up from their seats to come congratulate me before I'd really even had the chance to process it all.

Ethan and Holden both busted through the doors as if they'd been waiting and listening in the whole time, coming up to slap me on the back in congratulatory revelry.

"You guys are serious about this?" I finally got a chance to ask once everyone had calmed down a bit, but my question only sparked more laughter.

"How's this for serious?" Mac asked as he walked back over to his seat and pulled out two brand new leather cuts with our names on them, a Topsail Island rocker sitting at the bottom of both of them.

Reaching out for them, I could hardly wrap my mind around what I was seeing.

"You're gonna be my VP?" I asked as I watched him take off his Savannah cut and reach out a hand for his new Topsail one.

"I think it's only fair the new prez goes first, laddie," Uncle Lyn said to Mac as he took my new cut from me and slid it up over my shoulders. It fit perfectly, but I barely took the time to enjoy it before I was ripping Mac's out of his hands and telling him to turn around.

I put it on him, and he turned around, his eyes shining again for a second time that night.

"You know I had to get that hit in before you became my prez," he laughed out, and I joined in with him as all the guys around me started celebrating again.

A cooler of beer showed up out of nowhere, and as much as I wanted to partake, I knew I needed to call Kaliyah before the party really started.

Reaching into my pocket, I pulled out my phone, surprised to see I'd already missed a call from her.

Immediately, I checked the voicemail she'd left, and as I heard what sounded like a scream and glass shattering, my whole world fell apart in an instant.

"I know that face," Uncle Lyn said, a hushed tone falling over everyone, but I barely even heard him as I turned on my heel and started running through the warehouse, hating how slow my feet were, even though they were going as fast as they could carry me.

As soon as I busted through the doors, scaring the hell out of the prospects who'd been waiting there, more surprise rushed through me as Uncle Lyn, Mac, Kenly, Tito, that other kid, Ethan, Holden, and even the prospects started following right behind me, hopping on their bikes to follow me wherever it was I was going, simply because they thought I might need them.

"Lead the way, prez," Mac said as he started his bike up without question, and I barely looked back and nodded at him before I was taking off down the street, heading back to Topsail with my brothers at my back so I could try to save the woman I loved.

CHAPTER 30

KALIYAH

ighting off being disoriented, my hands rushed up to grab my nose but no sooner had I reached for it than Cam was grabbing me by my hair and pulling me into the empty space of my living room, where I proceeded to drip blood out of my face and onto the new carpet.

He pushed me down onto the floor, rolled me over on my back, and straddled me so fast it was hard for my brain to catch up.

Once I got my wits about me though, I started bucking, twisting, turning, flailing… whatever I could get my body to do to try and get him off me, but every move I made, he thwarted, pushing me aside as if I were a fucking ragdoll.

He grabbed me by my throat with both hands as my legs continued to try and kick myself out of his hold, but it was useless.

The look in his eyes was absolutely terrifying as his lips

lifted up in a snarl that showed his teeth while, at the same time, made it look like he was smiling.

I'd already been scared out of my mind, but once I saw his face like that, I became nearly paralyzed in sheer terror.

He was going to kill me, there was no doubt in my mind, and as he started to crush my windpipe in his hands, cutting off my brain from its oxygen supply, I had a moment where I was right back in our old apartment, cowering before him like always.

My mind started drifting in and out of consciousness as I hallucinated our apartment in Chicago that wasn't actually there.

Still, no matter how much I knew what I saw behind Cam wasn't real, all the things I felt were as real as they could get.

The panic, the fear, the utter hatred of myself as I let him continue to hurt me... all of it came back to me in that moment as my fingernails dug into the flesh of his hands.

'Just submit!' I thought at myself, knowing that was exactly what he wanted, but I knew that alone wouldn't be enough this time.

I'd wounded his pride, taken away his safety net, and made him feel alone in this world.

When I remembered that, it was like I knew exactly what I was going to do, even if he ended up killing me for it.

Smiling right back at his deranged face, I started laughing as best I could as his hands gripped me tighter.

I kept it up for a moment longer before black spots started seeping in at the corners of my vision, but that was long enough for him to back off and let me go.

He was still sitting on me, and my voice was coming out all raspy as I laughed, but I brought my hands up to my heart anyway, as if what he was doing was so fucking hilarious, I couldn't stand it.

His face actually did become funny to me then, so I didn't have to force that laugh for long.

"What are you laughing at, bitch?" he yelled in my face as each of his fists fell hard against the floor on either side of my head, but I didn't flinch or answer him; I just kept laughing.

When he was so caught off guard by my behavior that I knew I could make a move and he wouldn't catch it, I threw my hands up to grab his chin in both hands and spit the blood that was coating my mouth right in his face.

Some of it even landed in his eye, stinging him, and he crawled off me, falling to the side like he'd been mortally wounded while he called me every name under the sun.

But I didn't waste any time watching him; I got up as fast as I could, dizzy on my feet, and ran to the bathroom, where I reached to grab the gun I'd left laying there.

Only it wasn't laying on the counter where I'd left it.

Cam pushed me into the bathroom, and I stumbled forward, nearly pulling down the shower curtain before I was able to whip around and face him.

"Lookin' for this?" he asked as he pointed the gun right at my face, making me freeze instantly.

Slowly, I slid my hands up in the air, watching for even the slightest movement from him.

"That's right," he said as he wiped at his face with his other hand before he motioned with it for me to move where he wanted me. "Into the bedroom, now."

Never taking my gaze off of him, I started creeping forward as he backed up, always staying just far enough away that I couldn't reach out and try to take the gun from him.

When I got into the hallway, I started backing up into my bedroom, unsure of what else I could do to save my own ass.

"On your knees," he said, and it took every bit of strength I had left to do that without complaint.

I was no longer the same woman he'd known while I'd been with him. I might not have been able to explain the change or when exactly it had taken place, but I knew without a shadow of a doubt that I was better now, stronger, more capable.

"I should shove my cock in your mouth one more time before I kill you," he said, and immediately I knew I'd bite the thing off if he tried to make me do such a thing.

Seeming to read my thoughts, he said, "On second thought, stand up. Put your back up against the wall."

I didn't like where this was headed or the almost gleeful look in his eyes as whatever plan he had formed in his brain.

Still, I didn't want to get shot, so I moved slowly into the position he wanted me in.

He stepped closer, his head tilting to the side some as he said, "Take off your shirt."

Of fucking course, he'd want to humiliate me before he killed me; I should've fucking guessed.

Only barely able to keep the bile from coming up my throat, I did as he said, taking just my shirt off and holding it in my right hand.

I could tell he was getting excited as he gestured with the gun at me again, saying, "Bra too, we haven't got all night."

I moved slower at that command, preservation of self warring with preservation of pride inside me, but I did it anyway, reaching both hands up to unlatch my bra as his right hand slid into his pants, and I wanted to vomit all over him.

Sliding the garment off the rest of the way, I kept it in my right hand as well.

He stared at me for a solid minute, jerking himself off in his pants while I stood there, exposed and thoroughly violated.

But I'd gone to that safe part in my brain that I'd been to many times before with Cam. That place where the blows didn't hurt as bad, and the toll his hate took on me didn't cut so deep. It was the place where I could think straight despite whatever was happening to me, and as I watched him, I settled into that spot in my brain, thinking through scenario after scenario of how this could wind up turning out.

Seeming close to coming but wanting to drag out his pleasure, Cam took his hand out of his pants, unbuttoned them, and stumbled out of them with some difficulty, so within a few seconds' time, he was standing there, bare-assed in front of me, his dick as hard as a fucking rock as it stood at attention.

Without warning, he rushed me, pinning me to the wall with one hand while he shoved the gun in the side of my cheek.

I could feel his dick rubbing up against my thigh, and I nearly fell out of that safe headspace from the feel of it, but I got myself in check quickly and looked right into Cam's crazed eyes.

"Open your mouth for me," he said, and I knew right away his plan was to fuck my mouth with that gun, but I just couldn't let him do that.

Squeezing my lips together as tightly as I could and hoping like hell he didn't pull the trigger, I slung my shirt and bra around his arm, using the leverage I got from it to rip the gun out of his hand, sending it clattering to the floor between us.

As soon as it fell, he reached down to pick it up, only to have my uppercut to his chin knock him backwards because I knew that was what he would do.

I reached down and picked the gun up, pointing it right at Cam's face as I backed up from him.

The fear in his eyes was all I needed to see to know I had him.

"Back up," I said, forcing him back into the hallway.

I stepped forward, never taking my eyes off of him as I picked my shirt up off the ground.

Finger on the trigger, I took my sweet ass time as I put my shirt back on, starting by sliding my right hand through the armhole, gun and all. My eyes never left his through the process, even while I slipped it over my head and covered my breasts.

Such a thing might not have mattered to somebody else, but every second I held Cam at gunpoint, every move I made that wasn't what he was telling me to do, every breath I breathed without his permission was a fucking win; I was going to get as many of those from now on as I possibly could.

The coward didn't say a word the whole time, just stood there with his hands up and his shriveled-up dick out.

I felt like the most glorious monster who'd ever walked the earth, but I was only the monster he'd made me, so fuck him.

"Back up into the living room," I said, and as he did like he was told, I followed him every step of the way.

"Sit on your hands."

Sighing but still doing what I said, he sat on his hands right as I heard the most beautiful sound in the world.

Or... at least what I'd hoped would be the most beautiful sound in the world.

If those bikes I heard turned out to be from the Heathens instead of the Savages, I was done for regardless.

But as I saw even more fear creep up onto Cam's face as the bikes only got louder as they tore down the street, parking right below us, I knew we could both sense who was coming.

Declan tore through my front door, his Uncle Lyn and some other guys following right behind him, but they all stopped in the entryway to assess the situation before they said anything.

In their defense, I was standing there holding a gun on Cam, who just happened to be sans clothes below the waist.

"Kaliyah, are you good?" Declan asked as if he were weary of me; *of me?*

"I'm great," I said, still not trusting Cam not to try and make some last-ditch effort at escaping the inevitable.

"Aye, lass," Declan's uncle said, pulling my eyes to his as he moved over to Cam. "We'll take it from here, won't we, boys?"

Immediately, more men than I could count at the time came into my apartment, walked past Declan, and scooped Cam up, leading him out of my new home.

It wasn't until his body was being blocked by somebody else's that I let my arm with the gun drop to my side, and that seemed to be the cue for everyone to let out the collective breath they'd been holding.

Only three guys remained in my living room after the stampede had taken Cam away: Declan, his uncle, and some other guy.

"I knew I liked ya lass," Uncle Lyn said with a chuckle, making a blush form on my face.

Everyone still seemed on edge though, so I made a big show of putting the gun on the counter.

Declan stepped up to me then, wrapping me up in his arms without a word, and it was only then that I really started crawling back out of that place in my mind, realization dawning in my mind about everything that had just happened.

Like I said, I'm not perfect, and as the stress I'd been feeling reached its fucking breaking point, I felt the first warning signs of a full-on panic attack threatening to take hold of me.

Sensing some change, Declan said, "It's alright, it's alright," squeezing me tight, but his voice started to sound like he was speaking to me through a tunnel. "Kaliyah, hey," he pulled away so he could look me in my eyes. "Hey, you're okay. Say it. Say 'I'm okay.'"

I had to focus really fucking hard on doing what he said, but with more effort than I thought it would take, I heard myself croak out, "I'm okay."

"Say it again..." he prodded. "Come on."

"I'm okay."

And I was okay.

I might not have been back to my normal self by any means, but I was okay, and as the panic attack flew away, I heard some of the bikes outside fly away too. I didn't even need to ask what they were going to do with my ex-fiancé; I didn't care. It was enough for me to know that Cam was gone, and right then, we were all okay.

~

*T*he next few weeks passed by in a blur of excitement, and the news I had to share was just going to add to what was already turning into a beautiful life.

Nash came home from the hospital, forever scarred for his decision but alive.

Declan bought the Stevens house at a steal and set about demolishing both his surf shop and the old Stevens house so he could start from scratch, building a new surf shop and MC clubhouse in one.

The day Declan had finally let Nash come back to work on the demo, Declan had taken him aside as I watched on, trying to keep my smile from giving anything away.

"Here, prospect," Declan said as he threw Nash's new cut at him along with the keys to his bike. "Go wash the wheels."

Nash's eyes had nearly bugged out of his head when he caught it all mid-air, saying, "Are you serious? Fuck yes!" as he put on his new cut.

Mac was a good dude, I'd learned. Quiet sometimes, but he was always watching Declan's back, even when nobody was looking. I might not have chosen this life for Declan, but it made me feel good to know he wasn't doing it on his own, too.

The girls of Topsail were just as awesome as they'd always been, supporting all of us as we tried to move on with our lives after everything went sideways, and Mya had even asked that girl out that she'd been fawning over for years; they had a date coming up soon if I wasn't mistaken.

There was still the fact that Ray was out and on the loose,

but as far as Declan was concerned, with his failing health and seeing as how the whole MC had basically abandoned him under his uncle's leadership, he didn't think Ray was ever going to be on our radar again.

Every day, I got up each morning, had breakfast with Declan before he went across the street to work, and got to writing. It got a bit noisy sometimes with all the construction, but I'd just typed the last words on my first full novel, and I was about to tell Declan about it.

I was so freaking excited I could hardly wait for him to come home.

I'd printed out the whole thing, made him dinner, and had everything set up and ready for when he walked in the door.

"Hey, babe. How was your day?" he asked me as he strolled in without a shirt on, looking like a whole snack.

"Pretty good." I was nearly bouncing, I was so excited, but I kept myself in check as I motioned over to the kitchen table. "Come sit down; I wanna show you something."

Doing as I said with a suspicious look on his face as he saw the dinner I'd made, he asked, "What do you want to show me?"

Unable to hold it in any longer, I reached into the chair beside him and pulled out my printed manuscript.

A smile lit up his face as he said, "Oh damn! You finished it?"

I nodded and said, "Wanna read it?"

"What? Like right now?" he laughed, but he barely gave me a chance to answer him. "Alright, let's see...

Sorry to whoever wrote all the scripts for the fairytales I grew up watching in movies as a kid, but bro, you got it all wrong,' he read aloud from the book I'd written, but I cut him off before he could read anymore.

"Also, I'm pregnant."

The end...
    For now.

ALSO BY CILLA RAVEN

Beholden To Balance

Initiate

Reign

Hunter

Defender

The Fae Bounties

Shameless Fae

Reckless Fae

Lost Savages MC

Wake

Take

Raging Heathens MC

Drifter

Prowler

Hallows

A Date With Death: Part One

Shared Worlds

Sneaky As A Fox

Lexi

WAKE

A LOST SAVAGES MC NOVEL

I sincerely hope you loved Wake. If you enjoyed the book, I would really appreciate **an honest review** because they help so much! Thank you!

To get an immediate notification when I have a new release, please **sign up for my mailing list**!

To see the complete reading order for the **Lost Savages MC** and its companion series, the **Raging Heathens MC**, dive into all of my book worlds by **visiting my website**!

ABOUT THE AUTHOR

Cilla Raven is an indie author that lives in Montana with her husband, children, and a few fur babies.

You can find all of Cilla's books, merchandise, and more on her **website**!

Love Cilla's books? **Join her mailing list** to be notified of new releases, giveaways, and more!

She'd love to have you join her **Facebook group**: *The Raven's Nest - A Cilla Raven Reading Group.* You'll get exclusive updates and teasers, live streams with Cilla over coffee, and all the funny memes you can stand. **Join now.**